Issued to the Bride:
One Sergeant for Christmas

Cora Seton

Author's Note

Issued to the Bride One Sergeant for Christmas is the sixth volume in the Brides of Chance Creek series, set in the fictional town of Chance Creek, Montana. To find out more about Emerson, Wyoming, and their friends, look for the rest of the books in the series, including:

Issued to the Bride One Navy SEAL
Issued to the Bride One Airman
Issued to the Bride One Sniper
Issued to the Bride One Marine
Issued to the Bride One Soldier

Also, don't miss Cora Seton's other Chance Creek series, the Cowboys of Chance Creek, the Heroes of Chance Creek, and the SEALs of Chance Creek

The Cowboys of Chance Creek Series:

The Cowboy Inherits a Bride (Volume 0)
The Cowboy's E-Mail Order Bride (Volume 1)
The Cowboy Wins a Bride (Volume 2)
The Cowboy Imports a Bride (Volume 3)
The Cowgirl Ropes a Billionaire (Volume 4)
The Sheriff Catches a Bride (Volume 5)
The Cowboy Lassos a Bride (Volume 6)

The Cowboy Rescues a Bride (Volume 7)

The Cowboy Earns a Bride (Volume 8)

The Cowboy's Christmas Bride (Volume 9)

The Heroes of Chance Creek Series:

The Navy SEAL's E-Mail Order Bride (Volume 1)

The Soldier's E-Mail Order Bride (Volume 2)

The Marine's E-Mail Order Bride (Volume 3)

The Navy SEAL's Christmas Bride (Volume 4)

The Airman's E-Mail Order Bride (Volume 5)

The SEALs of Chance Creek Series:

A SEAL's Oath

A SEAL's Vow

A SEAL's Pledge

A SEAL's Consent

A SEAL's Purpose

A SEAL's Resolve

A SEAL's Devotion

A SEAL's Desire

A SEAL's Struggle

A SEAL's Triumph

The Turners v. Coopers Series:

The Cowboy's Secret Bride (Volume 1)
The Cowboy's Outlaw Bride (Volume 2)
The Cowboy's Hidden Bride (Volume 3)
The Cowboy's Stolen Bride (Volume 4)
The Cowboy's Forbidden Bride (Volume 5)

Visit Cora's website at www.coraseton.com
Find Cora on Facebook at facebook.com/CoraSeton
Sign up for my newsletter HERE.
www.coraseton.com/sign-up-for-my-newsletter

Chapter 1

WHEN THE DOOR opened at the top of the basement stairs, Sergeant Emerson Myers wasn't surprised. This early in the morning, the old house creaked and groaned with every step someone took across its floors, and whoever had woken up had made her way from one of the upper rooms, down the main staircase, through the big kitchen at the back of the house to the basement door. He was sure it was a woman. The footsteps were far too light to be any of the men, but since five women currently resided in the house, that didn't narrow it down too much.

He knew who he hoped it was, but Emerson figured she was still asleep. Wyoming Smith had moved to Two Willows several weeks ago when she'd lost her job. Best friends with Cass Lake—who'd been a Reed before she married and who had grown up on this ranch—Wye had happily joined the family to save money on rent and lend a hand around the house during Cass's pregnancy. But she wasn't usually the first one up in the mornings. Cass was. Emerson didn't think it was Cass at the top of the stairs, though. Six months along, she had a heavier, more careful tread these days.

It wouldn't be Sadie, either. She was always the last of the Reed sisters to get up. Jo had moved into the little house she and her husband, Hunter, had built. Lena, maybe? Had she heard him moving around and come to investigate? She was very protective of her home and family. Or maybe Alice?

Whoever it was pattered down the wooden stairs as he transferred his clothes from the washer to the dryer.

"Oh, you beat me to it," Wyoming said when she stepped off the wooden staircase into the basement, a basket full of clothes on her hip. "I was hoping to throw a load in before Cass got started with her laundry."

This was going to be a good day, Emerson told himself. Getting a minute alone with Wyoming was no mean feat with so many people living together at Two Willows. Any minute now, General Augustus Reed would wake up and start bellowing for his assistance. This was the General's ranch, after all, and they were all here on his sufferance. Emerson had served with the General for years before a missile strike had sent them both home stateside with injuries. The General's hip was healing slowly. Emerson's ankle still bothered him—a lot—but he was able to get around enough to be helpful to his superior officer.

"Just switching my clothes to the dryer," he told Wye, tossing the last of his things into the ancient machine and shutting the door. When he turned, he saw that she hadn't dressed for the day yet. Clad in sweatpants and an overlarge, very faded baseball jersey from some local team, she looked sweet enough to give him a toothache. Her curly auburn hair was piled on top of her head in a knot, strands falling down to frame her face. He wished he had the right to cross the room, hitch his fingers into the waistband of those baggy sweats and pull her close.

Instead he waved at the empty washing machine. "All yours."

Wyoming crossed the room and set her basket down in front of it. "You're up early."

"So are you." She was right; it was very early. No one else was stirring, and in a house full of military men and ranch women, that was saying something. He was glad for the time alone with Wyoming. He didn't get enough of that, and she'd been skittish around him lately. He'd never hidden his interest in her, and they'd been friendly since they'd met a little more than a month ago, but until recently she'd been too busy to notice him, caught up in a flirtation with Will Beck, who'd spent days trying to fix Two Willows' plumbing last month.

Unfortunately, it turned out Will wasn't a plumber at all. He was a drug dealer intent on wreaking vengeance against all of them for foiling his plans to use the ranch as a distribution center when he moved his operation into the area.

Will was dead now, leaving Wyoming devastated she'd chosen so badly, and for the first few days after the trouble with him went down, Wyoming had declared she was done with men forever. She'd calmed down since then and he thought once or twice he'd felt her considering gaze on him, but he didn't want to catch Wye on the rebound; he wanted her to want him in the same way he craved her.

Which was a lot.

His desire had hit him edgewise the first time he'd seen Wye, sharp and hot and all-consuming, as if he'd starved for weeks and caught sight of a three-course dinner. He supposed he shouldn't be surprised at his reaction. He'd watched the General send man after man home to marry his daughters, had watched Reed privately celebrate each nuptial. Had wondered long and hard why the General had never seen fit to send him—

Now he knew it was all for the best. The General's daughters were wonderful women, but they couldn't hold a candle to Wyoming, to his way of thinking. He was grateful she'd come to join him instead of turning around and heading right back upstairs. He was nothing like Will, and he meant her no harm. He had a feeling he and Wye could be good together if she'd relax around him long enough for them to get to know each other.

"We've got a wedding today," she said conversationally. "As soon as people wake up, it's going to be hectic around here."

"That's why I'm getting my laundry done now." Emerson made it a practice to minimize his effect on the family as much as possible. He was all too aware that his tenure here could be cut short at any time if the General stopped needing his services, and the uncertainty of his future pained him more than his busted ankle.

He couldn't return to active duty, and he had nowhere else to go. Emerson wasn't the panicking type, but he didn't even want to consider the pathways open to him if the General cast him off.

He definitely didn't want to leave Montana without getting to know Wye better.

"You're a handy guy around the house," Wye observed.

Emerson waited a beat, not sure if that was praise or a subtle dig. "The Army doesn't offer maid service."

She nodded. "You don't complain about it, though. Most men do."

He wondered if there was some man in particular she was thinking about. The other men at Two Willows had all served in the military, and although Cass tended to take on most of the household chores, that was a matter of choice, not one that was forced on her. Cass didn't like ranch work. She gladly cooked and cleaned in return for not being asked to muck stalls or other work with the ranch critters. Her sisters Lena, Sadie and Jo were much more apt to get their hands dirty with the men. Alice, on the other hand, tended to hole up in her studio above the carriage house and immerse herself in creating the costumes she sold.

"What's the point of complaining? A chore is a chore. Best to just get it done." Emerson turned the dryer on and leaned against it. "I think Cass is really glad to have you around to help her these days."

"I'm trying to do enough to earn my keep." Wye got the load of wash going. "I don't like that the Reeds won't let me pay rent."

"I hear that. I'm looking for ways to earn my keep, too." He'd give anything to get to stay at Two Willows long term, but if the General did his physical therapy exercises, soon enough he wouldn't need an assistant.

"I think everyone appreciates you running interference for the General. The Reeds are an interesting bunch."

"I like them." He admired the General, enjoyed the quirky companionship of the man's five daughters and the camaraderie of the men they'd married. But he liked Wye even more, and he was too aware she could leave at any time. It was obvious Cass wanted her to stay awhile but just as clear Wye found it embarrassing not to be working. Emerson wasn't sure how it would play out.

He needed to make the most of every day he had with her.

"You'll be run off your feet today helping Cass." Alice was marrying Jack Sanders this afternoon, and Cass was serving up a Thanksgiving-style dinner to all their guests. There would be a lot of them. "You let me know where I can lend a hand, all right? Think of me as backup."

Wye smiled gratefully. "That would be awesome. Cass was such a wreck last night, I'm not sure she slept. She wants the wedding to be perfect, since it will be the last one here."

Emerson swallowed a pang. He hoped it wasn't the last one at Two Willows. Maybe Cass and all her sisters would be married as of tonight, but he wouldn't be.

Neither would Wye.

He supposed it was much too early to consider marrying her, but something clicked in his heart the first time he'd laid eyes on Wye. Some instinct in him recognized her immediately: the one for him. Everything he'd seen in the past few weeks confirmed it. Wye was... special. Kind. Caring. Attentive to the ones she loved. Always looking for the thing that needed doing and doing it. Her sensible attributes aligned with the way he'd been raised, but that wasn't why he was attracted to her.

Wye... fit him.

He couldn't quite put what he meant by that into words, but his body understood it perfectly. He hadn't held her yet, but he knew with all his heart when he did it would feel right. He ached to get close to her and try it out, but he didn't need to perform the act physically to confirm his suspicion. He'd always thought the phrase "meant for each other" was silly, but now he understood why people used it. He was meant for Wye, even if she hadn't noticed it yet.

She was noticing him now, though.

She stood with her face tilted up toward him, her gaze scanning his as if searching to understand something. Could she tell what he was thinking?

A faint flush of color on her cheeks led him to believe she just might.

"There will be more weddings at Two Willows," he predicted.

Wye's eyes widened for a moment, and her lips parted, but she didn't say anything. Did she know he wished he could walk her down the aisle, even if that was putting the proverbial cart way before the horse?

"Cass is pregnant," he pointed out. "Someday her children will marry here, I would think."

"Oh... of course." Wye's flush deepened.

Interesting.

Had she hoped he was thinking of a different marriage? One between two people who were almost strangers but not quite?

"Wye—" He wasn't sure what he meant to ask her, but he needed to ask her something—anything—to get their relationship going.

She waited for him to continue, brows raised a fraction of an inch.

"I was wondering if—"

"Wye, are you down there?" Cass called from the top of the stairs. "I have a list a mile long, and I keep thinking of more things to do, and I'm losing my mind!"

"Be right there!" Wye called. "What were you wondering?" she prompted Emerson, moving an inch closer.

Her proximity increased the tug toward her he'd felt for weeks. Wherever she was, his body was painfully aware of her.

"I was wondering if you'd like to—"

"We'd better start with breakfast," Cass called down. "Is Emerson with you? Tell him I'm about to put the coffee on."

Hell. That was his cue. The General was very particular about his coffee. If he didn't get up there before Cass got going with the coffee maker, there would be hell to pay.

"I was wondering…" Hell, he didn't have time to spell it out. Before he could overanalyze his impulse, Emerson bent down and stole a quick kiss.

Wye sucked in a surprised breath, but she didn't pull away. Quite the opposite, actually. She put out a hand to brace herself against his chest. "Emerson?"

He couldn't help himself. He kissed her again, a kiss that lasted a fraction of a second longer. "Save me a dance later," he told her. "At the reception. And remember, I'm your backup today."

"O-okay," she said.

He covered her hand with his and shifted it so it lay over his heart. Could she feel it beating strong and loud—for her?

Lifting it high, he pressed a last kiss into her palm. He hadn't planned any of this. Had figured he needed to take his time to get to know Wye—to woo her.

Well, she knew where he stood now.

"See you later. Gotta get the General his coffee."

"Of course." Wye didn't move.

"Wye? Where are you?" Cass called plaintively from the top of the stairs.

"Coming."

Emerson, already turned toward the steps, grinned over his shoulder at her. "Let's go." He offered his hand.

She grinned shyly and took it. Heat—and hope—surged through him.

Things were looking up.

"WYE? YOU OKAY? You're not getting sick, are you?" Cass asked after breakfast as the two of them washed the dishes and got them put away.

"I'm fine. Just… woolgathering, I guess. I'm happy for Alice." Wye busied herself getting the last of the plates stacked in the cupboard. They needed a clean kitchen in order to take on the dinner they'd be serving in twelve hours or so.

Cass's expression softened. "I'm happy for her, too. All my sisters safely married and settled. Who would have thought it could happen so fast?"

"Who would have thought the General would turn matchmaker?"

Cass laughed. "Right? You're the only one left, you know." She set a clean frying pan in the dishrack.

"Me?" Wye squeaked. "I'm not getting married." She couldn't help but think of Emerson's kiss brushing her lips. She hadn't been able to get her mind off it since it happened. Sitting across the breakfast table from him had been torture. She was sure everyone could see what had happened between them in the basement, even if she wasn't sure exactly what that was. Why had Emerson kissed her—three times?

"I've seen the way Emerson looks at you." Cass plunged her hands back into the soapy water and pulled out a spatula. She got to work scrubbing it. "Have you ever considered him?"

"For marriage?" Wye fought to control her voice. "I haven't considered marriage at all. You know that."

Cass rolled her eyes. "I know your parents didn't have the best relationship."

Wye snorted. That was the understatement of the year.

"That doesn't mean you should stay single all your life."

"It doesn't mean I should go rushing into things, either."

"You could go on a date with Emerson. See what happens."

"He hasn't asked me," Wye said primly, wishing Cass would drop the subject. During the whole meal, Emerson had watched her with a look on his face she couldn't quite decipher. It wasn't triumphant or anything galling like that. It was… determined.

Wye had no idea why that tugged at something deep and primal inside her. Even if Emerson had set his cap for her, that didn't mean she was interested.

Although she had to admit she was—a little.

Hell, a lot.

Had she learned nothing?

"The last time I thought about dating a man, he tried to kill your whole family," she pointed out.

Cass waved that off. "Will fooled all of us, but Emerson is totally different. You can trust him."

"How do you know?" Although Wye felt the same thing. Emerson was the sort of man who was entirely himself. You knew exactly what you were getting, and although it pained Wye to admit it, she liked what he was offering.

Emerson was handsome in a way that had nothing to do with his features and everything to do with the quiet, absolute self-confidence he exuded while going about his business. The sort of man who came to a decision, made a plan and carried it out, politely but inexorably, until you didn't know how he'd come to take charge of everything. The kind of man who understood things.

She had the strangest feeling he understood her.

Which made no sense. They'd spent little time alone together.

She wouldn't mind spending more—

"The General trusts him utterly." Cass broke into her thoughts. "And the General doesn't trust many people. He certainly doesn't let them get close to him the way he does Emerson."

Was she thinking about the coffee? Wye suppressed a smile. Every morning Emerson made coffee for the General, then cleaned the machine so Cass could make coffee for everyone else, as she always had. Wye knew it galled Cass no end her father wouldn't accept a cup from her.

"The General is very set in his ways," Wye pointed out. "He likes everything done exactly the same every time."

"I know." Cass sighed. "Anyway, we're talking about you, not me, and I think you should give Emerson a chance."

Wye shrugged, drying the last of the dishes as Cass let the water out of the sink. Maybe she would.

"I'm not marrying him, though." She'd learned early to distrust the idea of happily ever after.

"Famous last words. Come on, let's go see what's next on the list."

EMERSON HAD BEEN in warzones less chaotic than the interior of the large white Victorian farmhouse after Alice married Jack. Vehicles of all sorts lined the long lane that led to Two Willows, and the first floor was crammed full of happy guests.

The General was looking decidedly mutinous, however. Settled into his easy chair in one corner of the living room, his cane set to one side, he was surveying the people around him with increasing irritation.

Time to fix that.

Emerson threaded through the crowd, careful not to put too much weight on his bad ankle, which still pained him considerably if he overdid it, and deposited a cold beer on the side table by the General's chair. He was getting around a bit better than he had a few weeks ago, when he'd first arrived, but it was unclear yet if his ankle would ever fully heal.

"Stop fussing, Sergeant. You're as bad as a mother hen." But the General picked up the bottle, took a long swig and nodded. "Could've got myself a drink if I wanted one," he pointed out.

"Of course. Got myself one, too." Emerson lifted

his to show him. The General hated the injuries that were making it difficult to negotiate the crowd filling his home. He'd borne the brunt of the blast that had torn through their bunker overseas and had required surgery to his hip before he was sent home. "Thinking about getting myself a few more appetizers. Want some?"

Emerson was risking the General's ire again, but his stomach was rumbling, and he didn't mind fetching food for the man. For one thing, it would allow him another glimpse of Wyoming, who'd parked herself in the kitchen with Cass, helping her to put the final touches on the meal they planned to serve to the wedding guests in a matter of moments. For another, it was his job.

"You know what I like. Get Jack and Alice, too, while you're at it. I want to talk to them—but before you do, I've got something to say to you—about your future."

Emerson, already heading for the door, turned back. There were enough people in the room to make it difficult to hear unless you were close to your conversational partner, but something in the General's voice had sliced through all the noise and warned him the man had a serious topic on his mind.

"You've served by my side a long time, and I commend you for all your hard work," the General began. In his fifties, his face was lined from long days in the elements and the cares that rested on the shoulders of someone responsible for the lives of so many men. Emerson braced himself for some kind of brush-off.

He'd begun to hope maybe the General would keep him at Two Willows to help out since they'd both taken work at the Army Reserve center in Billings. Wouldn't the General need a driver? Didn't Emerson help him daily in a hundred other small ways? He'd hoped that would be exchange enough for staying here.

"I've no doubt if you stayed at Two Willows you'd make yourself useful." The General echoed his thoughts, and Emerson's stomach tightened. Here came the kicker. The General was obviously sick of him. He already had a houseful of daughters, every one of them married to a man he'd hand-picked. Why did he need Emerson around?

"I'd try," Emerson assured him.

"You'll do good work at the reserve center," the General went on.

"I'll do my best," he managed to say. He wondered if Reed was going to suggest he should move into an apartment in town, closer to the center. Get full-time work. Make something of himself. He was still young, after all, even if he was injured.

He would miss Two Willows and everyone who lived here, though. He supposed he'd spent a lifetime looking for a surrogate family to replace the one he'd lost far too early.

"What's got you scowling like that, Sergeant?" the General demanded, looking him over.

"Nothing, sir." Just memories. Hard ones. He shook them off.

"Are you listening?"

"I'm listening, sir." Emerson gave the General his attention. "What can I do for you?" After all, in this moment he had a roof over his head, three square meals on the table and a job to do. This moment was all that mattered. Tomorrow could take care of itself.

"I said, if you want to stay here, you'll have to do your share. Pull your own weight and all that."

Regret tightened the muscles of his neck. That's what he'd been trying to do, but his ankle prevented him from doing the kind of ranch work the other men here were doing. Every day he had to swallow the bitterness of knowing he'd lost some of his usefulness. He tried to make up for it by doing his best for the General and anticipating his needs. He kept his paperwork and correspondence up to date and organized. His coffee hot and strong. Drove the General wherever he needed to go. Offered his arm when the man required it.

He'd done much the same kind of work overseas before the missile hit, but he'd never felt restricted by it the way he did now. He used to be able to cover ground at a run if the General needed something quickly. He couldn't run anymore.

Still, he'd do whatever he could if the General was willing to give him the opportunity to stay here.

"I'll do my share. More," he assured the man.

The General nodded. "I know you will. I mean to treat you like every other man I sent here. Same responsibilities, same privileges."

Emerson stilled. What did he mean? He'd sent the

other men to marry his daughters, and he planned to give them each a share in the ranch when he passed away.

The General nodded again. "You know what I'm saying. When I die, you'll get a share of the ranch, too, although I hope you're not in a big hurry to see that day."

"No, sir." Just knowing someday he'd have land—a place to call his own—for the rest of his life would make everything he'd gone through worthwhile. He'd always planned to save up to buy a spread eventually, and he'd known it would take him a decade or two to reach that goal. Ever since the explosion had sent him stateside with a limp that wasn't going away, he'd given up all thought of it. Owning a ranch had seemed out of reach forever.

Now it was within his grasp again.

"That's the payoff," the General said. "But there's a price."

"Price, sir?" Of course there was a price. There was always a price. He waited, wondering if his dreams were about to dissolve again.

"That's right. Marriage. You don't get to waltz in here without marrying one of my daughters. You of all people should know that."

Emerson blinked. "You don't have any more daughters, sir."

The General chuckled. "Maybe not official daughters, but Cass wants Wyoming to stay at Two Willows long term. An unwed woman is asking for trouble, by my way of thinking. Besides, I've seen the way you look at her."

"That's pretty old-fashioned thinking, sir." But Emerson's gaze moved toward the kitchen, as if he could see straight through the wall to where Wyoming was helping Cass. He'd marry her in a heartbeat. Did the General know that?

"I'm pretty old-fashioned. I want my daughters happy, and in Cass's case, that means keeping her friend close by, which means Wye needs to marry someone determined to stay right here, which means you need to marry her. Got it?"

Emerson stared at him. Twist his arm. "Yes, sir." He was more than willing to take on that task. Maybe some people would say he didn't know Wye well enough to stake his future on marrying her, but he knew all he needed to know. Wye was—amazing. A staunch friend to Cass and her sisters. Someone he thought loved Two Willows as much as he already loved it here. If Wyoming decided to marry someone, she'd be in it for the long-haul, and one thing Emerson knew about himself—he didn't want to be with anyone who'd leave.

Might as well be alone as choose that.

"And don't dawdle," the General was saying when he focused on him again. "I heard Wyoming talking to someone on her phone about a job. Didn't sound local."

"A job?" One that wasn't local? Hell, that didn't sound good. "I'll get on it right away, sir."

"Glad to hear it." The General looked him over.

"Thought I might meet more resistance."

"Hell, no." Emerson swallowed. "I mean—"

"I think I know where you stand, Sergeant," the General said. "Now get me those appetizers."

WYOMING FINISHED WHIPPING an enormous pot of mashed potatoes, the third pot of potatoes she'd prepared so far. Her arm ached, but she was glad to hide in here out of the crowd and hubbub of the living room. Not that it was much quieter here. All the Reed women's weddings had been crowded, but with the General home, even more people than usual showed up. All of their friends and neighbors wanted a chance to commend him on his service to their country.

Huge plates of turkey, stuffing, mashed potatoes and other holiday favorites lined the counters and large table, which bore bullet grooves from an earlier confrontation with drug dealers on the ranch. A testament to all they'd been through and overcome. People would soon file in to serve themselves buffet-style. She was having a hard time maneuvering about the room. Lord knew her Civil War–era dress barely fit into the house, let alone this kitchen.

Wyoming didn't have much opportunity to dress up like this, but Alice loved costumes. She ran a business designing and creating them for plays and movies, among other things, and she'd been trying to secure a contract to make the costumes for a Civil War–era production starring acclaimed actress Kate O'Dell when she'd met Jack. When the contract didn't pan out, she'd decided to throw a hoopskirt wedding. The dresses were fun to wear but not suited at all for a crush like this.

As Wyoming moved carefully around the kitchen, trying not to knock something over with her huge bell-shaped skirt, she wondered if she'd ever be the one getting married. Despite what she'd said to Cass earlier, she couldn't help wanting a relationship that would last. Still, every time she thought about Will and how wrong she'd been about him, her stomach sank. During the last few weeks, she'd run through all her interactions with him endlessly, cringing at memories of the times his veneer of cheerfulness had slipped and he'd shown his true colors. The times he'd grown impatient with his work. The times he'd scowled when Emerson came near.

He'd fooled her into thinking he was a fun, light-hearted, regular guy. Possibly someone she could make a life with when they got to know each other. His good nature had been a carefully crafted facade, however. One that had fooled everyone.

That did little to make her feel better. She'd always thought of herself as the last person to be taken in by a quick smile and a false intimacy. She had long relied on her intuition to help her navigate the world since she didn't have anyone else to guide her. Will had done more than hurt her pride—

He'd undermined her confidence in her own judgment.

Even worse, she couldn't seem to find a job, and there was a limit to the charity Wye was willing to accept. Without telling Cass, she'd begun to answer ads for positions in Billings and Bozeman. She kept telling herself it wouldn't be the end of the world to move to the city away from all her friends.

So why did it feel like it?

Wyoming squashed her dark thoughts. There was no time to feel sorry for herself. She had a wedding to help with. A job to find. A life to get on with.

So, she didn't have a mother who communicated from beyond the grave like Cass's mom seemed to, or a father who would send her a husband, like the General did—handsome, wonderful husbands—to each of his daughters. She had her independence. Her self-respect.

Wasn't that more important?

Her phone buzzed. She wouldn't have heard it if she hadn't fished it out of her ridiculous hoopskirt and placed it on the counter a few minutes earlier. Her brother's name flashed onto the screen. Wye wiped off her hands and took the call, plugging her other ear so she could hear above the noise as Cass directed the setup of the dinner buffet.

"Ward? What's up?"

"You haven't heard from Mindy, have you?"

"Mindy? No." She moved across the room to the back door to try to get away from the noise, but it wasn't much better.

"She's missing. She said she was going to the grocery store this morning, but she never came back."

"Where's Elise?" Wye asked quickly. Ward and Mindy's daughter was only ten months old.

"With me. Mindy wasn't supposed to be gone long."

His petulant tone made Wye sigh. She had no doubt if she wasn't at a wedding, Ward would try to lure her over to help. Not that it would take much luring; she loved her niece. This wasn't the first time Mindy had stayed away from home longer than expected, though. Wye tried not to judge, but Mindy wasn't the most maternal woman around.

"Did you call Mindy's friends?"

"Yep. No one's seen her. I called the grocery store. Hell, I'm about to call the sheriff."

Something twisted inside Wyoming, and she began to take the situation more seriously. "Do you think she got in an accident?"

"Wouldn't someone have called? I don't know what to do. She's got the car—it's a hike to the center of town with the baby, and it's cold outside. Could you—?"

Normally she could and would have taken over from here, running to the grocery store to check for Mindy there, then driving to her friends' houses, heading to the hospital, even, but she was needed here, and besides, it was barely half a mile from her brother's house to the grocery store—and the sheriff's department.

"No, I can't," she said firmly. "Call Cab Johnson and tell him everything. Call the hospital, too. If you need to get somewhere, take a taxi. Ring me back when you get news."

"But—"

"Ward, I'm at a wedding. You're much closer to the

grocery store than I am."

"Fine." He cut the call, leaving Wye to sigh again. It was obvious her sister-in-law wasn't happy with her lot as a small-town stay-at-home mom. Wyoming figured she'd driven right by the grocery store this morning and gone on to Billings to do some real shopping. She and Ward needed to work that out. It wasn't up to her to fix her brother's marriage.

Somehow Ward seemed to think it was, though, the same way he thought she should be available at a moment's notice to watch his baby daughter. It was like they were back in seventh grade. After their mother had left their father—left all of them, actually—Wyoming had been the one to pick up the slack. Her father hadn't sobered up for weeks, so she'd raided what little cash Randi had left in the cookie jar and walked to the grocery store every few days. She'd cooked meals that Ward had gobbled up and that her father had left mostly untouched. She'd done the dishes, the laundry…

And she hadn't stopped until she'd moved out.

A loud pounding sounded on the Reeds' front door and startled her out of her thoughts.

Someone was arriving late to the wedding.

Cass, carving one of the turkeys, groaned. "Who could that be?"

"I'll go get it."

Wyoming put down the phone and hurried to answer it. Her bulky skirt hindered her progress around the large kitchen table and chairs and made it hard to get past the other men and women who'd volunteered to help set out the meal, but she reached the front hall at last.

When she tugged open the wide wooden door, she laughed, some of her worry over her brother's missing wife slipping away.

"Emerson? What on earth are you doing out here?"

The sergeant stood in the doorway, his rangy, muscled body catching her eye like it always did. She hated to admit she'd been too infatuated with Will to notice Emerson much when she'd first met him, but these days she couldn't tear her gaze away—especially after those kisses he'd stolen. All day today she'd been aware of him whenever he got near and had held her breath, wondering if he'd kiss her again.

She admired the efficient way he completed each task. He wasn't as young as she'd first thought. Probably in his mid to late twenties. There were lines around his mouth and at the corners of his eyes she hadn't noticed. His gaze had depths not apparent to a casual acquaintance. He was a man who took his responsibilities seriously.

"Needed to see you, and I figured it was just as easy to go around the house as to try to push through the crowd. Besides, I wanted your attention. Looks like I got it." Emerson leaned against the doorjamb and added, "The General sent me. Are you going to let me in?"

"Sent you—to do what?"

Emerson grinned. "To marry you—what else?"

Chapter 2

WHEN WYE SPUTTERED, coughed, then laughed and burst out, "Marry me?" Emerson told himself to keep calm. He'd surprised her, that was all. She hadn't said no yet—that was a good start.

"That's right. What's wrong with that?"

"For one thing, I'm not the General's daughter. I'm not a part of whatever is going on in this place." She waved a hand to encompass the ranch. "I don't predict the future, or hear the garden plants talk to me, or anything like that, and I'm certainly not the type of person someone sends soldiers to marry."

"You are now." Although he was glad she wasn't as fey as the Reed women. Strange things happened at Two Willows, and he was content not to be a part of that.

"Am not."

"You think I'm lying?" Emerson had known Wye was too cautious to jump at a proposal like the one he'd just made her, but he had hoped to see a little more curiosity, at least.

Instead, Wye straightened as Cass called from the

kitchen, "Food's ready. Form a line, and don't worry; there's plenty for everyone."

Wye lowered her voice, as if anyone could hear over the din as everyone surged into the hall to form a line at the entry to the kitchen. "I think you're teasing me. And it isn't very funny, Emerson."

Uh oh. Wye was a proud woman. If she thought he was making her the butt of a joke, she'd be furious.

"I'm not teasing you," he assured her, becoming more serious, "and you're right—it wouldn't be very funny if I was." He took her elbow, drew her outside and shut the door so they could hear each other. This was too important to risk her misunderstanding him. Wye shivered in the cold, and he knew he didn't have much time to make this right. "I've been here long enough to know what I feel about you." He moved in closer, his hand still cupping her elbow. "I like you—a lot. Don't you think we could be good together?"

"Together… as in *married* together? You don't know me nearly well enough to even guess at that. And I don't know you, either." She reached for the door handle.

Emerson covered her hand with his, determined not to lose this moment with her. "Yes, as in married together. Maybe not now, but—"

"Of course not now. We haven't even gone on a single date!" She turned the handle and leaned in to push it open despite his interference, sending the back of her hoopskirt skyward. With a growl of frustration, Wye clapped a hand on her skirt to push it down.

"I'd like to start dating," Emerson said, biting back a

grin.

She turned a baleful look on him. "You could have led with that. Not with this marrying nonsense."

"Blame the General." He shifted to insert himself between her and the door. "He ordered me to marry you, not take you to the movies."

"Is that what this is about? The General? What if I don't want to marry you? Will he send me packing?" Wye stared up at him.

"You don't want to marry me?" He folded his arms over his chest, bracing himself for her answer.

"Oh, for heaven's sake." She tried once more to reach around him for the doorknob, but as the front of her hoopskirt pressed against his legs, the back of it tilted up again. "This stupid dress!" She retreated, her color high, and Emerson noticed she hadn't answered his question. Did that mean there was hope?

"So you don't want to marry me *today*," he clarified. "I'll let the General know, but I'm pretty sure I can guess his next question."

"What would that be?" Wye snapped. He could tell she was trying to figure out how to get to the doorknob without sending the back of her skirt upward again. He sent a silent thank-you to Alice for picking such an impractical style.

"When *will* you want to marry me?" He ducked when she shoved him. "Hey, you can't blame me for asking, can you? Like I said, I like you, Wyoming Smith, and more to the point, I have my orders. If I defy my superior officer, I could be court martialed."

"I don't think so." She crossed her arms, shivering a little. He'd better get her inside soon, but first he wanted an answer.

"Think of it as me serving notice of my intentions," he said placatingly. "We can take as long as we want to get to the altar, but at some point we have to get there." He nearly smiled at her incredulous expression. He had a feeling Wye had pegged him as someone as practical as she was, and this outrageous proposal had thrown her for a loop. He figured he might as well make the most of his advantage. "So pick a date," he said. "It'll make everyone happy—me especially—and it'll get the General off our backs."

Wye snorted in a decidedly unladylike manner. "That's the problem with men in a nutshell, isn't it? They're always *on* your back. They don't really want a partner in life; they want a servant."

"Hold on, wait a minute, that's not true at all." Emerson straightened up. He wasn't going to let her tar him with that brush.

"Isn't it?" she demanded. "If I became your wife, you'd expect me to cook and clean, take care of the kids, wash your laundry, iron your uniform—" Those were the kind of things her mother had done before she took off for greener pastures. That's what she'd done for her father for years once Randi was gone. Those years of caring for her father and brother had given her some insight into why her mother would take off the way she had. Her father never did have any respect for *women's work*, as he called it.

"No, I wouldn't." Emerson took Wye's hands, which were ice cold, and began to chafe them to warm them up. He really did need to get her back inside. "I don't know if you've noticed, but no one's taking care of me now, and they haven't in a hell of a long time. I'm the one playing nursemaid to the General, and I don't mind it one bit because he's a man who deserves respect—and help. I don't want you to be my mother, Wye. I want something entirely different. You can name the date any time you're ready, if that's all that's holding you back."

She jutted out her chin. "That's not what's holding me back, and you know it. I'm not like Cass or Alice or any of the others. You can't just arrive here and whisk me off to the altar and expect it to turn out all happily ever after. Things like that don't happen to people like me."

"Why not?"

"They just don't."

"You think Cass and her sisters have some kind of lock on romance?"

"You know what I mean."

He hated that he did. Wanted badly to make Wye believe she deserved a fairy-tale ending as much as her friend did. Her words struck home, though. He wasn't the kind of person happily-ever-afters happened to, either. "So we won't marry in December or January," he joked lightly, wishing he knew how to tell her he wanted to fight for a better future for both of them. "How about Valentine's Day?"

"You are pushing your luck, soldier." She yanked her hands away from his.

Time to change tactics. Jokes weren't working.

He reached for her hands again. Ran his thumbs over her soft skin. "I know you don't love me yet, and I know I'm going about this all wrong, but you know what the General is like. He was adamant I had to tell you tonight that he'd ordered us to wed, and if I hadn't, he would have been impossible. You don't want him to cause a scene at Alice's wedding, do you?"

Wye rolled her eyes, but she softened a little, too. "No, of course not."

"I've said my piece, and we can move forward. I want that, you know—to move forward in getting to know you. And not because the General told me to."

"Move forward in what way?"

"Dating. Spending time together. Seeing what this is between us." He wondered if she'd deny something was. "Do you think we could do that?"

"I... guess."

Emerson couldn't help smiling. Now they were in business. "I can be as patient as you need me to be. I could even wait until St. Patrick's Day for that wedding."

"You're impossible." Wye shook her head, but a little smile tugged at her lips.

"Memorial Day? The summer solstice?"

"Emerson!"

"July Fourth it is," He backed up when she took another swipe at him. "Seems like a fitting time to marry a soldier, don't you think?"

"You know what? That's it," Wye said. She shoved him aside, pushed the door open and escaped into the front hall, but just as Emerson cursed himself for going too far, she reappeared with their winter coats in her arms. "Come on." She tugged him right off the front steps, her hoopskirt trailing in the snow as she set off around the house, pulling on her coat as she went.

"Where are we going?" Emerson asked, shrugging into his own and then wincing when he came down hard on his ankle on the uneven ground while hurrying to keep up. The last thing he wanted was for Wye to notice his limp.

"To the maze. We're going to settle this right now."

Hell. Emerson tried to slow his steps, but Wyoming was nothing if not determined, and she dragged him right around to the back of the house, across the yard past Sadie's snow-covered garden to the hedge maze. He gave up fighting. The tall hedges loomed far above their heads, and when they entered the maze, they plunged into a gloom that was hard to penetrate despite the moonlit night.

Emerson had walked these passages a number of times, but that didn't stop the tickle of uneasiness that danced across the back of his neck. Like Wyoming had said, Two Willows was a place where strange things happened, and the maze was one of the ranch's most uncanny features. At least she'd slowed a little in the darkness and he could keep up without reinjuring himself.

"Use the flashlight function on your phone," Wyoming dictated.

"Shouldn't we go back and get our dinner?"

Wye ignored him. "Phone!"

He fished it out of his pants pocket reluctantly and turned on the light. Wye took it from him and led the way, even though he knew damn well how to reach the center. She used her free hand to lift her skirt, but it still dragged through the snow.

It was quiet out here. Clouds obscured the stars, and the air had a heavy quality to it, as if more snow would arrive soon.

"You don't have any gloves. We should go back."

Wye hushed him. "Nearly there. This won't take a minute."

She was right; one minute could dash his hopes for good. Despite having heard Wyoming state more than once that she didn't believe the standing stone at the center of the maze was anything more than a hunk of rock, he knew she was as superstitious about it as everyone else.

Cass and her sisters believed utterly that if you asked the stone a question, you would get an answer one way or another—and that answer was unfailingly right. Wyoming always argued that the women were making the stone's "predictions" come true themselves, but he'd also heard her say she'd seen things at Two Willows she couldn't explain. You couldn't hang around the place very long before you got sucked into its oddness.

It wasn't the women's stories that concerned him,

though. Brian had been the first one to tell him of his experience with the stone. "It said Cass would marry me, and she did" was how he put it.

All the other men confessed their own strange interactions with it. "If that stone says something," Logan had told him, using his fingers to make air quotes, "then you'd better believe it's going to happen."

Emerson searched for a way to distract Wyoming and get her out of the maze before the stone "predicted" she wouldn't want to have anything to do with him. Her reaction to his kisses this morning told him she saw him as a possible partner. The stone could undo the connection he'd built with her so far.

Unfortunately, he couldn't come up with anything other than tossing her over his shoulder and making a run for it—or rather, a hobble for it with his bum ankle—and he doubted that would go well.

When they reached the stone, she handed him his phone, and he shut it off and pocketed it. There was something so prehistoric about the standing stone it felt wrong to use such up-to-date technology around it. A slab of rock over a dozen feet tall, it stood as if it had grown here organically. No one knew who had positioned it here.

Emerson tried one last time. "We don't need a stone to make our decisions for us. You're right; I shouldn't have pushed. I should have asked you out first. I'm asking you now."

Wye rounded on him, her skirts swinging like a bell around her ankles, her curls wild in the low light. He could just make out the gleam of her eyes. "Emerson Myers, stop backtracking. You've got only yourself to blame for this. Five minutes ago you were trying to set a date for our wedding, so let's just settle this once and for all. Stone?" She turned to face it and put both hands on its wide flank before he could stop her. "Am I going to marry this man?"

They both waited as a whisper of a breeze brushed their faces.

"Don't let the stone ruin this, Wye," Emerson said.

She turned at the roughness of his voice. Dropped her hands.

"I shouldn't have joked about marrying you. I should have told the General to shove it when he ordered me to propose. That doesn't mean I don't want you. I do. Don't let a hunk of stone get in the way of something that could be good."

"I... ow!" Wyoming clapped a hand to her cheek. "What the hell, Emerson?"

"I didn't touch you." He stepped back, then leaned forward. "What is that?"

Wyoming opened her hand to reveal a folded piece of paper, her breath steaming in the cold air as she let it out. She opened the paper with shaking fingers.

"Oh... hell," she said slowly.

Emerson's gut knotted. He took the paper from her, afraid she'd ball it up and pitch it away before he got the chance to read it.

The stone had answered, just like everyone said it would.

What did it have to say?

He held up the paper, squinting at it in the low light. It was a photocopy of an old newspaper article. No, not an article—

A wedding announcement.

Emerson's heart hammered as he read the headline out loud. "Couple to be wed on New Year's Eve." He lowered the paper. Stared at Wyoming, who was staring back at him.

"Hell," he said slowly. "We're going to do it, aren't we? We're going to get married!" He laughed in disbelief, a weight sliding off his shoulders. If the stone said it, it had to be true. That's how things worked at Two Willows.

Wye was shaking her head. "It's just a coincidence it was a wedding announcement. It has to be. Or you did this! Did you plan this whole thing?"

"You're the one who dragged me out to the maze," he pointed out.

"You might have predicted I would."

"I'm not Alice." Emerson got a hold of himself. He had known Wye was the one for him the day they met, but Wye still had to catch up. The way she was looking at him now made him hope that was possible. Just like he'd thought, she wasn't immune to the mystery of the stone. "I had no idea that any of this would happen before tonight. The General told me to marry you twenty minutes ago, and I don't believe in magic or standing stones, either, but think about it. Every one of the men the General sent to marry Cass and her sisters has had something weird happen to him at Two Willows. Why should we be any different?"

"Because we don't belong here."

Her words punctured his enthusiasm, and he struggled to hold on to the confidence he'd felt moments ago. She was right; neither of them were born to this property. What right did they have to the stone's approval or anything else? "The General is going to give me a share in the ranch, just like the other men," he told her. "Marry me, and you'll belong here, too—forever."

"Forever?" she repeated. "You're going to own part of the ranch?" Her brow furrowed, and she glanced back at the stone, looming large over them.

Emerson realized that was the key to all of this. She wanted to belong at Two Willows as much as he did. More, maybe. She'd been living here for weeks and didn't seem in a hurry to leave, after all. She hadn't mentioned her parents in his hearing, although he had heard her mention her brother. Emerson thought he lived in town.

Did she yearn to belong somewhere the way he did? Was she searching for a family and a place to call home?

More to the point, could she ever love a man like him? He was younger than the other men at Two Willows. Not exactly poor, but a long way from wealthy. He'd been as good as abandoned by his family. Didn't have a large circle of friends. The General was the only one who'd seen something worthwhile in him. Could Wye come to see it, too?

He needed to find out.

Emerson stepped forward, cupped Wye's chin in his hands, bent down—and kissed her.

WYOMING HAD HELD her own until Emerson mentioned he'd inherit part of Two Willows. Then all practical thought escaped her head and an emotion she didn't want to name swept right through her.

Envy. Pure and unadulterated.

Ever since she'd met Cass, Wyoming had been entranced with Two Willows. She knew it was a sin to covet your friend's property, but she'd coveted everything about the ranch—its intangible assets as well as the tangible ones.

The property itself was wonderful, and she'd often enjoyed riding with Cass on the trails that looped through and around it. The rambling old house was beautiful. So were the extensive kitchen gardens, the maze, the carriage house and everything else.

Then there was the friendship shared between Cass and her sisters. Wye envied that more than anything else. Whether they were squabbling or laughing, they were part of something larger than themselves: family with a capital F.

Wye longed to be part of something like that. Wanted sisters. A beautiful home. A property. Somewhere to plant roots.

She wanted a husband, too, despite everything she'd been through. A partner in life—an equal partner—the way Cass had Brian. She'd thought, perhaps, she had found such a man in Will, but she'd been utterly mistaken, and now she didn't know how to trust her judgment.

At any rate, it would be completely inappropriate to try to horn in on her friend's life no matter who she married. She wasn't a Reed and never would be, despite the General's rash promises to Emerson. What would Cass think if the General announced he intended to make Emerson an heir? How would she feel if she thought Wye said yes to Emerson to gain a part of what wasn't rightfully hers?

Emerson was wrong to offer it to her, and she was wrong to even think of accepting.

Disappointment pierced her, all the more ridiculous because she'd never intended to marry anyway. Why on earth would she when she knew from experience how men showed their true colors the minute the ceremony was over? Her mother had escaped from all that but hadn't seen fit to rescue her, too. Her father had disowned her the minute she outlived her usefulness to him. Her brother saw her as little more than a babysitter and errand girl. And Will—Will had used her as cover in his quest to kill her friends.

Why should Emerson be any different?

She was about to tell him exactly what she thought of his proposal when he cupped her chin and kissed her, surprising her all over again. Sweet longing flooded through her as he moved his mouth over hers with a confidence that took her breath away, as if he'd known her forever—knew just how to twist her feelings into knots and turn on the emotions she'd tried so hard to turn off. She wanted those emotions to stay buried—it was the only way to keep herself safe and sane.

But somehow Wye found her fingers twisting in the fabric of Emerson's shirt as he pulled her closer into his embrace. He was warm in the frigid night, his arms strong around her. His kiss sent shivers of desire clear down to her toes. Under her hands, the muscles of his chest flexed as he tightened his embrace. Wye sighed, and he pulled back, examining her face as if searching for clues for how to win her.

"Let's get you back inside," he said softly. "It's cold out here." He took her hand as if it was the most natural thing in the world, turned on the light on his phone and led the way.

Wyoming wasn't sure if she was ready for the noise and crowds inside the house, but staying out here with Emerson was out of the question. He'd already turned her head and dissolved all the arguments she'd meant to make to stop him from pursuing her.

Besides, she was freezing.

Still, heading inside, facing Alice and Jack's happiness, felt like more than she could bear. Emerson was offering her everything she wanted, and she had to refuse it.

"Wyoming." Emerson's voice cut through her thoughts. "I know you're having a hard time taking this in. I should have explained it all better. Let you know a long time ago how I felt."

"Why?" she asked suddenly.

Emerson stopped, midway down one of the maze's passages. "Why do I want to marry you?"

Wye quailed at the thought of such an intimate conversation so hard on the heels of the stone's answer to her question and shook her head. "Why would you believe the Reeds would want us here? Why would the General give you part of the ranch?"

"Give *us* part of it," Emerson corrected her. "It's simple. The General wants Cass to be happy, and that requires you to stay put, which requires me to marry you." He smiled. "Which would make me happy, too."

"Would that make you happy?" she asked tentatively. "Marrying me on July Fourth?" She wasn't sure why she was asking. She'd already told him no.

Hadn't she?

Regardless, she found she wanted to know the answer.

"The stone seems to think we're getting married on New Year's," he reminded her, but his smile said he thought he was gaining ground.

"Not this New Year's! That's for sure."

His smile grew, and he pulled her close again. "Then July Fourth it is."

ADRENALINE SURGED THROUGH Emerson the moment he woke the following morning. Last night he'd taken a strong first step in his pursuit of Wyoming's hand in marriage, and he was eager to see her again and continue the campaign. He dressed quickly and headed downstairs to breakfast, going easy on the stairs—the last thing he needed was for his ankle to give way and to take a header down them—but Cass was the only one in the kitchen when he got there. Dirty dishes from the previous evening stood in stacks around the room, and he knew the refrigerator was stuffed with leftovers. Cass had sent food home with almost everyone who'd attended the wedding, but there was still more.

"Where's Wyoming?"

"Good morning to you, too," Cass said with a smile. "She had to run into town. Her brother needed her. Some kind of family problem."

Emerson remembered what Wyoming had said the night before—how men always needed looking after. Had she been talking from personal experience?

"What's her brother like?" He set about making the General's coffee. Cass raised a brow but didn't say anything. When he was done and had cleaned the pot, she'd make another batch—her way—for everyone else to drink at breakfast.

"Ward?" Cass shrugged. "He's kind of high mainte-nance, if you ask me. He got married a couple of years ago to a real piece of work. Mindy is only twenty-three, and I think she thought marriage was going to be more fun and games than it turned out to be—especially with Ward. He works at the radio station, drumming up advertising. Mindy has been staying home with their baby ever since Elise was born. I get the feeling from Wyoming Mindy is a bit of a shopaholic. Anyway, whenever she and Ward need a babysitter, they call Wye."

"Is she babysitting today?"

If Cass thought his interest in her friend was

strange, she didn't say so. Instead she grew serious. "Wyoming didn't spell it out, but from what I heard, it sounded like Mindy didn't come home last night." Cass shook her head. "She did this once before, and it really freaked out Ward. Rightly so," she added. "He's got work today, and Mindy left him high and dry with no one to take care of the baby. I don't know what she's thinking. I'm not sure that marriage is going to last."

"Sounds rough," Emerson said before he took the General his coffee. He came right back, since the General liked to start his morning in peace and quiet. He dumped out the coffee grounds, quickly washed the pot and filter, set them in the drying rack and accepted the plate Cass offered, heaped with bacon, eggs and toast. "You don't have to cook for me, you know." He took a bite of a piece of bacon as he sat down at the table. Cass made quick work of drying the coffeepot and getting a new batch started.

"I know." Cass smiled at him. "But I'd cook breakfast for an army if it meant I didn't have to muck out horse stalls." Her smile broadened. "Are you and the General off to Billings today?"

"Not today," Emerson said. "I'll see if the General needs any help this morning, but if you all don't mind, after that I'd like to take a ride." He'd hoped to ask Wyoming to come along, but that would have to wait for another time. Meanwhile, he couldn't help wanting to see the lay of the land, now that there was a chance some of it might belong to him someday. He wanted to see how it felt in the saddle, too. On the one hand, up on a horse he wasn't putting weight on his ankle. On the other hand, on past excursions, holding his feet in the stirrups had made his ankle ache after a while. He hoped today would be different.

"We don't mind at all," Cass said. "Just ask one of the guys if you need somebody to point you in the right direction. Take any horse except Atlas. Lena isn't one for sharing."

Emerson had gathered that much during his time here, but he didn't mind. He liked the frank way Lena talked and behaved. You always knew where you stood with her.

He wished he could read Wyoming as well.

After breakfast he spoke to the General and helped him with one or two work details before heading out to the stables. The General had let him know the night before that he wanted some time to himself today. He was going through some old paperwork he'd found in his office and didn't want to be disturbed.

"Make yourself scarce," he'd said when Emerson asked if he was sure he could spare him.

On his way to the stable, he met up with Brian. "Take Button," Brian said. "He's steady, and he could use the exercise."

Fifteen minutes later, Emerson rode south, his heart rising as the vista spread out before him. Keeping the far-off mountains in front of him, he went cross country for a while before picking up a trail and winding into the higher elevations of the ranch. For the next several hours he let the spare beauty of the place soak in, appreciating its size. Over the last couple of weeks, he'd spent most of his time close to home, closeted with the General, helping him with day-to-day tasks and trying to get him to do his physical therapy exercises. The General's health was improving, and he could make his way around the house without much help, but he'd be doing a lot better if he'd buckle down to those exercises.

When his stomach began to growl, Emerson turned, lunch on his mind, but on the way back he stopped at the Park, a flat stretch of ground about a quarter mile from the barns and outbuildings where a half-dozen trailers stood. Until recently they had housed hired hands, but Cass and her sisters had driven out those men months ago when they discovered they were trying to use the property as a distribution center for drugs.

Now the trailers sat empty, which was a shame. While some of them were older, most looked in good repair and should be put to use, to his way of thinking. They each sat a little distance apart, bushes and small trees between them adding to the sense of separation.

Emerson considered them from Button's back, flexing his foot to lessen the ache in his ankle, which had increased steadily during the last ten minutes. If he stayed, could he make his home in one of these? He could fix it up. Change out the tacky siding for something more attractive. Redo the interior.

Would the General appreciate his get up and go if he mentioned the idea? Or would he think he was already treating the place like his own?

Only one way to find out, he decided, and picked up his pace. The General knew him better than anyone else—he'd understand where Emerson was coming from.

Back at the house, he found everyone gathered for lunch. Still energized by his morning in the saddle, even if his limp was more pronounced after his ride, Emerson washed his hands and slid into the only empty seat at the table, catching a sharp look from the General.

"Sorry I'm late," he said. The General had a thing about punctuality, and he hadn't relaxed many of his military habits since he'd come home. Emerson looked around the table, noting that Wyoming still wasn't present.

"I don't think Wyoming will be back until dinnertime at least," Cass said, catching his eye.

"Have you set the date yet?" the General asked.

"What date?" Jo asked, swiping mayonnaise onto two pieces of bread before passing the jar to Hunter.

"His wedding date," the General told her. "I told him to fix things up with that little friend of yours, Cass, so she'll stay close. Figured you'd like that. Offered Emerson a share in the ranch if he marries her."

Cass's mouth dropped open in surprise, and Emerson saw the looks exchanged around the table.

Hell, the General obviously hadn't explained his intentions to any of them before offering Emerson part of the ranch. Would they think he'd begged for it?

"I… didn't know you'd done that," Cass said to the General.

Lena opened her mouth as if to say something, shut it again and huffed out a sigh. "Would've been nice to be asked if we want to share the ranch, at least."

"This is still my spread," the General said. "If I want to hand out a hundred shares in it, I can."

Emerson's gut tightened. The General was going about this all wrong, riling up the very people he should be soothing. "I don't need the handout," he hurried to say. "I'll marry Wyoming regardless and make a home for her somewhere else."

"No, you won't!" the General snapped. "You'll live here, or you won't marry her at all!"

The man was building into one of his towering rages. It was rare he really lost his temper, but when he did, heads rolled. Emerson knew he needed to stop this—now.

"Let's have our lunch," Emerson said. "We're all hungry, and the dinner table isn't the place to discuss business matters—or personal ones."

Sadie snorted. "That doesn't leave much for us to talk about."

"Emerson is right," Cass said. "Let's discuss this another time. We like having you here," she added, reaching across the table to touch Emerson's hand. "It's just we're still working out the logistics for how *we* can all live here, work together and share the ranch."

"If we're basing our futures on this ranch, we need some say in what happens here." Lena didn't seem ready to give up the argument.

"Seems fair to me." Emerson tried once more to

diffuse the situation.

"Seems like a load of hogwash to me," the General said. "Emerson is a good man, and he's served by my side through thick and thin. He's injured because of me. Lost his career in the Army because I was targeted. I'll give him the whole damn ranch if I want to." He slammed his hand on the table hard enough to make the silverware bounce.

"General," Emerson began.

"Don't General me." The man stood up, wavered a moment, grabbed the back of his chair to steady himself and found his cane. "I've had enough of this insubordination." He hobbled out of the kitchen. "Bring me my lunch," he hollered over his shoulder.

Emerson hurried to do just that, but as soon as he settled the General in his office with his sandwich, he returned to the kitchen table, interrupting the discussion that had broken out in his absence. "I didn't ask for a share, and I would never take it if I felt I wasn't wanted," he announced to the room at large. He needed them to know this wasn't his doing.

"Look, that's not it," Jack told him. "We'd be glad to have you."

"We need to sort things out with the General, though," Cass said. "And if Wyoming marries you, it has to be because she wants to, not because I want her to stay here."

"Oh, for heaven's sake, you know darn well if the General has sent her a husband, it's pointless to fight against it," Sadie joked, taking a bite of her sandwich.

"The lass is right," Connor said in his overdone Irish accent. "Orders are orders."

Logan chuckled. Alice smiled. Emerson relaxed a little, but he wished the General had discussed his plans with his daughters and their husbands rather than throwing it in their faces as a done deal. Didn't he realize they'd resent that?

"When do you figure you'll marry Wyoming?" Brian adopted a lighthearted manner, but Emerson didn't think it represented his true state of mind.

"July Fourth. Or New Year's Eve. That's when the standing stone said we'd get hitched." Emerson snagged a couple of pieces of bread from a platter in the middle of the table, bracing for the attack he knew would come. He reached for the mayonnaise and mustard next, and Sadie handed him another platter stacked with leftover turkey, even as she exchanged surprised looks with her sisters.

"The stone said you'd get married?" Cass asked slowly. "Wyoming never mentioned anything about that."

"She was probably waiting to see if I changed my mind overnight." He bit back a smile at Cass's instant outrage. Brian caught his eye and shook his head, but a smile tugged at the corners of his mouth. He must not be too pissed off about sharing the ranch, then, if he could still summon a sense of humor, Emerson thought.

"If you changed *your* mind?" Cass asked. "Somehow I doubt that's going to be the problem."

"You're right. I won't change my mind, but we've

still got plenty of other problems to solve. Wyoming and I do need a place to live when we marry. Like I said to the General, if we don't live here, I'll find another home, so you don't need to worry about that. I'm not chasing her to get a piece of your ranch. That's not who I am." He would miss Two Willows if he had to leave it, though. Miss all of this, too—the constant bustle of a large family. The friendly kidding around and bickering.

"If you did stay, where would you settle?" Jo asked curiously. "I suppose you could build a house in the springtime, like Hunter and I are." She and Hunter currently lived in a temporary tiny house they'd built together, but they planned to build a bigger one when the weather warmed up.

"I had an idea about that," Emerson admitted. "All those trailers at the Park are sitting empty. I could renovate one of those. Be out of everyone's way."

Cass's frown deepened. "Wyoming won't want to live in a trailer."

"Wyoming is pretty practical," Lena pointed out. "She might not mind as much as you think. If they have to share the ranch with us, it would be a workable solution."

"I would fix it up," Emerson assured them. "I could switch out the siding, even. Make it look like a little cabin rather than a trailer. I don't like seeing things go to waste. I could fix up the rest of them, too. Help rent them out, if no one objected. The rental income would be my contribution to the family income, although I'd do what I could to help out in other ways, too."

No one told him to get lost, but no one hurried to assure him they'd like to share Two Willows with him and Wyoming—not even Cass.

Emerson sat down and ate his sandwich in silence.

It would be hell living here if the others didn't want him.

WHEN SIX O'CLOCK passed and there was still no sign of Ward, Wyoming lost what little remained of her patience. He'd promised he'd be back by four thirty, and she'd told Cass she'd be home in time to help with dinner. It was driving her crazy the Reeds wouldn't accept any rent money from her. She needed to pay her way with chores, at the very least, or she'd feel like she was abusing Cass's friendship.

Worry about Mindy ate at her, too, although she didn't want to admit it. At first, she'd assumed her sister-in-law had run off to have a little fun, but she still hadn't returned, and Wye was afraid something had happened to her on the road yesterday. What if her car had broken down and she'd taken a ride from a stranger who turned out to be dangerous? What if she'd been in an accident? Wyoming kept telling herself someone would have called them if that was the case, but what other explanation was there for her prolonged absence?

When Ward called her this morning to ask her to babysit, she'd been happy to spend the day with Elise, but she didn't understand why he hadn't taken the day off to search for his wife—or at least the afternoon. He'd claimed he couldn't afford it. "If she's off gallivanting around, she can find her own way home," was all he'd said before he left this morning, walking to work since Mindy still had the car.

Wyoming had spent the day putting her brother's house in order. There had been a sink full of dirty dishes in the kitchen. Four or five loads of laundry to do and no clean rompers for the baby. While Elise was napping, she mopped the kitchen floor and swept all the hardwood floors. Mindy still didn't come home.

With nothing in the cupboard to make for dinner, Wyoming bundled Elise in her car seat, drove to the grocery store and stocked up on all the basics that were lacking back at Ward's house. Upon her return, she whipped up a stir-fry.

That was two hours ago. By the time Ward arrived home at half past six, Wyoming was furious.

She met him at the front door, Elise in her arms. "Your dinner is in the refrigerator. Just heat it up in the microwave. Elise is fed. I've got to go; I'm late." She tried to hand him the baby, but Ward held up his hands to fend her off.

"Are you serious? I just got home. Can't you give me one minute to relax before you shove that baby in my arms?"

Wyoming reared back. "You've got to be the one who's kidding! I've been on my feet since I got here. I cleaned your whole house. I shopped, watched your daughter and made your dinner. And now I'm late for the dinner Cass made for me. By the way, you owe me $130 for groceries."

"I don't have that kind of cash on me. This week is going to be tight. I had to rent a car today." Ward reluctantly took Elise when Wyoming held her out again and sighed. "Get here at seven thirty tomorrow morning, so I can be to work on time."

Wyoming stared at him. "Get here at seven thirty?" she parroted. "Don't you mean, 'Please, Wye, could you come babysit my daughter at seven thirty tomorrow morning? I'll love you forever if you do.'"

"Oh, come off it. It's not like you have anything better to do. You don't have a job or anything, right? You got canned."

"So you think I'm at your beck and call?" His accusation stung. Yes, she'd been laid off, and yes, she was having trouble finding a new job. That didn't mean he had to be rude to her. Nor did it mean she was responsible for his child.

"My wife is gone, Wye. Disappeared. I can't believe you're acting this way."

Wyoming gave up. She supposed she could do one more day, but she hoped Mindy decided to come home soon. She had a feeling Ward couldn't do this on his own—and as much as she loved spending time with her niece, she really did need to find a paying job. "Are you going to be okay tonight?" she asked despite her better judgment.

"You think I can't handle my own kid?"

"That's not what I meant and you know it. You look tired. Did you talk to Cab today?" The sheriff should be able to track a runaway wife.

"He said she has to be gone forty-eight hours before they can do anything," Ward said. "But he'll keep an eye out. Nothing like the whole town knowing your business," he added tiredly.

Wyoming softened. She knew her brother loved his wife, and he had to be worried about her. "I'm sorry this is happening. I'll be here tomorrow at seven thirty."

"Thanks," he said grudgingly. "See you tomorrow."

On her drive to Two Willows, Wyoming tried to shake off the bad feeling that had settled in her gut. Her confrontation with Ward reminded her of living with her father—his foul moods and the way he believed that no one suffered quite as much as he did. Back then she'd had no escape. She had taken afterschool jobs in order to save enough money so she could move out as soon as possible, but it was years before she accumulated enough to create the kind of savings that would keep her from ever having to return home. Besides, no one would rent an apartment to her until she was seventeen. Even then it had taken some fast talking to persuade a landlord to take her on.

Now somebody else's drama and bad choices were sucking her in again. Neither her father nor Ward ever seemed to grasp the connection between their actions and the consequences.

She would never marry a man like that, she promised herself. Never marry at all.

Her thoughts turned to Emerson. He'd been on her mind all day—except for the last two hours when her anger at Ward's thoughtlessness had overpowered everything else. Ward got off work at four. He hadn't brought home any groceries—she'd done the shopping. She knew he'd stopped in to see Cab on the way to work—so what had he been doing since he left the radio station, besides renting a car?

Had he driven around town looking for Mindy? Or had he gone to a bar? She hadn't smelled alcohol on his breath. Who knew what he'd done to fritter away the time?

Would Emerson leave a woman hanging like that?

She didn't think so—but men often sweet talked until they got what they wanted, then they showed their true natures.

She should have refused Emerson when he brought up marriage. Should have told him in no uncertain terms she wouldn't have him—even if the standing stone decreed she'd marry him on New Year's Eve. She wasn't a Reed. She wasn't bound by the same ties to Two Willows that they were. Even though the General was home, she noticed Cass and her sisters still unconsciously made sure one of them was always on the ranch, the way they and their mother before them had when the General was away serving his country. She came and went without ever giving it a thought.

And she wasn't going to marry anyone now that Ward had reminded her the way men acted when they had the upper hand.

As soon as she got back to Two Willows, she'd seek out Emerson and tell him to back off.

An image of him leaning against the doorjamb last

night filled her mind, and Wye shook her head to try to dislodge it. Why hadn't Emerson simply asked her out? They could have had a good time for as long as it lasted rather than saddling their relationship with the weight of forever. How much easier it was to simply divide your things, load up a car and drive off if love didn't last. For her and for any man she chose to spend time with.

Not that she could see Emerson packing up and driving off when times got tough. She had to admit he exuded staying power. There was something about him that said he'd honor any commitment he made.

It was kind of hot.

Wyoming let out a gusty sigh, disappointed with herself. Enough of that, she thought.

As soon as she got home, she would tell him no.

Chapter 3

"THE GENERAL'S PHONE," Emerson said, taking the call late that afternoon when the General's cell phone piped a military tune.

"Myers? Is that you? Buck Mayflower here," a man's voice said on the other end. "You're the person I'm looking for, actually."

"What's up?" Buck was one of the reservists he and the General were training, a hearty, friendly young man who was also a volunteer fireman and worked as a cook for his day job.

"Wanted to know if you'd heard about any apartments in Chance Creek? I'm moving in with my girlfriend, and neither of our places is big enough. She's starting work at the bank there, anyway, and I don't want her commuting from Billings during the winter. I know you've settled there with the General, and I thought you might have the inside track on a situation."

Emerson thought about it. "I haven't heard about any apartments," he said slowly, making sure the General wasn't paying attention. He turned his back and lowered his voice. "But I might have a line on a trailer.

It'll need some fixing up, though. Let me get some more information and get back to you." He hadn't discussed his ideas about the trailers with the General yet. The General had been surly since he'd left the kitchen table, and he had been muttering over paperwork ever since.

Emerson wanted to cut this conversation short until he'd had it out with the General—and the General had had it out with everyone else.

"A trailer? Does it come with any land?" Buck asked.

Emerson looked over his shoulder and caught the General watching him. "Possibly," he said tersely into the phone. "Don't want to get your hopes up, though. It's far from a done deal."

"Thanks, man. I'll wait for your call." Buck's excited tone said Emerson's warning hadn't sunk in.

Emerson hung up.

"Who was that?" the General demanded.

"Buck Mayflower. He's looking for a place to stay." Emerson hesitated but decided he might as well push forward. "I mentioned we've got several trailers sitting empty down at the Park. I could fix up one to rent him. Help bring in a little money—if I'm staying."

"Of course you're staying. We've been over that."

Emerson shrugged. "You need to work out a few things with your daughters before that's a done deal, sir."

"I told them and I'm telling you, I call the shots around here. Marry Wye, and you've got yourself a slice of the ranch."

"Pardon my frankness, sir, but that's not going to work. You can't shove Wye and me down your daughters' throats and expect one big happy family—unless you're looking to start trouble. Is that it? Are you bored?"

The General's eyebrows shot up, but just as Emerson had hoped, his blunt assessment of the situation cut through the man's ire. "Hell, yeah, I'm bored. But I'm not starting any feuds because of it. My daughters know what you've done for me. So do their husbands. How can they object to my giving you a share of my ranch?"

"Amelia's ranch," Emerson corrected him. "I know what you mean," he added as the General moved to protest. "Amelia's property is yours, of course, but your daughters feel a strong connection to their mother here. Giving her land away is like giving a piece of her to a stranger."

"Wyoming isn't a stranger."

"No, she's not, but they hardly know me, and you've got to learn to suggest things rather than order people around. I can't stay here if I'm not wanted, and I'm sure Wye feels the same way."

The General leaned back in his chair and studied him.

"I suppose you're right, son," he finally said. "Rankles a man to ask his children their opinion, though. What if they don't agree with you?"

"Then I guess you have to try and win them over." Emerson hesitated, knowing what he needed to say might ruffle the General's feathers but knowing he had to say it anyway. "I appreciate the sentiment when you call me son, sir, but I don't think your daughters do. I wonder if you should stop."

The General considered this, peering at Emerson over the rims of the reading glasses he wore when his office door was closed. "I guess all those years my girls were fighting me, I started to think of you as the one child I hadn't lost," he said slowly. "My girls should understand that."

"I don't think they do." Emerson was firm. "You've been more of a father to me than my own father ever got to be, or my uncle cared to be, and I'll always be grateful for that. But I need to hang in the background for a while. Not steal your own children's thunder. It's the only way my living here can possibly work. Out of sight, out of mind, right? If I move down to the Park, your daughters might stop thinking of me as a threat."

"They need to understand you're going to be just as much a part of this ranch as everyone else. You and Wyoming. That's my decision."

"At least give it time," Emerson argued. "Let me prove I can be an asset rather than a liability to the operation."

"I'll parent as I see fit," the General said, ending the discussion. "Go get me a bowl of ice cream."

"Yes, sir." Emerson knew better than to keep arguing when the General got stubborn. He'd try again tomorrow.

He got to the kitchen in time to see Cass answer her phone. "Hey, Wye, are you on your way? I've been holding dinner for you." She paused to listen. "It's no trouble. I figured you'd be here soon."

"Is that Wye?"

Cass nodded and held up a finger. "No, I think I've got everything I need. I'm going shopping tomorrow anyway."

"Can I talk to her?"

Cass was listening to something Wye said. "Emerson wants to talk to you." She was quiet a moment. "Oh. Okay. I'll tell him."

"Tell me what?" He held out his hand for the phone, but Cass had already ended the call.

"She's on her way, and she doesn't want to talk while she's driving. She'll be here in a few minutes. You can wait, can't you?"

"Sure." But wouldn't a woman want to talk to a man if she was seriously thinking of marrying him?

Emerson's spirits sank.

"LONG DAY, HUH?" Emerson asked, startling Wye. She'd just parked and gotten out of her car, not noticing that he was standing at the base of the back steps. He was half-shadowed in darkness, and she wondered if he'd done that on purpose. Was he afraid she'd pull right back out if she spotted him there?

"It was a long day," she agreed. "My sister-in-law still hasn't come home, and my brother is pretty worried."

"Has she ever taken off like this before?" Emerson took the cloth bag she'd brought with her to her brother's house. It had an extra sweater and a novel in it and was easy enough to carry, but she appreciated his solicitude. Especially when he took a step and she saw him wince. She'd noticed that his ankle still bothered him sometimes even if he tried hard not to show it. She knew better than to mention it, though.

"Once or twice she's stayed out with friends, but nothing like this. Ward has called everyone he can think of, and no one saw her last night."

"Do you think she ran away?"

"God, I hope not." Wye hadn't let her thoughts stray that way. "What kind of a woman leaves her child behind—" She broke off and shook her head. "She wouldn't be the first woman who did," she said bitterly. "It's still hard to believe her capable of it."

"I hope she turns up soon."

"I keep wondering if she's been kidnapped—or worse. Half the time I'm thinking awful things about her, and the other half I'm scared stiff."

"Your brother called the sheriff?" When she nodded, he went on, "Cab Johnson seems like a capable guy."

"He is. I trust him to do everything he can. I've got to go back tomorrow and watch Elise again—unless Mindy turns up overnight."

Emerson hesitated, one foot on the bottom step. "You're a good sister. I hope your brother knows that."

Wyoming stood with him, noticing the glittering stars above them for the first time. It was a beautiful night despite all the trouble in the world. "I think he does on some level, but he's not one for showing it."

"That's what you said yesterday. Sounds to me like he takes advantage of you."

What did Emerson know about her family? "I'm happy to help in a situation like this," she said tightly. "He's my brother—family sticks together, right?" At least, that's what everyone said. She certainly wouldn't know.

Emerson shrugged. "I suppose so."

Wyoming blew out a breath. The strain of the day had left her with little energy. "Look, I'm tired and hungry. I'd like to go inside." He didn't shift to let her past, and she had a feeling he would bring up the standing stone and the possibility of marriage again. That was the last thing she wanted to discuss right now. "It's just... my brother didn't even pay me back for the groceries. He acted like I should be grateful he let me cook for him. He's always been like this." Wyoming stopped herself before her rant escalated and she ended up ticking off her father's offenses, too. "Sorry. Like I said, it's been a long day."

"And I'm keeping you standing out in the cold. Come on. I'll take your things upstairs." He reached for her purse. "You go find Cass. She'll get you sorted out."

"Thanks." Now she felt like an ass for snapping at him. "You're a good guy, Emerson."

"I don't know about that. If I was a good guy, I wouldn't do this." He bent down and brushed a kiss over her cheek, then captured her mouth with his. She knew she should push him away, but the spark that lit between them had her leaning in for more, instead. Up close, she could smell the soap he used, something masculine and fresh. His flannel shirt was soft to the touch, his muscles hard underneath. Kissing him felt good.

Emerson pulled back. "Dinner first, then we'll put your feet up. Find something good to watch on TV."

Before she could protest, Wye found herself inside Cass's warm kitchen, a beer in her hand, her butt in a chair and the room filling with all Cass's sisters and their husbands as they came to greet her and hear about Mindy. Her tension melted away among their questions and chatter. Emerson took a seat next to her a few minutes later, having stowed her things in her room. He leaned in close.

"Tell your brother tomorrow he can't keep commandeering you forever. You've got people here who need you, too."

"People?" Wye leaned back so Cass could set down a plate of food in front of her.

"Me. Look—whatever happens between us, I'm in your life now, and it makes a difference to me if you come home or not. If you're happy or not. You tell your brother you have people who need you here—or I will." He took her hand. "We need to talk. When you aren't so tired. Things have gotten a little complicated."

Did he mean because of Mindy's disappearance and the time she was spending at Ward's—or something else altogether? Had he changed his mind and decided he didn't want to marry her after all?

Why did the thought make her wince? Hadn't she promised herself she'd break things off with him?

"No more talking tonight—please?" she asked. "I've had about as much as I can take today." She wasn't sure if she was putting him off to avoid telling him they were through—or because she was afraid he might end the relationship himself.

She didn't want to examine her motivations, either.

"Okay," Emerson agreed. "I can wait."

THE NEXT DAY passed much like the previous one had. Emerson busied himself helping the General and staying out of everyone else's way. The General continued to fuss about the insubordination of his daughters and their husbands and refused to do any of his physical therapy exercises, even when Emerson pointedly did his own in full view of him. Everyone else was perfectly polite to his face, but he couldn't help wondering what they were saying behind his back. Late that afternoon, he found himself searching online for apartments to rent in Billings—and looking for a full-time job to take on in addition to his reserve work.

He kept hoping the General would talk to Cass, Brian and the others and that together they'd decide about letting him—and Wye—stay, but no one seemed in a hurry to debate the topic.

Which left him hanging in an unpleasant way.

Wyoming missed dinner again, an awkward meal at which the General said little and everyone else said too much to try and fill in the gaps. When she did arrive later in the evening, she was on her phone. Emerson caught her heading in the kitchen door. Wye lifted a finger to tell him she'd be off in a minute.

"That's good news," she said. "Where is she?" She listened a beat. "Idaho? Is she coming back?" She listened some more, the furrow between her eyebrows deepening along with her frown. "Okay. See you tomorrow."

"What was that about?" he asked.

"Mindy has been spotted in Idaho," Wye said tiredly, shedding her coat, purse and carryall. Emerson helped her put things away. "She sped through a light, and an automatic camera took her photo. The local police passed it on to the Chance Creek sheriff's department. Cab called Ward just now, and he called me."

"She's coming home?"

Wye shook her head. "No one even knows where she is now. Seems she was just passing through Boise. There was no one else in the car," she added. "Not that they could see, anyway."

Emerson processed that. "So she's on her own."

"At least she hasn't been kidnapped—and she's still alive—although I'm not sure that's going to make Ward feel any better."

"Why were you so late?"

"Ward kept me waiting again."

"Was he out looking for Mindy?"

She shook her head. "I think he was drinking. I thought so yesterday, too, but today I could smell it on his breath. He said he had only one beer, but I stayed to make sure he ate a meal and drank a few cups of coffee before I headed out. He was completely lucid the whole time, and I'm probably making a mountain out of a molehill, but I had to be sure he was sober enough to care for Elise. I wish I'd brought her home with me."

"You want me to go back there with you and get her?"

She scanned his face. "You'd do that?"

"Of course."

She thought about it. "No, like I said, Ward was fine when I left."

"How about when you talked to him on the phone just now?"

"He was definitely down after that call from Cab. He said he planned to go to bed early, so hopefully he'll get some sleep, and I'll be there first thing in the morning."

"If Mindy doesn't come home, how long are you going to keep watching Elise?" Emerson asked carefully. He respected Wye for how she was stepping in to help, but Ward didn't seem the least bit grateful for what she was doing—nor did he show the least amount of respect for her time. Wye deserved better.

She pocketed her phone. "I don't know," she said. "Until he figures something out, I guess. I'm sure she'll come back—sooner or later."

And Emerson was just as sure Wye would keep filling in for her sister-in-law, no questions asked, until then.

Which made her a good person, he reminded himself.

"Why does it bother you so much that I'm spending time with my niece?" she asked him.

Hell, was that what she thought? "I'm not bothered by that at all. I'm bothered by Ward taking advantage of you." He struggled to explain. "Reminds me of someone I used to know. It's not important." He waved it off, but the truth was Ward's behavior bothered him a lot. It reminded him of the way he'd worshipped his older cousins growing up at his aunt and uncle's house. The way he'd rushed to help with their chores and to fetch and carry things for them because he wanted to tag along on their adventures. The way he'd covered for them so they wouldn't get in trouble with their parents.

The way they'd cut ties the minute his uncle kicked him out. One day he was part of a big family. The next he was on his own.

"Cab Johnson told Ward he can't treat the case as if there was foul play. 'Looks like she drove off on her own accord,' is how he put it. Ward's furious." She made a face. "He demanded to know if Cab thought Mindy ran away from him."

"What did Cab say?"

"'Wouldn't be the first time it happened.' Kind of cold, don't you think?"

"Seems about right to me." If Ward treated Mindy the way he treated Wye, who could blame her for leaving? Although it said something that she'd left Elise behind.

"What if Mindy is clinically depressed? It seems like someone should track her down and make sure she's okay," Wye pressed.

"I guess they have rules to follow. A person isn't a criminal just because they leave home."

Wyoming played with her keys. "What if Ward doesn't go to bed? What if he drinks more and doesn't wake up when Elise cries?"

"Give me the word, and we'll drive right back there. Is there any chance he could get violent?"

"Ward? With Elise—or me?" Wyoming asked.

"Either of you."

She found her purse and deposited the keys into it firmly. "No, that's not his style at all, and he loves Elise. Ward's a little full of himself, and he's definitely having a pity party right now, but he's not a bad guy. I could just kill Mindy; the least she could do is call and let everybody know she's okay." She set her purse on a nearby chair. "I don't know about you, but I need a cup of cocoa. Want some?"

"Sure. Maybe Mindy is afraid that if she calls, someone will persuade her to come back."

Wye had just opened the refrigerator and was reaching for the milk, but she looked over her shoulder at that.

"Not because Ward is a bad guy or there's anything wrong with her life here in Chance Creek. Just because she's obviously overwhelmed," he hurried to explain.

"Or lazy," Wyoming said. She shut the door with a thump. "Sorry, now I'm the one being harsh." She poured two cups full of milk into a pot and turned on the burner. "When things got hard for my family, I didn't have the option of running away and weaseling out of all the work I needed to do."

"You're like me," Emerson told her. "We couldn't run off knowing we were hurting someone at home. Maybe that's because we know how it feels to be on the receiving end."

Wyoming nodded. "I guess you're right." But she didn't explain her answer. Emerson wished he knew more about her past, but he'd wait for another time to ask.

The following morning Emerson watched her head out, squashing the urge to kiss her again, knowing the time wasn't right.

"I'll let Cass know when I'm going to be home today," Wye told him.

"How about you call and let *me* know." Emerson touched her hand. "I like to hear your voice," he added.

Wyoming smiled a little. "I guess your voice isn't so bad either," she said. "See you later."

"See you."

He realized he still hadn't told her about what'd happened at dinner the other night. Had Cass mentioned the argument to her? Somehow Emerson doubted it, and the knowledge of a looming showdown made him feel the need for some fresh air. He decided to walk out to the Park again this morning and make some notes on what needed to be done. He could always leave them behind for someone else to take on if he ended up moving somewhere else.

He made sure the General was up, dressed, fed his breakfast and settled at his desk before he left. Once more Emerson did his PT exercises ostentatiously in the General's presence. Once more the General balked at doing his own. "Be back in an hour," Emerson said to him when it was obvious nothing would change the man's mind.

The General only grunted.

"Taking a walk," he told Cass when he passed her in the kitchen.

"Hold up," she called as he went to put on his coat and boots. "Last night the General asked me to find these and give them to you." She held out a ring of keys. "They're for all the trailers. He figured you'd want to see inside them at some point." When Emerson took them from her, she added, "We're happy to have you and Wye here if that's the way it works out, you know."

"You all discussed this with the General?" He was surprised; when had they had the time?

"No, not exactly," she said.

"He ordered you to give me these."

"Don't take it like that. It'll work out in the end, you'll see. Our argument is with the General, not you, and it's about his lack of communication with us, not the decisions he's making."

"Still." He tried to hand back the keys, but she wouldn't take them.

"It's fine, Emerson. None of the rest of us want to live at the Park. And you don't have to, either, you know. You're not a hired hand. Is that really where you want to settle?"

"No sense letting perfectly good houses go to waste."

"He's right," Lena said, coming into the room from the hall. "I think Emerson is smart to see the opportunity there."

Emerson checked her expression to see if she was being sarcastic. He had no doubt Lena resented the amount of time he spent with her father, and she'd been angrier than anyone else at the General's high-handed tactics. She didn't understand that the General was comfortable with him precisely because he wasn't a member of their family. The General had gotten so used to fighting with his daughters and being called out by them for all his flaws, he still struggled to relax around them. At least he was no longer doing daily muster sessions, the way he had during his first weeks here, even though his daughters had told him it would be okay to continue the routine. Once he got settled in, the General had realized that everyone chatted about their day over dinner, anyway. They didn't need to go over the same ground twice.

Emerson doubted Lena would want to do any of the jobs he carried out for the General, but every time she came upon the two of them together, she still acted like he was horning his way into her family. He would've liked to help out more with ranch chores, but she had a way of making them uncomfortable, too. While his ankle was healing, it still slowed him down, and Lena went out of her way to move extra fast when he was around, getting things done with a quick efficiency that left him feeling like a child rather than a man. A couple of the other men had noticed, including her husband, Logan. Emerson had a feeling Logan had taken Lena aside and chastised her about her behavior, but just as he might've expected, that did nothing to warm her toward him.

"I'm only planning to make a list of what needs to be done to fix up the trailers. I'm not trying to take over the job."

"I just told you; no one else wants to live in them," Cass said. "Right, Lena?"

"Right."

"The General and I have discussed renting out some of the others. All the income would go straight into the family coffers," he added.

"Which works out nicely for you since you're wedging your way into the family," Lena quipped.

Hell.

Emerson watched her go, all his interest in the trailers disappearing with her.

"Don't let Lena get to you; you're not the one she's mad at. She and the General were starting to get along and then he got all high-handed again."

"Of course." Emerson walked out the back door more frustrated than he could say. Cass was right. Lena had made it clear how much she resented that her father never trusted her to run Two Willows, even though she was obviously more than qualified to do so. He'd watched her and the General come to something approaching a truce in the last few weeks, but it was a tentative one and needed nurturing. Instead, the General was pitching hand grenades across enemy lines. Emerson hesitated on the back porch and considered taking a drive to town to clear his head but decided against it. He wasn't going to let Lena knock him off his course when he wanted to contribute.

The cold air braced him, and by the time he reached the Park, he'd simmered down some. He knew Lena had long resented her father's interference in her running the ranch, and Logan had told him how hard it had been to persuade her to share the job with the men her father had sent. They'd shown themselves to be worthy of her respect.

Emerson wasn't sure she'd ever respect him.

He paused by the first of the trailers. He could solve this right now—by leaving. Would that be the smarter play?

He thought it probably would be, but he didn't want to go, and no one—especially not Lena—would respect him for running away. It was obvious Wye wanted to stay, and he meant to do all he could to make her happy.

Maybe taking on this chore that no one else wanted was a start.

He was pleased that his ankle was only minimally sore after the walk. For once he'd managed not to step wrong, or maybe those exercises were finally paying off. He let himself into the newest trailer first, a white one, and was almost disappointed to see that inside it was nearly spotless. It had little charm, however, and what Emerson really wanted was a project that showcased his skills. He'd always felt that people missed a trick when they built trailer homes. He understood they were supposed to be a frugal alternative to buying a single-family house, but that didn't mean that they couldn't be cozy or elegant.

He envisioned taking a trailer, cladding it in wood outside and installing his own cabinetry and flooring inside. Maybe this wasn't the one for him to start with. He went down the row, letting himself into each trailer in turn, until he found one he thought could work. It was one of the older ones, striped with broad bands of blue and white. Probably built in the 80s, its carpeting was worn and ragged, as was the upholstery on the built-in banquette. The cupboards looked like the ones in his grandmother's kitchen, and the Formica counter-tops were chipped and burned in several places.

He could gut this trailer without guilt, rebuild it from the floor to the ceiling and truly make it his own. He couldn't wait to get started. Fixing the siding might need to wait until spring, but that was okay. He could take his time with the interior and meanwhile fix up the interiors of the rest of the trailers, as well. He could reach out to Buck and offer him the white one that was already habitable.

He drew out the pad and pen and began to make a list of supplies he'd need to renovate the one he wanted for himself, adding little sketches to remind himself at the store what he had in mind. When he caught himself whistling, he chuckled. For the first time since the blast that had changed his world, Emerson felt truly happy. He had a project, he had a woman to woo. Maybe things would work out after all.

WYOMING COULDN'T BELIEVE she hadn't found the note before.

During the past few days, in between playing with Elise, feeding her and changing her diapers, and taking her outside on errands or short walks in the frigid weather, she had cleaned most of Ward's house from top to bottom. After that first day when she'd whipped the kitchen into shape and got on top of the laundry situation, she had tackled each room in turn, getting into corners, whisking away cobwebs, vacuuming under beds and sofas, scrubbing everything in sight.

Today she tackled their tiny dining room, and in the process of getting into all the corners with a vacuum cleaner, she'd gotten down practically on her belly to vacuum under the big hutch that stood along one wall—which was when she discovered the envelope lying beneath it.

Even before she pulled it out, her stomach sank. Once she was back to standing again and saw Ward's name written in Mindy's handwriting on the envelope, she knew what it had to be. Mindy must have propped the letter on the hutch, assuming Ward would see it on his way through the house to the kitchen the day she left, and somehow it had fallen down and slid under the hutch where no one had noticed it until now.

The flap of the envelope was tucked in but not fastened. Wyoming battled with her conscience, knowing the contents were for her brother's eyes only but wanting desperately to know what Mindy had said.

She wasn't proud of herself for opening the letter, but she didn't want to get Ward excited about the discovery if this was only an old birthday card or something like that.

Mindy's note was short and simple. She was unhappy. She didn't want to be a mother, didn't want to live in a boring backwater town like Chance Creek all her life, so she was heading to California to start over. She would be in touch through her lawyer when she was ready.

She'd written no words of apology for abandoning Ward or their daughter, or any explanation for what had gone wrong, outside of the fact that she felt hemmed in.

Wyoming's hands shook as she slid the note carefully back into the envelope and considered her next move. Although she tried not to overreact, hot anger welled up inside her at her sister-in-law's callousness. Didn't she know how much it hurt to be abandoned like that? Was she so unfeeling she could walk away from her husband and child without a second look?

She needed to call Ward, but Wye found herself hesitating. When she did, she'd kill any hope he had that Mindy was coming home, and he'd have to face a life as a single parent. Was it fair to call him in the middle of his workday? Or should she withhold the information until he came home?

No matter what she did, Ward would be crushed. She wasn't the only one who knew what abandonment felt like. Maybe her brother didn't talk about it, but she knew their mother's leaving hurt him as much as it had hurt her.

Wyoming didn't realize what she was doing until her phone was in her hand and she'd tapped out a message to Emerson.

You there?

A moment later her phone trilled. She answered it.

"What's wrong?" Emerson asked. "Do you want me to come over?"

His instant offer of help and companionship warmed her. "It's Mindy. She did leave a note, and I just found it. I know I shouldn't have read it, but I couldn't help myself."

"Of course you couldn't. What did she say?"

Wyoming told him, clutching the phone like a life-line, blinking back the tears that gathered in her eyes. "Ward is going to be devastated," she said when she was done. "I don't know what to do. Should I wait for him to come home or call him at work?"

"I think you have to call him," Emerson said. "Do you want me to come over?" he asked again.

"You'd better not. Ward won't want anyone outside of the family around when he finds out. He's going to be so angry."

"What about you? Are you going to be okay? What about the baby?"

"I don't know," Wyoming confessed. "I'll call Cass,

too. Maybe I'd better bring Elise home with me tonight. Or maybe I should stay here."

"Bring Elise to Two Willows," Emerson told her. "Seems like your brother is going to need to let off some steam tonight. Does he have a friend you could get in touch with? Someone who can be there for him?"

Wyoming thought about that. "Yes. I think I know who to call." Ward still hung out with the same buddies he'd had in high school. They weren't her favourite people, given the way they'd teased her when they were all young, but they weren't bad guys. They might be a little rough around the edges, but they were just the type to show up when someone needed help.

"When he's home and you're ready, pack up Elise and bring her here. We can all help you with her."

Wyoming didn't doubt that would be true. Cass loved babies, and so did most of her sisters. It wouldn't be much trouble to have Elise tonight.

She wondered what tomorrow would bring, however. How would Ward keep going to work knowing Mindy wasn't coming home? How would he handle the day-to-day stress of a full-time job and taking care of his baby? He would need to hire a nanny, she thought. Could he even afford one?

"I have a feeling I'm going to do a lot more babysitting," she said. "Not that I mind," she hurried to add.

"Of course not," Emerson said. "When you call Cass, tell her to give me a ring if she needs any help getting set up for you."

"Thanks, Emerson. I knew I could depend on you."

More grateful than she could say for his help deciding her plan of action, Wyoming hung up, called Cass and gave her the lay of the land, then braced herself for the most difficult call of all.

"Hi, Celia, it's Wyoming. Can I talk to my brother?" she asked the receptionist at the radio station.

"Oh… Hi, Wyoming," Celia said flatly.

Wye waited, a little disconcerted by her tone. Usually Celia was as chipper as she'd been as a cheerleader at Chance Creek High, where they both attended school.

"Is Ward available?" Wye prompted her when she didn't go on.

"Uh… not really. He's… in a meeting and can't be disturbed right now."

"It's pretty important," Wye said. She didn't think she'd ever had a problem getting Ward on the phone when he was at work.

"He said he can't be disturbed," Celia said again.

"What kind of meeting?" Wye pushed.

Celia hesitated. "An… advertising meeting?"

She sounded uncertain, and suddenly Wye knew Celia was covering for Ward. "What's going on? Talk to me, Celia."

"I don't know. It's just…He's not… He can't take your call right now. I'll have him get back to you as soon as he can." Celia hung up before Wye could ask any more questions, and Wye shoved her phone in her pants pocket.

That was strange.

Celia was lying, but Wye wasn't sure which part she

was lying about. Was Ward not in a meeting? Or was he in one but not taking her calls? Or was he not at work at all?

If she went looking, would she discover him at the Dancing Boot or Rafters, Chance Creek's two watering holes? How drunk would he be when he arrived home tonight? When would he even get home?

Wyoming decided not to wait. She pulled out her phone again, called Steve Merks, one of Ward's closest friends, and filled him in on the whole situation. Then she packed a bag for Elise. When Steve arrived, she gave him a note of her own along with Mindy's letter, and sent him to town to pigeonhole Ward, wherever he was.

It was better this way, she thought as she drove to Two Willows, Elise gurgling in her car seat in back. She would have liked to be the one to tell her brother the news, but he'd made that impossible, and she had a feeling he'd prefer it if Elise wasn't around when he discovered that his wife wasn't coming home. He needed time to process what Mindy had done—time to be angry and then calm down. Tomorrow, when he was ready, she would sit down with him and make a long-term plan.

Chapter 4

"EMERSON?" CASS CALLED and appeared in the doorway of the General's office a moment later. "Wyoming just pulled in, and she's got Elise. She doesn't look happy."

"Thanks. You mind, General?"

"Go help your fiancée." He waved Emerson off gruffly. Emerson caught Cass rolling her eyes as he slipped past her through the doorway.

"She's not his fiancée yet," Cass told her father.

"She will be."

"You can't keep ordering everyone around."

"Like hell I can't."

Emerson kept going toward the kitchen. Cass followed him more slowly, grumbling, and went back to work as he crossed to the door and opened it just as Wyoming approached. He took Elise from her arms, grabbed her purse and set it on the nearest chair. "You okay?" he asked her.

"Fine."

"How did Ward take the news?" Cass asked, taking her coat when Wyoming struggled out of it.

"I don't know. I couldn't reach him." Wyoming told them everything that had happened as she kicked off her snowy boots and settled in at the table. Cass moved around the room whipping up a snack for her.

Emerson sat in the chair beside her, holding Elise on his knee. The baby reached up and grabbed for his nose.

"I think you did the right thing," Emerson told her, evading Elise's sticky grasp. "Let your brother come to grips with what happened."

"Meanwhile, we get a playdate with Elise!" Cass said happily. She patted her own growing belly. "Got to practice before my baby comes."

"Guess so," Wye said. She looked tired—and worried—and Emerson vowed to help as much as he could tonight.

Everyone else at Two Willows seemed to have the same idea, and they all got to play with Elise before it was her bedtime, gathering in the front room and taking turns rolling a ball to her or playing with the stuffed animals Wye had brought with her. Jo went one better and brought one of the dogs in for Elise to pet for a minute. She sent Isobel out of the room when Elise pulled on her ear one too many times.

"I think that's enough for one night, anyway," Wye said, lifting Elise and balancing her on one hip. "We're going upstairs."

"I'll come, too." Emerson scooped up the baby bag she'd set in one corner of the room.

"Thanks."

"No word from Ward?" he asked when they reached the room Cass had set up for her nursery. She'd said Elise could use the crib she'd put together in anticipation of her baby's birth.

"No. Steve texted that he found Ward at Rafters. He took Ward home and ordered pizza. Said not to expect much more tonight. Sounds like Ward is taking it hard."

"Guess that's not surprising. How about you?"

"Me?" Wye looked up from changing a wriggling Elise into a new diaper and sleeper suit. "Like I said before, I'm fine."

"Mindy isn't just Ward's wife," he pointed out. "She's your sister-in-law, too."

Wye thought about that. "We were never close, though," she said sadly. "I mean, we had dinners together. Spent Christmas with each other. We live in the same town and weeks went by without us saying a word, you know? I'd hoped… well, I'd hoped having her around would be like having a real family."

Emerson nodded. They seemed to be alike in that— wanting family around. "You think Cass, Brian and the rest of them know how lucky they are?"

"Yes—and no," Wye said after a moment. "I don't think you can know unless you've done without."

Emerson agreed with her.

"I'm pretty tired," Wye said when she'd settled Elise into her crib. "I think I'll hang out with her until she's asleep, then hit the hay myself."

"Good night, then." Emerson leaned in and kissed her cheek, not even thinking about what he was doing until he'd done it. He didn't apologize, though; it felt right.

"Night," Wye said softly.

The next morning the General surprised Emerson when he asked to come along to the Park. Wyoming was long gone. She'd gone to Ward's house to talk with him about what he planned to do next. Emerson would have liked to sit in on that meeting, but then Wye would have to explain who he was, and that would open another can of worms. One crisis was enough for now, he supposed.

Although the trailers were only a quarter mile away, he drove the General in the pickup truck he'd leased after arriving at Chance Creek. The General was footing the bill, but he wouldn't be able to drive himself until his hip healed. When they arrived at the Park, Emerson kept close when the General got out of the truck and hobbled over the uneven, snowy ground, leaning heavily on his cane. He was afraid the man might trip and hurt himself all over again.

"This is the one." Emerson gestured at the blue-and-white-striped trailer he had chosen to work on first.

"Ugly son of a gun, isn't it?" the General said, looking it over.

"That's what makes it perfect," Emerson told him. "That one down at the end is too new to tear apart. I figure it's perfect to rent to Buck."

"If it's new, why don't you want to live in that one?" the General asked.

"It doesn't have any soul. This one I can make my

own—if I stay."

"You're staying," the General asserted.

"I will if you talk about it with the others and they all agree to have me, sir." Emerson wasn't going to back down on that point.

"You've picked well," the General said, ignoring him. "You start with something perfect, and it will never be truly yours. If you pick something a little rough around the edges, you can buff it up just the way you like it."

Emerson wondered if that was how the General saw him. Maybe it was the way he saw all the men he had handpicked and sent home to marry his daughters. Every one of them flawed, every one of them able to be buffed up into something better. He hoped the General liked the way he was turning out.

Hoped everyone else would in the end, too.

"I'm pretty sure Buck will want that first one," he said. "I'll find a contract online, and you can tell me what you want for rent."

"You'll need to take a percentage as a management fee," the General said.

"I don't think that's a good idea. There's no reason you should be paying me to do the job when any of the other men could do it just as easily and save you the fee."

"The others have enough ranch work to keep them busy," the General countered. "A man needs an income, especially a man who's looking for a wife. How's that going, by the way?"

"Fine. Or it would be, if I ever got to spend any time with Wyoming."

"Cass told me about her brother's wife. Sloppy work there," he added disgustedly. "A man ought to keep watch on his woman, make sure she doesn't wander away."

Emerson turned to hide the smile he couldn't quite suppress. "I'm not sure Ward was expecting his wife to wander away, sir."

"Vigilance. That's the trick," the General said. He looked the trailers over again. "I see what you mean about this one, and I have no doubt you could make something special out of it, but I don't like the idea of you and Wyoming living all the way down here. Jo and Hunter are building a house close to the main one. I wouldn't be surprised if another house or two gets built, as well. That's where you should build, too—close to the others."

"Wyoming and I will do just fine down here. If we marry. And if we stay." And it would keep Lena happier, Emerson thought privately. Maybe she'd even agree to giving them a share in the ranch.

"Do I stink or something?" The General turned on him testily. "Need to keep your distance?"

"You know it's nothing like that, sir."

"Well, whatever it is, I don't like it."

The man knew exactly what it was. Emerson decided not to argue with him. He'd get nowhere when the General was in this kind of mood. "You don't want me to fix up the trailer?" he asked instead.

The General glowered at him. "Never said that. Go ahead. Just don't get too attached to it. You and Wyoming need a real house. You talk to her, figure out how many kids you are going to have, how many bedrooms you'll need. We'll get it sorted out."

Children? Emerson wanted kids, of course, but they were getting a little ahead of themselves. First he needed some time alone with Wyoming. Then he needed to convince her to actually marry him. Then Cass, Brian and the others needed to buy in to the idea of them staying.

How was he supposed to know ahead of time how many kids he wanted, anyway?

"Just ask her," the General said as if he'd read Emerson's mind. "Get a ballpark figure. Five? Ten?" He shrugged.

This time Emerson didn't hide a smile. "Ten? That seems excessive."

"Especially if you're going to live in a trailer," the General said.

WYOMING SHIFTED ELISE to her other arm and knocked on Ward's door again. When he still didn't answer, she fished her keys out of her purse and let herself in, figuring he must be in the shower. It had probably been a long night. Had he and Steve stayed up late talking?

The minute she stepped into the house, she wrinkled her nose. It smelled like a bar in here. As her eyes adjusted to the dim light, she noticed the bottles on the coffee table in Ward's small living room. She moved from window to window, raising the shades, set Elise down on a blanket on the floor and began to collect the empties.

She hoped the number of them meant some more of Ward's friends came over to console him. She set the bottles on the kitchen counter to rinse later and hurried back to check on Elise. The little girl was mobile enough to get into trouble at a moment's notice.

"Ward?" she called. "You here?"

There was no answer. With a sigh, she picked up Elise again, settled her on her hip and headed down the short hall to the bedrooms. Ward slept in the largest at the end of the hall. The door was firmly shut, so Wye rapped loudly on it with her knuckles.

An indeterminate noise emanated from the bedroom.

"Ward? I'm here with Elise. We'd better talk about schedules, don't you think? Aren't you going to work?"

Ward groaned again. She thought he said something about being sick.

"We need to talk," she said again. She understood Mindy's desertion must be hard to process, but Elise hadn't seen either parent in days. "I've got Elise with me," she added again for good measure.

No answer.

She moved to the kitchen, settled Elise in her high chair, gave her a toy to distract her and started pulling out the makings for a big breakfast for Ward. Surely the smell of bacon would rouse him.

Thirty minutes later and still no sign of her brother, Wye was losing patience. She called Steve.

"Morning," he answered cheerfully. He wasn't any worse for wear after a hard night's drinking, Wye thought.

"Steve, it's Wye. I'm worried about Ward. He won't get up."

"He really tied one on last night. Better let him sleep it off."

"Did you talk to him? Did he say what he's going to do?"

"Honey, the last thing your brother wanted to do last night was talk. We watched the game."

While she took care of Elise and worried about him? She bit back a caustic reply. "He isn't going to work."

"Won't need that fancy house without Mindy to have to impress," Steve remarked.

Wye looked around her. This was a fancy house in Steve's opinion?

"He's still got a daughter to raise. She needs a roof over her head and food on the table."

For the first time, Steve seemed uneasy. "Yeah, I know. Don't think Ward's in a mindset to do much fathering. You might need to pitch in a little."

That was obvious. "I guess I'll take her back to Two Willows."

"That's a great idea. I'll stop by after work to see Ward."

She wasn't sure if she should be comforted or worried. "Don't let him drink. He needs to go to work, and he needs to hire a sitter."

"Sure. No drinking." Steve chuckled.

Wye hung up and shook her head at Ward's breakfast getting cold on the table and the dirty dishes she'd made.

He could deal with the aftermath of the meal, she decided, if and when he ever decided to get up.

"Come on, Elise. We came all this way to town. Might as well get some errands done."

She took her time, stopping in at the bank, the post office and the library. It seemed everyone she met wanted to greet Elise and coo over her, and once she got over her irritation with Ward, she began to enjoy herself. She stopped in at Fila's Familia restaurant for lunch, and both Fila Matheson and Camila Whitfield came out of the kitchen to greet her and play with the baby. Fila warmed Elise's bottle, then went back to cooking while Camila insisted on feeding Elise her baby food while Wye enjoyed a plate of fajitas.

It was early afternoon—time for Elise's nap—when she reached Two Willows. To her surprise Cass was nowhere in sight when she came in the back door, but Emerson was elbows deep in sudsy water, cleaning up from the midday meal.

"Hey, what are you two doing back so early?" Emerson approached and touched Elise's nose with a sudsy finger. Elise shrieked happily.

"Wye? What's going on?" Cass appeared in the doorway. "Emerson, what are you doing with my dishes?"

"Cleaning them." He returned to the sink and got busy again.

"That's not your job. I was just switching a load of laundry into the dryer. I was coming right back."

"I'm happy to help," Emerson said, setting another plate on the drying rack. "I've always liked getting things back in their places."

"Do you even know where their places are?" Cass asked, fluttering around behind him as if angling to get to her accustomed position at the sink. "You haven't been here that long."

"I've been here for weeks." Emerson faced her, clearly taken aback. "It's no big deal, Cass. Like I said, I'm happy to help."

"Which is very nice of him," Wyoming added pointedly. "I don't know about you, Cass, but I appreciate it when someone gives me a break from chores."

Cass bit her lip. "You're right," she admitted wryly. "Thank you, Emerson," she added. "It just feels wrong to me when a guest does housework. But Wyoming is right; I have plenty of other things I can do, including hanging out with my husband. But first, why don't I get Elise down for her nap and you two can talk."

"Thanks." Wye gave Elise a kiss and a snuggle and handed Cass the baby and her bag. When she was gone, Emerson braced his hands on the counter and sighed.

"She didn't mean that," Wye hurried to assure him, knowing instinctively which part of the conversation with Cass was bothering him. "She didn't even realize what she said."

"But that's how everyone sees me. As a *guest*."

"That's how they see me, too, despite what Cass says. But what can we expect?"

"The General assured me there's a place for me— and you—on the ranch. I'm not ready to give that up yet, but if push comes to shove, I'll work as hard as I can to make us a home somewhere else. I want you to know that."

Wye wasn't sure what to say. On the one hand, his assurance that she wanted him to make her a home was galling. On the other hand, it was... She didn't know what it was, but it was something. Something that tugged at a place in her that wasn't rational.

The handsome soldier washing Cass's dishes wanted to make a home for her.

Who else had ever wanted to do that?

"Let's worry about one thing at a time," she said. "I need to sort things out with my brother. You need to help the General—and fix those trailers."

Emerson perked up. "How about tomorrow we can go out there, and I'll show you what I'm planning. We could bring Elise." He cocked his head, fishing another dish out of the soapy water and washing it. "Did things go well with Ward?"

"No, not at all. He drank so much last night he couldn't get out of bed this morning. I finally gave up," she admitted, hoping Emerson didn't notice how worried she was.

"He did get some pretty bad news."

Wye was pretty sure Emerson wouldn't get drunk in

similar circumstances, but all she could do was shrug. "I'll call him later. He's got to get up sometime. Tell me about what you're doing at the Park." She fetched a towel from one of the drawers and started drying the stack of clean dishes.

"I picked one of the trailers to start with." Emerson seemed to understand she wanted to talk about something different. "I'll swap out the siding, take the interior down to the studs and rebuild it. It won't look like a trailer at all by the time I'm finished with it."

"That sounds like an interesting project. What will happen to it when you're done?"

He gave her a funny look. "I'm hoping you'll move into it with me," he said.

Suddenly the events of the morning and her frazzled emotions caught up with her, and Wye set the dish she'd been drying down on the counter with a thump. "Too soon," she told him. "I've got too much on my plate to talk about things like that right now."

Emerson gave her a long look, but in the end he only nodded. "Guess you're right. But it'd help to know your opinion on the matter. Could you be happy in a refurbished trailer? Or do you need something nicer?"

How on earth was she supposed to know what would make her happy? Her whole world had turned upside down in the last month and a half. She'd lost her job, given up her apartment, was living as a guest at her friend's house and entertaining thoughts of marriage to a man she didn't even know, just because her friend's father had decreed it. Her brother's wife had run away, and Ward seemed to view her as a stand-in for Mindy. She wasn't ready for any of it.

"I have no problem with living in a trailer that's made to look like a cabin," she said carefully, "but I do have a problem, a big problem, with being pushed into a situation for which I'm not ready. Do you understand that?"

Emerson set the last dish on the drying rack and dried his hands. "Yeah, I got it," he said and walked out of the room.

"I MAKE A pretty mean cup of coffee, you know," Cass said early the following morning.

Emerson lifted the tray he had just assembled and turned to face her. "I'm sure you do, but the General is very particular. I've been making his morning coffee for years."

"It just seems silly to make coffee twice in one morning," she pointed out. She leaned against the counter in a warm, quilted robe, fuzzy slippers on her feet, one arm cradling her belly. They often met up like this since Cass liked to get a big breakfast on the table for her family. The General had always been an early riser and didn't seem likely to give up his military ways anytime soon.

"I've been careful to clean the coffee maker after I use it," Emerson said. "Am I getting in your way?"

Cass opened her mouth, seem to reconsider her words, and said, "I appreciate that you clean the coffee maker after you use it. All I'm saying is, maybe if the

General tried my coffee, he'd get used to it, and then we'd only have to make it once."

"Or I could just make enough for everybody," Emerson pointed out.

"Or I could." Cass lifted up her hands in exasperation. "I'm just as good at keeping house as you are."

Emerson winced. He was hardly *keeping house*. He was the General's aide; this was his job. Working to hold his temper in check, he tried to see things from Cass's point of view. He supposed he was stepping on her toes, but he prided himself on keeping an exact schedule. If the General could depend on the small details of his day unfolding like clockwork, he could save his brainpower for the important ones—like directing troops during wartime, or…

But the General wasn't serving at USSOCOM anymore. Neither of them were. He supposed his attention to the General's coffee and schedule seemed ridiculous here on the ranch, but a man like the General hated to be sidelined, and Emerson felt sticking to a military schedule kept his spirits up, as did his forays to Billings to work with the reservists.

"I'm not trying to step on your toes. I'm trying to show the General I appreciate everything he's done for me. He didn't have to bring me here—or get me work at the reserve base. The least I can do is make his coffee the way he likes it." He lifted the tray an inch. "I guess from your perspective it would have been better if he'd left me back at USSOCOM."

"Would they have let you stay on?" Cass asked curiously.

"I'm not sure. The Army tries to find work for wounded soldiers if it can, but..." He shrugged. He didn't know if he'd have passed muster.

Cass softened a little. "I don't mind you being here, but you have to understand this is my kitchen, that's my coffee maker and that's my father you've got holed up in his office. I'd like to make his life easier, too. That's how I show people I care, Emerson—by cooking for them. And by making them coffee."

"The General loves your cooking," Emerson assured her. "But I get what you're saying. If I stay, I promise I won't live under your roof forever. I'll move down to the Park as soon as possible, fix up the trailers and manage them. That income will go straight into the communal kitty. I want to pay my way around here."

Cass sighed. "I know. I'll try to be patient about the coffee." She frowned, holding a hand to her abdomen.

"Are you okay?"

"Yes, I'm fine. This little bugger keeps kicking me. Speaking of which, time to check on Elise. She's bound to wake up any minute. I think Wyoming is still sleeping, and she needs it. She hasn't had a full night's rest in a week."

Emerson just managed to stop himself before volunteering to get the baby himself. He figured Cass wouldn't like that.

She laughed. "You were about to offer to get Elise, weren't you?"

He scratched the back of his neck. "You caught

me," he admitted. "I was one of eleven kids in the house growing up, and we all did our share. Picking up a baby, washing dishes, harvesting the hay—it was all in a day's work, and woe to anyone who didn't prove their worth."

He hadn't meant to sound so bitter, and he wondered where that anger had come from. He was lucky enough his aunt and uncle had taken him in even though they had so many mouths of their own to feed. So what if they'd cast him off when he'd grown up?

"I don't think kids should have to prove their worth, do you?" Cass asked sharply. She circled her belly protectively with her arms again.

"No. Definitely not." He pulled himself together. Cass didn't need his life story—not this early in the morning. "I'm going to take this tray into the General before his coffee gets cold. Is there anything I can do to make your life easier today?"

"You're incorrigible." She smiled at him, though, and he thought that was an improvement.

"I know." He smiled back.

"You probably have your hands full with the General, but if you want to come out later and hold Elise while I vacuum, I won't turn you away."

"Sounds good."

Emerson headed to the General's room and found him sitting at his desk as usual. He looked up with a scowl that softened when he took in the coffee on the tray Emerson was carrying. "Good man," he said. "I'm not myself before my first cup of coffee, as I'm sure you know."

"None of us is."

"These days I'm not myself," the General complained. He thumped the desk with his hands. "Look at me, sitting all the time. It was bad enough at USSO-COM, but it's even worse here. There's a whole ranch out there, and I can't do anything with it."

"Then let's get started with those physio exercises your doctor ordered. If you want to be out working the ranch, you need to do them. I've already done mine today."

The General waved him off the way he'd waved him off every day they'd been here. Emerson bit back a sigh of frustration. He wanted to be out on the ranch, too, working on his trailer, coming up with ideas for what else he could do to help around the place. Instead, he'd end up spending his morning here, helping with the paperwork and pleading with the General to do the exercises that were his only chance at getting back the range of motion it would take to have an active lifestyle again. He needed to help Cass with Elise so she could do her vacuuming, too.

The morning went just as he predicted, and it was only an hour before lunchtime when he escaped to the Park. He wasn't sure where Wye, Cass and Elise had gone. The men were out doing chores. So was Lena. Jo was with her dogs, Sadie at work in her greenhouse. The lights were on in Alice's workshop in the carriage house's second story, so she was probably designing something or other.

As he walked slowly down the track to the Park, careful not to slip on the snowy ground and do his ankle more damage, he decided something had to change. The General was getting more and more frustrated with his injuries. He'd snapped at Emerson twice this morning, not entirely an uncommon occurrence but still a harbinger of worse things to come.

There had to be away to make the General see that the pain of doing his exercises was worth the outcome down the road. After all, it wasn't the pain the General was afraid of—it was the possibility that even if he put in the work, he wouldn't get the results he wanted. A self-fulfilling prophecy, if there ever was one.

He'd think about it tonight, Emerson promised himself. Meanwhile, he was getting out while the getting was good.

Before he made it to the Park, however, his phone rang. Emerson took the call.

"Buck—how are you doing? I've been meaning to call. I've got that trailer for you, like I said I might."

"Hey, do you have any more trailers for rent?" Buck asked. "I've got a friend who needs a place, too. He's on a bit of a budget, though. You got anything that's a little banged up?"

"I might," Emerson hedged. "Let me get back to you on that." He couldn't imagine the General or anyone else would balk at the chance to make more money. Maybe it was time for him to operate on faith. "Let's set a time to meet late this week, and I'll have more answers for you," he added.

"Okay."

"YOU WANT KIDS, don't you?" Cass asked, sitting in the rocking chair in the nursery room, where there was a crib and changing table for Elise. "If you don't, you'd better tell Emerson now. I think that man wants a houseful."

"You talked to Emerson about babies?" Wyoming finished changing Elise's diaper and lifted her into her arms. She swallowed a familiar rise of irritation. She and Emerson had yet to go on a single date. Why did everyone insist on jumping the gun?

"Hard not to when we've got one in the house," Cass pointed out. "Did you know he was one of eleven kids? I've never heard him talk about his family. Somehow I thought he was an orphan."

"I don't think those were his brothers and sisters." Wyoming bounced Elise in her arms, swaying back and forth. "I think he got put with another family when his parents died. We haven't really talked about it, though." There was a lot she didn't know about Emerson, Wyoming realized. The first few weeks he was around, she'd paid far more attention to Will. Since then she'd been too busy with her own family's problems.

"Are you serious about marrying him?"

"I'm not serious about anything except getting through the day," Wye said in exasperation. "I need to talk to Ward this afternoon. He still hasn't answered my calls, so I'm going over there, and I'm not going to let him avoid me any longer. Do you think I should bring

Elise along? Or get someone to babysit?"

"You know I'd happily babysit," Cass said. "But won't he want to see her?"

"He hasn't even asked about her." Wye lowered her voice as if Elise could understand what they were talking about and get her feelings hurt. "I don't know what to think. I don't blame him for being upset, or for being scared, which I think he is," she added. "Suddenly he's a single father. I wouldn't want to raise children on my own, either."

"Good thing you have Emerson, then." Cass grinned at her. "Much as I dislike sharing my kitchen with him, he's really a good guy."

"Whatever." She didn't have the time—or energy—to think about a relationship, or kids, for that matter. "I'm calling Ward again."

This time he answered, although it took several rings. "Hey," Ward said dully. "Come on over. Bring Elise. Let's talk."

An hour later she pulled into the driveway, and he met her at the door. He'd showered and dressed carefully. Shaved, too.

"Glad to see you back on your feet." She handed him Elise's car carrier. The baby had fallen asleep on the way over, and she hadn't wanted to wake her.

Ward made a face, took the carrier, ushered her inside and led the way into the living room. He sat on the couch and put the carrier on the floor beside him. "Sorry about dumping everything on you yesterday," he said, gazing down at his daughter. "Guess I kind of lost it the night before. My boss is pissed I missed another day at work. I told him I'd be in this afternoon at one. Look, Wye, I know it's asking a lot, but I need you to help me for a few more weeks, just until I've got my head together. I've got to get to work, prove that I'm not going to start day-drinking all the time. I'm probably going to have to do some overtime to show them I'm really going to play ball. So I was thinking… What if you move in here? Just temporarily," he rushed to add when she made a disbelieving noise. "Just so you don't have to drive back and forth."

Wye took a moment to answer, telling herself not to overreact. On the one hand, it was a reasonable proposition, she supposed, but on the other hand, it wasn't. She had no doubt what would happen if she moved in. She'd be the one up at all hours with the baby—

"Wyoming, please. I wouldn't ask if I wasn't desperate. I know I need to hire someone to live in, and honestly, I don't know how I'm going to stand a stranger in the house—taking care of my baby—when I just lost my wife. I'm hanging on by a thread, and my boss has made it clear that any more drama on my part and I'm out of a job. What the hell would I do then?"

His anguish was all too clear, and Wyoming gave in. After all, she loved her brother and Elise, and she was sure he'd do the same for her in a pinch.

Well, maybe not sure. *He wouldn't do a thing.* The traitorous thought wormed its way into her consciousness, but Wyoming brushed it aside. She would feel awful if Ward hired someone sight unseen to care for her niece.

And she couldn't believe his boss was being so heavy-handed. Had Ward used up his patience in the past with other absences from work she didn't know about?

"I'll move in for two weeks," she said. "That will give you plenty of time to assess your situation, take out an ad for a nanny or look into other childcare options. I want to be back at Two Willows by Christmas. Got it?"

"Got it. Except—it might be easier to find someone after the holidays—"

"Ward!" That was exactly what her father used to do. Ask for something, then ask for a little more, and a little more…

"Fine. I'll find someone by Christmas," he assured her. "Why don't you get your things? I'll make sure there's clean sheets on the guest bed for you."

"There are. I put them there." Wyoming stood and gathered her purse.

"Wyoming," Ward said before she reached the door. "What about Elise?"

"What about her?"

"I told you. I have to get to work."

She pulled out her phone and checked the time. "At one—which is in two hours."

"I need to get ready. Get my head on right."

Wyoming bit back the scathing reply that sprang to her lips. "Right. I'll take Elise. You get your head on right."

She scooped up the baby in her car seat and walked out the door.

"YOU'RE BACK," ALICE said from her perch on top of the refrigerator when Wyoming walked into the kitchen, awkwardly lugging Elise in her baby carrier.

"Alice, you're an old married woman now. What are you doing up there?" Cass asked, coming in from the front hall. "Wyoming, you're back already."

"Just for a few minutes."

"I'm doing what I'm always doing up here. Drawing. And staying out of your way." Alice lifted her sketchbook to show them. "If Kate O'Dell ever does get in touch with me, I want to have some ideas ready to show her."

"Does Kate O'Dell have any say in what she wears in movies?" Wye asked.

"She does when she's co-directing them. I looked it up, and it turns out she's half in charge of that Civil War movie she's in. I hope I hear from her."

Wyoming was happy to see Alice so contented. She'd spent months creating costumes on spec for a period drama that hadn't panned out, but it sounded like it was still possible Alice could work with her favorite actress.

"What's going on? What happened with Ward?" Cass asked Wye, tugging at the refrigerator door. Alice peeped down as Cass withdrew a can of pop and opened it.

"Pass me one?" she asked.

Cass did so.

"I'm packing up and heading back to Ward's place. I'm moving in there for a few weeks." Wye hoped her disappointment didn't show. She'd been looking forward to decorating for Christmas with Cass and spending the holidays at Two Willows. Despite her brother's assurances, she thought it wasn't likely he'd hire anyone by then.

"You're moving to town?" Cass looked as disappointed as Wye felt.

"Who's moving to town?" Jack asked, coming in from outside, trailed by Emerson.

"Wyoming is. She has to stay at her brother's place for a few weeks," Cass told him.

"And Cass isn't happy about it," Alice said, nimbly climbing down from the refrigerator to greet her husband with a kiss.

Emerson stopped in the doorway. "You're really leaving?"

"I really am." Wyoming didn't think she could take much more of this. Bad enough to have to leave without everyone going on about it. "I'll be back as soon as I can, but Ward needs me."

"You'll come back every day, though, right?" Cass asked. "The nursery is all set up, so you can take care of Elise here, where you'll have help. Your brother can't have a problem with that, right?"

"I guess not," Wye mused. That would be a lot more fun than being alone with Elise all day. "I'll need to stop in town in time to cook something for him for dinner, though. He can't order out every day and still afford a nanny."

"Can't he learn to cook for himself?" Emerson

asked.

"He wasn't raised like you," Wyoming said. "It's only temporary, and Cass is right. I could come here every day—if you really want me," she said to Cass.

"Of course I want you. I asked you to move in, remember?"

"What's going on out here?" The General thumped into the room on his cane. "Sounds like a riot."

"No riot." Cass explained everything again.

The General turned a baleful look on Wye. "So you're going AWOL."

"I'm helping my brother." Surely they understood she didn't want to leave. She'd far rather be here where something was happening all the time than in a house alone with Ward, who wasn't going to be very good company.

"Make sure you're back by 0900 hours each morning. Cass depends on you. We all do. Don't let us down."

"I—" The General stomped off before she could answer. "I'll be back by 0900 hours, I guess," she said to Cass helplessly.

Cass hugged her. "You wouldn't want to let the General down. See you tomorrow. Don't work too hard tonight."

After Wyoming had packed her bags and carried them downstairs, Emerson took them from her and loaded them into her VW. He waited while she got Elise into her car seat.

"I'll miss you, you know." He leaned against the car

and took her hands, drawing her nearer. "I hardly ever get to spend time with you as it is."

Despite herself, she let him. She'd miss him, too, if she was honest with herself. "I'll be back tomorrow morning."

"That's not soon enough." He bent down to kiss her, and Wyoming didn't back away, enjoying the feeling of his mouth on hers and needing one thing to be about her today rather than her brother. Emerson's kiss started out soft but soon grew more insistent, and an answering thread of desire wound its way through her. Emerson was strong and steady. Dependable when nothing else seemed to be.

"I've got to go," she said finally, pulling back.

"See you tomorrow."

He stood watch while she backed up, turned around and left.

Chapter 5

"**T**HE TRAILER YOU offered me looks great, but I'm not sure how Gary will feel about this one," Buck said later that week as they surveyed the green trailer Emerson had gutted along with the blue-and-white one he was working on for himself. He'd already given the white trailer a once-over so it would be ready for Buck come New Year's Day, when the man wanted to move in. Now he'd prioritize the green one, since despite all his hints, the General hadn't hashed out things with his daughters or their husbands on the matter of him staying here long term. The General maintained that he got to determine who lived on the ranch—and inherited a share in it. That wasn't good enough for Emerson.

"I've got two people interested in renting trailers at the Park," he'd told everyone at breakfast today. "You all need to decide if that business is a go or not." He'd gone back to eating his French toast and bacon as the others discussed the matter, agreeing that collecting rent from the abandoned trailers was a good idea.

He hadn't brought up the possibility of living in one

himself, and no one else had either—least of all the General, so Emerson decided he'd proceed as if his time at Two Willows was temporary. That meant starting a serious search for a full-time job and alternate housing. He tried to suppress the disappointment that surged through him whenever he thought about the situation. The General had never left him hanging like this before. Then again, the General wasn't used to anyone gainsaying his orders. He seemed to think it was all a done deal.

"It doesn't look like much now, but it will," Emerson said, shaking off those frustrating thoughts and leading Buck inside. Time enough to sort out all that later. The only thing he could do now was show he could be an asset to the ranch.

Buck whistled. "It's going to be a while before this one is inhabitable, huh?"

"Not as long as you might think." But longer than he'd like. As he'd expected, the General had been fractious all week, putting off his exercises until later and later each morning, if he did them at all, coming up with busy work to occupy both of them instead, and Emerson couldn't get down to the Park until it was afternoon. This late in November, it was dark well before dinnertime, and while he'd rigged up some work lights, he found it hard to get much done at night.

Wyoming hadn't been around nearly as much as he'd hoped, either, and Elise, who'd decided to cut a tooth, demanded all her attention when she was. Wyoming had been handling the baby's doctor's appointments and riding herd on a string of workmen at

Ward's place when his furnace gave out. Each time Emerson saw her, she was more frazzled.

He wished he could help.

On the bright side, his daily walks to and from the Park had gotten easier, and he'd noticed that although his ankle was still sore at the end of the day, it wasn't as bad as it had been.

And now it was Friday. Tonight he'd booked dinner for the two of them at DelMonaco's. Cass had said she'd babysit Elise if Ward didn't get home on time. She thought Wyoming needed a break, too.

"He's taking advantage of her," she'd told Emerson earlier that morning.

"I know."

"I don't know what to do about it."

"I'm not sure there's anything we can do," he told her, and they'd both gone back to work.

"The plumbing is in," Emerson told Buck now. "So's the electricity. That's the hard part. I can have this place ready to go by New Year's. Bring Gary out any time to take a look. It'll be all brand new when I'm done, clean as a whistle." Personally, Emerson thought Buck might feel he'd gotten the worse side of the deal when the green trailer was done. His shiny white one might be up-to-date as far as trailers went, but Gary's would have character, and that was better, to his way of thinking.

"You're okay with me moving in on the first of January?" Buck asked.

"I've got the paperwork with me, and the General's

signed off on having you here. There's only one thing I have to make clear first. Just because I know you doesn't mean I'll go easy on you if you're late for rent, or partying or anything like that. I hope this is going to be my home, too, and General Reed and his family don't need any more trouble here."

"Got it." Buck grinned. "Lighten up, Emerson. I won't screw up the good thing you've got going here."

"I hope not." Emerson grinned back, relaxing a little. He didn't expect any trouble with Buck.

At the main house later that afternoon, Emerson whistled on his way up the stairs but came face to face with a frowning Cass at the top of them.

"Something wrong? Where's Wye?"

"She ended up staying in town all day. Elise has been crying nonstop, and Ward's going to be late tonight. I don't think this is the night to surprise her with dinner plans."

"You didn't tell her about them, did you?"

"No. I figured that was for you to do."

Emerson was glad of that; it gave him some leeway. "I'm going over there."

"I don't think she needs to entertain you on top of everything else." Cass followed him down the hall.

"I don't need *entertaining*." Emerson turned on her. "Hell, Cass, is it just me, or do you think all men are helpless?"

Cass wrinkled her nose. "Sorry. I think I'm nesting, and it's hard having so many men all over the place. I'm not used to it. I want everyone out of my house so I can get it cleaned and organized the way I want it. I'm at the end of my rope."

He supposed he couldn't blame her for that. "I'll try to stay out of your way," he said shortly. "Meanwhile, I need to get ready to go. I'll bring some food to Wye," he added when it looked like Cass would argue again. "I'll help her with Elise. We can watch a movie or something. She shouldn't be stuck there alone on a Friday night."

"I guess you're right about that," Cass admitted. "Okay, go. Just... make sure you're really helping."

"I will."

An hour later he knocked on Wyoming's brother's door, bags of takeout in his arms. He could hear Elise wailing from all the way out here. He figured Cass would have given Wye a heads-up by now, but when she opened the door, she looked surprised to see him.

"What are you doing here?"

Not quite the welcome he'd hoped for. Elise's wails went on and on from inside the house. "I brought you dinner."

But her gaze had already fallen on the bags from Burger Shack. "Oh, you wonderful man," she exclaimed, and her entire countenance brightened. "I need a burger—desperately. I don't suppose you brought fries."

"Of course I brought fries. And a chocolate shake."

Grateful tears welled in her eyes as she let him into the house, but Wyoming laughed. "This day has been so awful I didn't think anything could go right, but a chocolate shake might do the trick."

Elise, sitting on a blanket on the floor, toys spread around her, cut off mid-wail when she saw him, her big blue eyes brimming with tears, but the silence was short lived. A moment later her cries rang out anew. Emerson handed Wye the bags of food, shucked off his outer gear and headed for the baby.

"Come on," he told Elise. "Let's get you to bed."

"Hah. Good luck with that," Wyoming said as he made his way through the small house to the bedrooms in back. It was easy to figure out which one was the baby's. "I just changed her," Wyoming called after him.

"Great."

Lullabies were playing in Elise's room, and he began by leaning her against his shoulder and patting her back as he bounced and swayed lightly to the music, humming a little now and then. When Emerson had lived with his aunt and uncle, he'd been tasked many times with watching the children of his older cousins and had learned that one way to calm a baby was to calm himself. He emptied his mind and breathed deeply, slowing his heart rate. While Elise continued to cry and fuss, she also yawned once or twice—a good sign.

It took nearly an hour, but in the end Elise lost the war of wills and fell asleep. Emerson laid her down carefully in her crib and tiptoed out to find Wyoming on the couch watching TV.

"I know I should have come and helped. I just sat down for a minute and then couldn't get up again. Did you do it? You got her to sleep?" Wye said hopefully.

"For now. Better keep things under control out here."

She gestured to the TV. "I'm hardly causing a ruckus."

"But you might."

"Eat your burger."

Emerson sat down on the couch next to her and did so gladly, not caring that it had gone cold.

"You're amazing," Wye said.

"I was hoping you'd notice that."

"I miss you—all of you. I wish I was back at Two Willows."

"So do we."

"I'm not sure Ward is even trying to find someone to help," she admitted. "I don't know what to do."

"For now, how about we watch a movie. Later we'll get it all figured out."

AFTER WATCHING AN hour of television with Emerson, Wyoming began to feel almost human. During a commercial break, he fetched a cooler from his truck and handed her a beer. "I thought about picking up wine, but I figured this would go better with the burgers."

"It's perfect." Wyoming took a long sip. "Thank you. I didn't realize how much I needed someone to come and help."

"No problem." He shifted on the sofa to face her and set his beer on the ground carefully. "Give me your feet."

"My feet?"

"You heard me. Get them up here."

Wyoming leaned against the armrest and lifted her sock-clad feet tentatively, but she moaned with pleasure when he began to knead them with his strong fingers.

"I'll do your neck next. I'll bet you're sore from carrying Elise around."

"More like tense from her crying all day."

"Is that why you stayed away from Two Willows?" He dug down deep into the arches of her feet.

Wyoming squirmed, but it felt good. "I didn't want her to bother the General. I know Cass and her sisters would be fine no matter how fussy she gets, and the guys could all scatter to the barn—Lena, too," she added with a smile. "But the General is stuck in his office, pretty much."

"He's going to have to listen to Cass's baby soon," he pointed out.

"Not until March. And that's his grandchild. Elise isn't a relative."

"You know, it'd be a good thing for the General to want to get out more." He relayed the problem he was having getting him to do his exercises.

Wyoming laughed. "Tell him Cass's baby will be riding before he will. That ought to light a fire under him."

Emerson switched feet, nodding. "You might be right."

"I'm slacking off, too, these days. I should be job hunting," she moaned, closing her eyes and wriggling down until she could rest her head on the arm of the sofa. "I can't keep sponging off the Reeds forever. And I don't want to be Ward's nanny, either. I need a real income."

"Do you want a job?"

She opened one eye. "What's the alternative?"

"Marry me."

Here they went again. "Look—"

He waved off her complaint. "I'm just asking, Wye. I need to know things about you. If you don't want a job, and you want to marry me, I'd do my best to make it so you didn't need one, but if you do want one, I'm not going to stand in your way. I want you to know that."

He kept offering her so much. Wye wished life would slow down long enough for her to get to know him so she could decide how to proceed. She had too many decisions to make these days, and she didn't feel capable of making another one.

"I like working. The thing is—you can't tell Cass about this, by the way."

Emerson pretended to zip his mouth closed, then went back to work on her feet. He had the most amazing technique, Wye decided, but she forced her thoughts back to the present when they slipped to wondering what he could do with those hands on other parts of her body.

"The thing is, there aren't any jobs for a paralegal around here. All the openings are in Billings or Bozeman, and as nice as she's been about putting me up,

I'm probably going to have to move."

"Or marry me."

She shook her head in exasperation. "Fine. You're right. My other alternative is I could marry you."

He stopped massaging her feet and instead gripped her ankles. "Would it really be so bad?"

"I don't know. I know nothing about you."

"WHAT DO YOU want to know?" Emerson asked, not letting himself slide his hands up her legs, the way he wanted to. If he had his way, he'd explore every inch of Wye's body, but that had to wait until she felt the same way about him.

Meanwhile, he waited as patiently as he could for her to answer. He knew he shouldn't promise to support her until he found his own full-time job and that he'd be lucky to find something in town. He, too, might need to move to Billings or Bozeman.

"Everything. Start at the beginning." Wye took another draw on her beer.

The beginning. He didn't like that part.

"I was born outside Spokane, but my parents died in an accident when I was seven."

"I'm sorry to hear that. That's very young to lose your folks."

Emerson kept going. He'd learned long ago not to dwell on that time. The wound was as fresh now as it had been back then. He'd never forget the moment his principal had come to fetch him from class, sat him down in her office and explained in short, clear sentences that his mother and father were dead and never coming back.

"Not ever? Not even if I'm really good?" he'd asked. He didn't know where that idea had come from. It was just something to say to fill the awful gap left by her words, but sometimes he thought he'd been trying to be really good ever since, on the off-chance…

He cleared his throat. "My aunt and uncle took me in. They lived on a farm in southern Illinois and were quite religious," he explained. "Quite conservative, too. Believed in leaving the size of their family up to God, so I have a lot of cousins, who have a lot of kids themselves."

"Is that what you believe? That God should determine the size of your family?"

Was she afraid he'd make her have eleven kids? "No," he said. "I'm all about free will and planning ahead."

She smiled. "So it was like having siblings when you moved in with them."

"To an extent." He wasn't sure how to explain it so she'd understand how crowded the house was—and how lonely sometimes. "It wasn't like they mentioned my parents or the difference between me and their own children, but that difference was there all the time no matter what I did. I think my cousins would have accepted me fully if it wasn't for the distinction my aunt and uncle made. As we grew older, it got more pronounced, but it wasn't just me who bore the brunt of their behavior," he added, hating how self-pitying he sounded. "My aunt and uncle were strict with all of us. Their motto was 'everyone contributes,' but it wasn't a 'we're all in this together' sort of thing as much as a 'what have you done for me lately?' type of situation. I think we all were a little worried we might get taken for a ride in the family car and dropped off on the side of the road like an unwanted puppy."

"Emerson, that's awful!"

"They were farmers, Wye. Far from wealthy. They had eleven kids. The money pressures must have been hard."

"Even so!"

Her outrage on his behalf warmed him. When he thought back to those days, the muscles in his neck tightened. It was only later that he realized how tense he'd always been. "When I turned sixteen, my uncle took me aside and made it clear it was time for me to leave."

"Did you graduate from high school at least before he kicked you out?"

"I got a job. Got my GED. Then I got on with my life." Tears shone in Wye's eyes, and Emerson's gut twisted. He hadn't meant to make her sad. "Hey, it wasn't so bad," he assured her. "The Army was the making of me. Taught me all kinds of things. Gave me a career. I would never have known the General without it—or you."

"I just think kids deserve their childhoods," Wye said stiffly.

"Look at it this way." Emerson shifted toward her

on the couch, sliding himself along under her legs until he was close enough to pull her onto his lap. "I'm hardworking. I know the value of a dollar. And I don't expect anyone to wait on me, because no one ever has. That makes me pretty good husband material, right?"

Wye sat still, bracing one hand on his shoulder. "If so, I guess I'd make a pretty good wife."

"In what way?" He wanted to know more about her. Would she open up to him?

"My mom walked out on us when I was twelve. I was instantly promoted to head housekeeper," she said wryly. "Dad saw no reason a girl my age couldn't fill my mother's shoes. I cleaned, I cooked, I shopped and I treated my father and brother like the kings they thought they were."

Emerson stroked her arm. "That was a lot for you to take on."

"I went from being a kid to an adult overnight. No one seemed to think I might miss my mom—or need to mourn her. We never talked about her again. It was as if she never existed. She didn't call or text or email. No Christmas cards—she was just gone. I began to think that if I didn't do my new job perfectly, maybe I'd disappear, too. Over time, I began to wish I could."

"I bet." Emerson wished he could go back in time and tell that little girl she was worth far more than the way her family was treating her.

"I got a job as soon as I could. Started saving my money. Moved out when I was seventeen, which pissed off my dad no end. Ward was gone by then—went to school on a hockey scholarship, although he never went any further with that."

"I haven't heard you mention your father before now," Emerson said softly. "What's he like?"

Wye laughed, but it wasn't a happy sound. "The day I moved out was a Sunday. I'd taken three loads to my new place before he even woke up. He shuffled out of his room in his robe, blinked at me a couple of times and bellowed, 'What the hell do you think you're doing?' I told him I was moving." Wye wouldn't meet Emerson's gaze. "'Who's going to keep this place up?' he called after me as I hauled the last box down the walkway to where I'd parked on the street."

"What did you tell him?" Emerson asked.

"He'd have to do it himself. Ward had already moved on. You know what he said?"

Emerson shook his head.

"'Then you can fuck off, just like your mother!' He slammed the door before I could come back and say a proper goodbye. I thought about going in for the last couple of jackets, scarves and gloves I'd left on my bed, but I decided it wasn't worth another confrontation. I got in my car and drove away."

Emerson found he could picture the whole thing, and his chest burned with indignation. "Did you find a way back to each other?" he made himself ask evenly.

"No." She shook her head. "Dad sold the house and left town several months later—without giving me a forwarding address. I've never heard from him since."

"Hell, Wye." Emerson sought for words that could

encompass his disbelief. "He doesn't deserve you. Neither of your parents do." He wrapped his arms around her, wishing he could protect her from every kind of harm. How could people leave their children? He'd never be able to do that.

"You didn't deserve to have your parents die," she said.

He had no answer to that, so he bent to kiss her.

Wye gave a little sigh as his mouth moved over hers, and all the desire Emerson had been holding back lurched up inside him. He tightened his arms around her, sliding one hand down to the base of her back. Things always felt right when Wye was close to him.

Very right.

To hell with her parents—and his aunt and uncle. To hell with anyone who didn't understand what real love meant.

He promised himself then and there he'd be everything Wye ever needed. A whole family in one person. He'd never let her down.

Emerson deepened the kiss, savoring the feel of her mouth under his. Warmth spread through him along with a need that threatened to overwhelm his better nature. A moment later he bowled her gently over, laid her out on her back on the couch and covered her with his body. He kissed her thoroughly, and when she threaded her arms around his neck, he took that as an invitation. She was soft underneath him.

Wonderful.

Bracing himself on one elbow, kissing her all the

while, Emerson began undoing the buttons of her blouse. He had just exposed her bra when the front door crashed open, sending both of them scrambling to sit up and set their clothes to rights.

"What the hell is going on here? Where's Elise?" Ward bellowed.

OF ALL THE times for Ward to come home, Wyoming thought as she rose to her feet, quickly buttoning her shirt again. She was sure her face was flaming. At least her brother didn't look drunk—just angry.

"Ward, this is Emerson Myers. Emerson, this is my brother, Ward," she managed to say.

Ward ignored Emerson's outstretched hand. "You're screwing on my couch when you're supposed to be watching my daughter? What are you thinking, Wye?" His gaze roved between them, his jaw set in a familiar way. He was gunning for a fight.

"We weren't screwing around." Wye kept her voice even, refused to rise to the bait. "Elise is sleeping, and you'd better not wake her, because she cried all day. My friend brought me dinner. I don't see any harm in that."

"You're supposed to be babysitting." Ward finally entered the room fully, dropping his coat on the floor she'd vacuumed only hours ago. He'd better not expect her to hang it up. He wasn't a toddler.

"I held Elise for ten hours today. She was teething the whole time. I thought about calling you home from work."

Ward winced, like she knew he would. "I told you, I

can't take any more time off," he muttered.

"How many people did you talk to about the nanny position today?"

He waved off that question as he crossed the room. "I can't do personal business on work time."

"You took a lunch, right?"

"I work hard; I need a break at lunch." He headed for the kitchen. Wye followed him.

"I worked hard today, too, and I didn't get lunch off."

Ward turned on her. "You sound just like Mindy. Whine, whine, whine—"

Indignation rose inside her, but before she could chew out Ward, Emerson stepped between the two of them. "Hey, back off. Your sister is doing you a huge favor, so the least you can do is act grateful. Apologize!"

"Who the fuck do you think you—"

"Apologize!"

She thought Ward might punch Emerson, but he must have seen something in the other man's face that stopped him, because instead he stepped back and raised his hands placatingly. "Okay, okay. Chill, man. Sorry, Wye. You know how I get. It's just been a long day."

"For both of us," she pointed out.

"And it's time for us to go," Emerson said. "Wye, grab your things."

"But—"

"She lives *here* now," Ward spoke right over Wye. "She's not going anywhere."

"Why should she live here?" Emerson demanded. "She's got a houseful of friends at Two Willows who'd like to spend time with her."

"She needs to live here because she needs to take care of the baby," Ward said slowly, as if Emerson was stupid enough to need it spelled out for him. "She needs to get up with Elise when she wakes in the middle of the night."

Emerson's eyebrows shot up, and he turned to her. "Are you kidding me? Wye, are you the one getting up…?"

Wye couldn't blame him for his surprise, but what could she say? She was a sucker for her niece. As soon as the baby started crying, she needed to comfort her, and as soon as Ward realized she'd pop in to tend to the baby, he'd made sure to wait a few minutes before he got up—and then stopped getting up at all.

"What the hell am I saying? Of course you are," Emerson said disgustedly. "That stops today. You"—he turned to Ward—"will start acting like a father and take charge of your baby's needs. And you"—he looked to Wye—"are moving back to Two Willows, where you'll get the help you deserve. Every morning your brother can drop off Elise as early as he needs to. We're all up before dawn, anyway." He turned to Ward again. "Every evening, directly after work, you can pick up your daughter, take her home and care for her. You get off work at five, right?"

Ward just stared at him.

"Four, actually," Wye said.

"Four? Then you have until four-thirty to pick up Elise, or you'll pay Wyoming double."

"He doesn't pay me at all," Wyoming said, then wished she hadn't when both men turned on her. Was Emerson counting to ten? He looked like he was counting to ten. His eyes locked with Ward's.

"That stops right now. The going rate for daycare in Chance Creek is…" He named a weekly sum. "Paid in advance so you don't run out on the bill."

"Are you fucking kidding me?" Ward started, but Emerson spoke over him.

"Come on, Wye. Go get your things. Cass will love having you back. You'll see Elise tomorrow—as long as your brother brings the cash."

Wye hurried to do as he said, and Emerson swept her out the door, ignoring Ward's protests.

Outside, by their vehicles, Emerson took a breath. He wiped a hand over his mouth, hoping he hadn't angered Wye. "Sorry if I spoke out of turn. I probably should have asked you what you want to do instead of telling you."

"Normally I'd be pissed if someone took charge that way," she admitted, unlocking the door of her car and setting her bag inside, "but if I'd gotten involved, I'd still be back there—working for free."

A smile spread over Emerson's face as he realized she appreciated the way he'd stuck up for her. "Should we send someone over to help him tonight?"

She shook her head. "Ward's actually really good with Elise. He's avoiding her—and the responsibility for her—because he hasn't wanted to face what's happening. This is good for him. It'll get him moving on making some decisions." She went up on tiptoe, braced her hands on Emerson's chest and kissed the corner of his mouth. "Thank you."

"You're welcome."

Chapter 6

STANDING UP FOR Wyoming had felt better than he'd expected. Emerson knew people thought he was mild mannered and that sometimes he got over- looked because of it. What they didn't realize about him was he found it handy to hide in plain sight. Most of the time he was perfectly happy to be helpful and take a back seat to the action. When he needed to settle a score or protect a boundary, however, like he had tonight, the element of surprise worked to his ad- vantage.

Ward wasn't the only adversary who'd looked at him differently after a confrontation. Emerson was solid in his self-confidence when it came to that kind of thing. Men like Ward enjoyed bossing people around, but they also wanted to be liked and respected. When you pushed back, they surrendered quickly.

It was fun being a white knight for Wyoming, and the way she'd smiled at him afterward had him buzzing all the way to his toes. He'd be glad to be her protec- tor—when she needed it.

They each drove their own vehicle to Two Willows

and parked next to each other behind the house when they arrived. When they got out, Wye hesitated by his truck. "Do you think we'll ever truly belong here?" she asked softly.

He sensed she wanted to talk more before joining the others indoors. She'd had a long day with Elise, and the moment she stepped inside they'd be surrounded by the usual Two Willows hubbub.

"The standing stone likes us," he reminded her.

"Maybe it does," she said. "I wish I was more like Cass and her sisters sometimes."

"In what way?"

"More… I don't know. Impulsive and in the moment rather than always choosing the practical path."

"Cass is practical. Lena, too, don't you think?"

"In one way. But in another they're so…" She shrugged. "I don't even know what to call it. When they're mad, they get really mad. When they're sad, they cry. They *feel* things."

"We feel things. Don't we?" He moved to stand closer to her and took her hand.

"The difference between us and them is that in a minute, we'll go into the house, have a snack, clean up and go to bed at a decent hour so we can be rested and refreshed for work tomorrow. Cass and her sisters would… I don't know… do something crazy under the moonlight."

"I can be up for crazy." He tugged at her hand. "Let's see what the stone is doing."

"Now? It's pretty dark in there."

"It was dark last time, too. Come on."

"It's cold."

"None of the Reeds would ever say it's too cold to see the stone," he teased her.

Still, Wyoming hesitated. "What if something crazy actually happens, though? Cass told me a strange story about being in the maze once—how it wouldn't let her out."

In the moonlight, Wyoming's wild curls and pixie face gave her an otherworldly look, and Emerson was compelled to touch her. He lifted a hand to cup her chin. Smoothed her curls away from her face. "Then we'd just have to stay there. I bet we could figure out how to pass the time."

Her eyes widened, and for a moment he thought she'd say she wanted to go inside. Wye chewed on her lip, sent another uncertain gaze toward the maze and said, "Okay, let's see the stone."

Emerson's pulse thrummed as they made their way to the maze's entrance, still holding hands. Was he fooling himself, or had she just given him permission to get a little closer?

They were silent as they traversed the pathways. He was far steadier on his feet than he'd been the first time Wye dragged him through here, but he still stepped carefully, knowing how much damage one wrong move could do to his ankle. When they reached the center, a shiver traced down his spine. The stone looked a little wild in the light of the moon.

"Should we ask it a question?" Wye asked quietly.

Emerson led her close to it. "Like what?"

She leaned against the stone, facing him. "You could ask if I'd let you kiss me."

He probably should ask, Emerson thought, but he couldn't wait for an answer. Instead he braced his hands against the stone to either side of her and lowered his mouth to hers.

His kiss was slow, probing, and her response was sweet enough to take his breath away. He framed her feet with his own, wrapped his arms around her and leaned in. When they finally came up for air, they were both breathing hard.

"What else should I ask the stone?"

An impish smile played with her lips. "If I'd let you undress me?"

"What happened to it being too cold?"

"Shut up."

He chuckled and unbuttoned her coat slowly, pushed it back over her shoulders and helped her out of it.

"It is cold."

"We'll have to take care of that."

He lifted her sweater over her shoulders next, and Wye shimmied out of it. She quickly unbuttoned her shirt and shrugged it off.

"You'd better warm me up," she told him.

"Yes, ma'am." Emerson undid the catch of her bra and tugged it off to bare her breasts. He longed to be naked himself.

Soon.

When he palmed her breasts, sucking in a breath at their delicious heaviness, Wyoming sighed and leaned into him. Emerson caught her mouth in a kiss and began to struggle out of his own clothes.

Wyoming helped him strip down, until he stood in jeans, boots and nothing else. He wrapped her in another embrace, trying to keep her warm with skin-to-skin contact.

"You feel good," she groaned a moment later, "but I'm freezing."

"Should we go inside?"

Wyoming hesitated, freezing in his arms. "If they can do it, we can, too."

"Do what? Who?"

"You can't tell anyone I told you this," she whispered. "Cass would kill me—but they've all had sex out here in the maze. Every last one of them. Even when it was cold."

"And if we're going to live here…" He let the statement hang.

She shrugged. "It's like… in the rule book. Don't you think?"

Definitely. Emerson surveyed the situation, scooped his winter coat off the ground, hung it around her shoulders and backed her up against the stone again.

"What about you? Aren't you cold?"

"Don't worry about me." He'd be warm in a matter of minutes. "Wye, are you sure?"

She nodded.

"I need to hear you say it." He never wanted to do

anything she didn't want him to do.

"I'm sure," she said. "Look, I've spent years holding men at arm's length, not wanting to get involved. Not wanting to risk letting anyone treat me the way my father did. Then you came along. Emerson, no one... no one's ever stood up for me the way you did tonight. It was... amazing." She went up on tiptoe and kissed the underside of his chin. "So I'm sure—about this, anyway. I'm not making any promises about forever, though. Not yet. Maybe not ever. All I'm saying is I trust you. I know being with you will feel good. And I want..."

"You want to feel good?" he supplied.

"I want to get to know you better."

Was she blushing? He wished he could tell, but the light was too dim. At least it illuminated her curves—and her wicked little smile. God, Wye was hot as hell.

And she wanted him—inside her. His whole body heated at the thought of it.

Emerson worked at the button of her jeans, unzipped them and tugged them down.

"It'll be easier if they're off." Wyoming stepped out of one boot, then the other, balancing on top of Emerson's feet so as not to touch the snowy ground. She wriggled out of her jeans, her movements turning him on even more.

If that were possible.

He decided to join her. In for a penny, in for a pound, he thought. He hoped like hell no one came looking for them, or they'd get an eyeful of his bare ass.

When he'd shucked off his jeans and boxer briefs, Wyoming ran one hand lightly over him, tracing the scars he'd earned in the explosion, including a long one over his right hip where shrapnel had sliced his skin. He was grateful it hadn't gone deeper.

"Does it hurt?" she whispered.

"No. Only my ankle once in a while. It took the brunt of the damage."

Wyoming threaded her arms around his shoulders and pulled him close. "I could have lost you before I ever found you."

Emerson could hardly breathe. He knew exactly what she meant. He'd built a good life for himself in the Army, but the last few days had been sweeter than anything else he'd known.

"I'm right here, and I'm staying here, I promise," he told her, encircling her with his arms. He didn't ever want to let her go.

Wye pressed close against him, making it clear she wanted much more than kisses and hugs. "Emerson—"

He knew what she was asking for. Wanted it, too. His hands explored her curves, his erection hard between them.

"Protection?" he breathed in her ear as he edged her up against the stone again, the coat buffering her from its cold flank.

"We're covered. The Pill," she told him.

Good. Not that he'd be opposed to children when the time came, but first things first. He needed Wye to know how good things could be between them. He needed her to want forever.

"Oh," Wye breathed as he lifted her up, braced her against the stone, positioned himself between her legs, nudged against her, then pushed inside.

His own groan mingled with hers. Hell, he'd be lucky if he lasted a minute. He'd waited for this for so long.

Well, for a month, anyway.

His chuckle was lost in the kiss she pressed against his mouth, and Emerson tangled his hands in her hair as he entered her fully, needing to feel all of her. Wyoming wrapped her legs around his waist. Emerson had a bad moment, wondering if his ankle would hold, but it seemed to be doing fine. If fact, he wasn't sure when he'd last felt so strong.

Now he had full access to her, and it was everything he could do to hold back as they began to move together.

He wanted the moment to last forever. Wyoming in his arms was more than he'd ever hoped to deserve. Could they really make a life together here?

Could the universe be that kind to him?

He'd learned early the only safety lay in depending on yourself and yourself alone, but the General had chipped away at that stoicism, gradually letting him know he had a champion, at least. When he'd brought him here to Two Willows and encouraged him to woo Wyoming—and make his home here—Emerson hadn't known whether to trust him entirely.

Still didn't trust it would work out.

He hadn't let himself imagine a scenario in which Wyoming fell for him, either. He'd been ready to work hard to get her to consider him as a partner, but he hadn't suspected he'd succeed.

Here she was wrapped around him. He was inside her.

And she was—

Emerson lost the ability to think when Wye tilted her head back and her nipples brushed his chest. He wanted to spend hours exploring her breasts. Wanted to taste her. Bring her to completion again and again—

But it was late, and cold, and sooner or later someone would notice their vehicles behind the house and wonder where they'd got to.

He increased his pace until Wyoming's soft moans had him on the brink. She felt so damn good he couldn't stop.

"Wyoming?"

She opened her eyes. Gazed into his.

As her orgasm overtook her, Emerson lost control and rode the wave of her release with her, pulse after pulse thrumming through him until he thought it would never end. When it did, he gathered her up, breathing hard, and leaned with her against the stone.

"You all right?"

"I'm fabulous." Her voice was rough, though, and Emerson pulled back when he saw the glint of tears in her eyes.

"You sure?"

"Yes." She nodded with a little laugh. "I think—it's

the relief. Of finding this with someone. It's been a while."

"For me, too." He might never have found "the one" before, but he was no saint, either.

He wanted to stay right there, but he knew they'd both be shivering in moments, so he pulled out of her, Wyoming's small moan of disappointment a balm to his soul. She wanted more of him.

Well, he wanted a hell of a lot more of her, too.

They dressed quietly, helping each other balance until each of them was back in jeans and boots.

Emerson caught her in an embrace before they went back to the house and gave her the kind of kiss that should let her know exactly what he was thinking.

She breathed out when he was done. "I knew I liked you," she said. "But I had no idea I'd like you like this when we met."

He'd known he'd love her right from the first time he laid eyes on her, but he wouldn't tell her that yet. Instead, he took her hand and led the way out of the maze.

IT WAS FAR more fun to be a Reed than it was to be a Smith, Wyoming decided when she woke up the next morning. She'd dreamed of Emerson, of making love to him again in the maze.

That had been unexpectedly wonderful, she admitted. She needed to get naked with Emerson a lot more often.

He'd known exactly how to fire her up. When she

thought about the way she'd shattered in his arms, she felt her cheeks warm but in a good way—in anticipation of doing it again rather than any sort of shame.

Emerson wasn't a love-her-and-leave-her kind of man. He'd been with her because he liked her. Hell, he'd told her he wanted to marry, even if she hadn't entirely taken him seriously before.

Could she marry him?

Wye shifted in her bed uncomfortably. What would it be like to have a partner? She wasn't sure she believed in marriage. Would have told anyone who asked before the last few weeks that marriage wasn't in her life plan. Watching her parents' marriage disintegrate—and now Ward's, too—made it difficult to believe in a fairy tale in which people stayed together. Even if she'd watched every one of the Reed women fall in love and marry.

Wasn't it safer to keep to herself?

Lots of women lived on their own these days, after all. Had careers. Bought themselves everything they wanted and needed, from houses to jewelry and more. Chose when and where to date men—or women. Didn't feel the need to weigh things down with more permanent arrangements.

What was in it for her in a long-term commitment? Emerson was wonderful now. Helpful. Supportive. The way he'd sorted out Ward last night was wonderful, but long-term?

Wouldn't he sink into the same kind of self-absorption most men exhibited?

She'd hate to be married to a man like that.

Wyoming climbed out of bed, wrapped herself in a robe and moved to find clothes for the day. Out in the hall, she ran into Connor, who was already dressed and looked to be heading out to do his chores. He lifted a finger to his lips.

"Sadie's sleeping. She had a headache last night. I'm hoping she can sleep in."

Wyoming nodded and fondly watched the big man tiptoe down the hall. Cass and her sisters had found men that didn't seem prone to being self-absorbed.

They were all still in the honeymoon phase, though, she reminded herself. Who knew what would happen in time?

"Wyoming?" Emerson's voice had her turning around. He was lounging in the doorway of his room, wearing sweatpants but nothing else. The strong planes of his chest made her fingers itch to explore his body all over again. Heat pulsed inside her, reminding her of how good it had felt to take him inside her last night.

"Just getting in the shower."

A grin tugged the corners of his mouth. "I could join you." He shrugged. "Don't have to if you're not a morning person."

She was a morning person. "Give me two minutes. I need to freshen up." She ducked into the bathroom, closed the door and got ready for a close encounter with the sexy soldier. She opened the door a crack, checked to see if he was still there and opened it more widely, like an invitation. "Come on in."

Emerson looked up and down the hall and hurried

past her. "We'd better be fast. Someone else will be up and wanting a chance in the shower."

"I can be fast." She knew she'd be hard pressed to last a minute if Emerson made love to her again.

She worked the knobs of the shower, and soon the water temperature was right, she disrobed. Half a minute later, they were both under the stream of water.

When Wyoming had wet her hair and squirted a dollop of shampoo in her palm, Emerson took over, scraping the shampoo from her hand and sudsing her hair. When he began to massage her scalp, she moaned. "You can do that every day."

"I'd like to." He dropped a kiss to her neck. "Rinse."

"Mmm." She did as she was told as he quickly washed his own hair and leaned in to rinse it. When he lathered his hands with soap and began to scrub her body, she turned and leaned her back against his chest, enjoying the lazy circles he made around her belly, hips and breasts.

Turning her again, he soaped her back and bottom as he bent to take one nipple in his mouth. Teasing her and eliciting more moans, he rinsed his hands, then dipped them between her legs.

Wyoming clung to him, unable to do anything else, but when her foot slipped, Emerson looked up. "Not sure we can do this without one of us sustaining an injury—and that's the last thing either of us needs. Come on. I want all of you."

"Me, too."

He helped her out of the shower, turned it off, wrapped her in one towel and himself in another, and opened the door a sliver.

"Coast's clear."

They scuttled across the hall into his room, where he picked her up and tossed her lightly onto the bed.

"Brace yourself," he growled playfully.

Wyoming shrieked when he jumped after her, and he covered her mouth with his hand. "Shh, you want to wake the whole house?"

She shook her head. "Not until we're done, anyway." She rolled over onto her belly and propped herself up on her elbows, wondering if he'd understand, but Emerson had already lowered himself on top of her, the salient part of him nudging against her, ready to go.

Their foreplay in the shower meant she was slick and ready for him, and as he slid inside her, she pulled one of his hands beneath her to cup her breast.

Emerson began to move, and she knew soon she would feel as good as she had last night. There were so many things she wanted to try with him. Different positions, different tempos…

Maybe it wouldn't be so bad to spend a lifetime with one man.

Emerson gripped her hip with his free hand and worked in and out of her with an intensity that soon had her panting with need. Braced on her elbows, she pushed back against him, needing all of him inside her. He obliged gladly, and soon it was all she could do to hold on. She wanted to feel this way forever—wanton.

Desired and desiring. Hungry—on the brink of being satisfied.

Loved.

Wyoming's eyes flew open at the thought, but her release overtook her at the same time, and the way Emerson pumped into her sent it crashing over her until all she could do was ride the waves of emotion.

Was she crying out? She tried to hold it in, but she didn't know if she succeeded. Emerson thrust inside her one last time and collapsed on top of her. Wyoming lay panting until her heart slowed again, her mind still tangled in the conundrum her emotions had served.

Was she loved by Emerson?

Surely not—it was way too soon.

When he slid out, she felt the same sense of being bereft she'd felt the previous evening. She craved that connection with Emerson, no matter how short a time she'd known him.

Love at first sight.

The phrase echoed through her mind.

Was it real? Or was it a trap? Mother nature determined to perpetuate the species at all costs?

Emerson turned her gently to face him. "You're thinking," he accused with a smile.

"I'm made to want you, aren't I? Even if it isn't wise."

"Maybe it's the wisest thing of all. I'd spend my life caring for you, Wyoming."

"How can you know what you'll feel like in twenty years?"

He smiled, but it was a sad one. "Because I know what I felt twenty years ago. I'm gambling, too, you know. I got my heart broken once before."

By his parents, she understood. They might not have meant to leave him, but they had.

"I think love is worth the gamble." He took her hand and kissed her fingers one after the other, then placed a final kiss in her palm. "You don't have to make up your mind today," he assured her.

"Have you made up yours?" She hadn't meant to ask, and she held her breath, waiting for his answer.

This time his smile reached his eyes.

"Hell, yeah. I asked you to marry me, didn't I? I wasn't kidding around, Wye. I know what I want, and it's not a slice of Two Willows. It's you. It'll always be you."

And he kissed her again.

EMERSON KEPT HIS eye on the time and made sure they were dressed and downstairs for breakfast by the time the General began to bellow for him and Ward showed up with Elise.

Ward was gruff this morning, and he didn't meet Emerson's gaze, but he handed the baby to Wye tenderly, kissed Elise's head and said, "Thanks for taking her today." He hesitated, put his hand in his pocket and pulled out a check. "Your friend's right; I should be paying you. Wish it could be more."

"We're family…"

Emerson closed his eyes but didn't interfere. Wye

needed to learn to stand up for herself with her kin.

Ward shook his head. "This is a lot bigger deal than asking you to watch her for a few hours on a Friday night. This is a full-time job. See you tonight."

"See you."

When he was gone, Wye looked to Emerson in astonishment. "Did you see that? He gave me a check."

"Better cash it quick." He regretted his joke almost immediately. "Just kidding." He touched her arm. "I knew your brother would be reasonable. He was too caught up in his own grief to think about anyone else until now."

"Did I hear a baby?" Cass said, bustling into the room and pulling on an apron. "I've got to get breakfast started, but first I need a snuggle."

Wye got Elise out of her carrier, and Cass took the baby in her arms. "You are darling, aren't you?" she asked the little girl.

"When you aren't teething," Wye clarified, looking over Cass's shoulder and making funny faces that caused Elise to giggle.

"And we get her all day?" Cass began to move around the kitchen, gathering ingredients for the meal, baby still at her shoulder.

"That's right." Wye took back Elise. "So you'll get plenty of time with her."

"Good. Emerson, you haven't made coffee—"

"Where's my coffee?" the General bellowed from his office.

"Hell, you're right. Falling down on the job." He

winked at Wye, then got busy.

Luckily the General was in a good mood and didn't seem to mind his coffee was late. When it came time for his exercises, however, he was as elusive as ever. Emerson had hoped he could take Wye to the Park to see his improvements on the trailers, but the way the General kept dragging his feet, they wouldn't have time.

"You were right, Cass," Emerson called out when he couldn't take it anymore. "At this rate your baby will be riding a horse long before the General gets back in the saddle."

Cass appeared in the doorway of the General's room, her features slack with surprise. "What are you talking about?"

"Your father refuses to do his physical therapy exercises. Instead of getting more limber, he's getting stiffer. All I'm saying is it's a good thing he'll have grandkids soon to get all the chores done, because he's not going to do any of them himself."

Cass put her hands up as if to say she wanted no part of this and ducked away without saying a word. Emerson didn't blame her when he caught the General's expression.

"Are you saying a passel of babies are going to run my ranch?"

"Pretty much. If they don't take their cue from you and sit around on their asses all day, sir."

It was a risk, but he knew the General would suffer more long term if he didn't do those exercises than he would if he simply buckled down and got to them.

"You think that reverse psychology bullshit is going to work on me?"

"What *will* work? Because we need you up and on your feet, General. I know you're sore and frustrated, but you're not an old man, even if you're acting like one. You could have decades ahead of you to enjoy your ranch and your family. What's it going to take for you to see that?"

"Whatever it is, it won't be your nagging that does it—" The General stopped midsentence, and Emerson followed his gaze out the window, craning his neck to see whatever it was that had arrested the General's attention.

He smiled when he caught sight of Brian leading Button and Jack balancing baby Elise on the horse's back. Elise was squealing with delight. Wyoming was following them with her arms half-raised, obviously worried that Jack might let go.

The General scrubbed a hand over his jaw. "Hell." He shook his head. "Well, what are you waiting for, Sergeant? Get over here and help me exercise. No baby is going to steal a march on me."

"ELISE LOVES YOUR costumes," Wye told Alice. She and Cass had brought the baby to her carriage house studio, and Alice had heaped a number of costumes around her. The different textures of cloth they were made from entranced the little girl.

"Everyone loves costumes," Alice said.

"Wye? Are you up here?" a voice called, and a moment later, Emerson came up the stairs and poked his head into the room. "There you are." Coming into the large space, he greeted the women and bent down to chuck Elise under the chin. "I came to see if you want to go to the Park for a bit," he told Wye.

"Sure. Let me grab Elise's backpack carrier from the house," Wye said.

"Why don't you leave her with me for an hour?" Cass put in. "That way you can help Emerson."

"You don't mind?"

"Not at all. It's time I got back to work. Elise can help me fold the laundry."

"I'll help, too," Alice said.

"Seems like cheating to get paid for taking care of Elise and then getting Cass and Alice to do the work," Wye joked a few minutes later as she walked with Emerson down the track past the outbuildings. She was dressed for the weather in her coat, a white knitted cap and gloves, but the sun was out, and she didn't mind the cold.

"I'll have you earning your keep in no time." Emerson stopped and dipped a hand in his pocket, pulling out his phone, which was vibrating. "Emerson Myers here," he said when he lifted it to his ear. He listened a moment. "Yes, I will have a couple of trailers coming up for rent soon. Three of them?" He made a face at Wyoming. "I've got three, but they all need renovating. I hadn't planned on renting them until February at the earliest." He listened again. "January fifteenth? That's cutting it pretty close." A pause. "Okay, how about you give me a few days. Come out on Thursday." He hung up. "Buck's been talking out of turn. Seems like someone in Chance Creek is taking a fourplex off the market—turning it into a few condos instead of renting them out. One of the current inhabitants is leaving town, but three of them are friends of Buck's and want to stay close to each other."

"You've got all the trailers rented before they're even ready. You're some businessman."

Emerson shook his head. "That's a lot of work to do in a short time. I'm going to end up renovating while people are living in them."

"I guess that's better than them ending up on the street. Let's make a list of what needs to be done, and we can make a plan."

"We?"

"Sounds like you need help," Wye pointed out. Besides, she liked the idea of renovating the trailers. It was a finite project, and when it was done, someone would enjoy the results. No other problems in her life were so easily solved.

"I'd love help." Emerson snagged a kiss.

"No more of that; we've got work to do."

By the end of their inspection, Wye wasn't as upbeat. Several of the trailers needed to be completely gutted, and one she wasn't sure could be fixed at all. It had a stuffy smell she thought would be hard to get out, even though Emerson assured her it was possible.

They returned to the main house for lunch. Afterward, Cass had an appointment, so Emerson carried

Elise's portable crib to the Park so they could get back to work. While the baby slept at one end of the best trailer of the bunch, Wye and Emerson sat at the other end, itemized their to-do list and constructed a calendar for the operation, Emerson ducking out now and then to confirm information or take a measurement in one of the other trailers.

"I wish I could help more," Wye said after they'd trudged back to the main house for dinner, Emerson carrying the portable crib again and Wye carrying a wriggling Elise. When Ward arrived a few minutes later and whisked the baby away home, Cass pressed a storage container of lasagna on him, since she'd made a double batch for dinner. "We could work at night, when Elise isn't around."

"We'll probably need to do that regardless," Emerson said. "But don't worry; I appreciate whatever help you can give."

"You need some help at the Park?" Jack said as he came into the kitchen and took a seat at the table. "I'm happy to lend a hand. I'm pretty handy, and I'm working only part-time with Cab at the station."

"Hunter and I are old hands at building things," Jo said as she and her husband joined them. "We'd love to help. It's winter, so things are kind of slow around here anyway."

"Jo's right. We need practice for when we build our big house come spring," Hunter said cheerfully. Wye thought he was one of the most contented married men she'd ever seen. She'd thought Hunter and Jo an odd couple when he'd first come to Two Willows, but now she was convinced they were made for each other.

"What's going on?" Lena asked, coming in from outside and hanging up her coat.

"We're all going to help Emerson and Wye with fixing the trailers," Jo told her.

Logan came in next and started to pull off his outer gear. "Emerson and Wye are fixing up the trailers," Lena relayed to him. "We'll help, right?"

"Sure. Tonight?"

"I guess," Lena said at the same time Emerson said, "No. Not tonight."

"I thought you just said…" Cass began and trailed off when she took in Emerson's expression. She shifted her gaze to Wye and raised an eyebrow. Wye just shrugged. She wasn't sure why Emerson's mood had shifted so quickly. Hadn't he just been saying he needed to get on with the project?

"I appreciate the offer," Emerson said, his gaze dropping to the floor. "It's just… this is my project. I need to contribute around here, and if you all do the renovations for me, I'll be back to square one."

The other men exchanged glances, and Wyoming knew they didn't understand, but she did. She felt the same way, after all.

"You all have chores on the ranch," she explained. "Emerson and I would like to do something to help out, as well."

"The General is insisting I take a percentage for managing the trailers, but—"

"Of course you'll take a percentage," Jo said. "It only makes sense."

"I think we should give Emerson a competitive wage, not just a percentage," Logan said.

"That's not—"

The General shuffled into the room, leaning heavily on his cane. "What's the hubbub all about?"

When it seemed no one would answer, Brian spoke up. "We're figuring out how to pay Emerson for his work on the trailers—a percentage or an hourly wage."

Wye saw Emerson's face fall and knew why. They were back to treating him like a hired hand, not one of the family, like the General said he'd be. Brian, Logan and the others might think they were being helpful, but in reality they were killing Emerson's dream of belonging here.

Which meant they were killing her dream, too.

And she found she wasn't ready to let go of it without a fight.

"You know what, Emerson?" she spoke up loudly. "As good as this lasagna smells, I think you should take me out to dinner tonight, and I think the rest of you should talk about whether you actually want Emerson and me here long-term or not. The General told Emerson he'd get a share in the ranch and that if he married me, I'd be family, too. I don't think anyone else agrees with him, though. Everyone keeps pretending we're welcome here, but I get the feeling we're not on those terms. Here's your chance to talk among yourselves and figure it out once and for all."

"Wye," Cass began but Wye cut her off.

"Talk to your family, Cass. Really talk to them. Figure out what you want—because it's not fair to keep us in limbo like this. We'll be back later, and we'll abide by your answer no matter what it is. Come on, Emerson."

He followed without a word.

Chapter 7

"WHO'S THE BOSS now?" Emerson teased Wye on the way to town, although he'd been grim for most of the drive. "You put the Two Willows posse on notice back there."

"That's the problem with so many adults living under one roof—too many people who think they're in charge."

He relaxed as the heat warmed the truck's interior. It was a cold, clear night. Stars twinkled overhead in a sable sky. If this were a true date, he was sure he'd be enjoying himself, but Logan's and Brian's careless words at Two Willows had cut him to the quick. He'd been smart not to count on the General's assertions that there was a place for him there. Obviously, there wasn't.

"It'll get better in the spring when people start building their own homes, I guess." Emerson kept his gaze on the snowy road ahead of them as the headlights cut through the gloom. At least he knew what Wyoming felt.

"I'm sure it will—for them. You aren't mad I took over the situation?"

"Not at all." That was the one bright spot in the situation, actually. Wyoming scolding the General and everyone else was something to see. Proof that she cared for him—and was thinking long term when it came to their relationship.

That was good.

"The General should have talked to the rest of them well before he made you any promises. I don't know what he was thinking. How are you feeling?"

He grunted. "I'm okay."

She slid him a look that said she knew he was lying. It hurt to know that Brian, Logan, Jack and the other men felt they deserved a slice of Two Willows, just for following orders and marrying the General's daughters, but they couldn't see their way clear to allowing him the same reward for his service to the man. He'd worked side by side with the General for years. He hadn't ever screwed up and faced a court martial like all of them had, either. They had to realize he wouldn't rest on his laurels. Always pulled his weight. Always went above and beyond. He would be an asset to Two Willows. Why couldn't they see that?

"At least we get a chance to be by ourselves."

It was his turn to slide a look her way. "Is that a good thing?"

"You know it is." Wye grinned. "Keep your eyes on the road, Soldier."

"I'm watching where I'm going," he assured her. "I've got a question for you, though."

"Oh yeah? What's that?"

"Will you still be interested in dating me if they say no?"

Wye studied the dark landscape outside her window. "I'm not fragile, Emerson. I won't run at the first sign of trouble. You and I still have a lot of getting to know each other to do, but if things don't work out between us, it won't be because you don't have a share in Two Willows."

"Good to know."

Just as they were seated at DelMonaco's, Wye's phone rang. She pulled it out and frowned.

"It's Cass. Should I answer it?"

Emerson nodded. Might as well learn the worst.

"Hi, Cass." Wye listened a moment before going on, her side of the conversation punctuated by long silences. "That's good to hear. Okay. Uh-huh. All right. Yes, I guess so. I mean… sure. I know how the General is." She looked up at Emerson. "I don't think he'll mind. See you later? Bye."

"What'd she say?" Emerson pretended to look over the menu, but he wasn't even reading the words. At first he'd thought it was good news, but the longer the call had gone on, the more uncomfortable Wye looked.

"They've decided they want both of us to stay," Wye said. "Which is good. The General has made it clear he views you on equal footing to the rest of the men and views me as an honorary daughter. Cass says they had a full discussion, and as soon as the General agreed to hear them out, everyone fell over themselves saying they want you to join them—but they want the

General to stop acting like a dictator. They want a democracy. Cass says it got a little dicey. I'm not sure the General believes in democracy."

"The General believes in the Army, and the Army doesn't believe in democracy—not within its ranks, anyway," Emerson corrected her.

"Anyway, the upshot is we're in. You're an honorary son, like all the other men. I'm an honorary daughter."

He sensed something was bothering her. "But…" he prompted.

"I guess… I don't understand why he'd do that—I mean, I get why he wants you around; you're obviously very important to him. I'm riding on your coattails."

"I don't think that's true. I think you qualify because of the way Cass feels about you. I think the General appreciates the good head on your shoulders and the way you've been a steady friend to her."

"That's not enough to earn a share in a ranch like Two Willows." She played with her fork. "I just don't want to believe in something that could be pulled out from under my feet at any moment. And I'm not talking about the share of the property, either."

He knew that. She was talking about family. "You're afraid if you relax your guard and allow Cass and the rest of them to love you, they could take that love back at any moment."

Wye swallowed and nodded. "That's it exactly. Why would they stick with me when my own parents…" She shook her head. "There's more," she added.

"What?"

"I'm supposed to help you with the trailers. We're supposed to run them together, and I'm supposed to do the books for them and help with the books for the ranch, too. I think the General's mixed up my paralegal job with accounting."

"Are you good with numbers?"

"Actually, yes," she conceded.

"But you want to keep doing paralegal work?"

"I've been looking for jobs in Bozeman and Billings. There simply isn't enough work here in town to go around."

"You like paralegal work, though?" he pressed. She hadn't answered him straight.

"I don't dislike it," Wye said after a moment's hesitation.

That wasn't saying much. He leaned back. "You wouldn't mind the commute?"

"I hadn't intended to commute," she said softly. When Emerson didn't answer that, she met his gaze.

"You make me wonder if I've made myself clear," he said softly. "I'm looking for a lifetime with you, Wyoming. I'd like to share my future with you. I'm happy to share running the Park with you. I'm happy to support you if you want to work in Billings or Bozeman, although I'll worry about you driving that commute in winter." He flashed her a smile. "I know the General is trying to box you in, trying to sort things out too fast for you. You don't have to make up your mind yet, although I'd hoped you already had." He reached out, took her hand and stroked a thumb over her palm. "I've been in love with you since the moment I saw you. I know that's the oldest line in the book, but there it is: it's true. How about we give living at Two Willows and being a part of it a try? You help me with the rentals, and I'll help you with Elise, and we'll see what happens."

"Cass said we should keep a percentage of the rent we earn and pay the rest into the general operations account for the ranch. The others would like to help us with renovations one day a week. You provide the list of what needs to be done, and they'll provide the labor."

"You didn't answer my question."

"I do want to try," Wye admitted. "I just... don't want to fail."

"Honey." He wanted to draw her into his arms, but that would have to wait for later. Instead he squeezed her hand. "Maybe we don't have to fail."

She nodded.

"Wye. Look at me." He waited until she did so. "How about we decide to succeed?"

After a moment, she nodded again.

EMERSON WAS STILL thinking about their conversation when he drove the General into Billings the following day. Wyoming had shared his bed last night—but for only part of the night, slipping back to her own room after they'd been together.

"I'm not ready to share our status with everyone else," she'd said.

Emerson doubted anyone was unaware of what they

were doing, but he'd held his tongue. Wyoming valued her independence, and if he pushed her, he might not like the consequences. He couldn't blame her for being wary of trusting him or the General and his family all that much; he knew her own family had let her down. Her concerns plucked at his own. He might talk a good game about trusting the General, but he knew how quickly someone's patronage could slip away.

"Looking forward to this?" he asked the General as they neared the reserve station.

The General grunted, but Emerson knew he was. The man needed to be useful. He sat ramrod straight in the passenger seat, alert and ready.

While most of their time at the reserve station had been spent on preparation and paperwork so far, today was the beginning of the unit's once-a-month training weekend. The General took his duties seriously, and as usual, Emerson functioned as his right-hand man, making sure he had everything he needed, being his legs when something was out of his reach, transmitting information to the other officers who headed up the active training sessions.

The work gave the General a renewed sense of purpose, and Emerson liked it, too, even if his injuries sidelined him from serving in a more active way. He could almost forget his bum ankle as he hustled around, and when the reservists learned that he'd been overseas when he was injured, most of them treated him with a kind of deference that soothed something bitter in him he hadn't realized he was harboring.

So when he exited the General's on-site office at the end of the weekend, tired and happy from the experience, it was a blow to overhear some of the trainees as they prepared to return to their homes.

"I can see why they hired the General. The man's a legend. I don't care if he's injured; he knows stuff worth listening to. But Sergeant Myers? What's his deal? There's plenty of men around who can do the General's errands for him."

"I heard he's never even been in the field," another man said. "Spent his whole time at USSOCOM in Florida. Pretty cushy, if you ask me."

"He got that limp overseas, you idiot," a third man said.

"His first time overseas."

Emerson pulled back into the General's office and closed the door, figuring he'd wait to leave until they were gone. Confronting them would make him feel like a fool. They'd back right down, of course. They couldn't insult him to his face when he worked for the General. He'd prefer knowing how they really felt.

"Why are you malingering there?" the General said when he'd packed his briefcase. "Thought you were going to load our bags into the truck."

"Yes, sir," Emerson said. He opened the door again. The reserve men had scattered, and he exited the building, all his satisfaction in the weekend gone. This was just one more place he'd never really belong.

"ISN'T THIS THE cutest thing you ever saw?" Cass held

up a pale-green baby onesie dotted with tiny dinosaurs.

"Everything in this store is the cutest thing I've ever seen," Wyoming told her truthfully. They'd driven to Bozeman to go shopping, and Wye was discovering that baby clothes were like candy—absolutely delicious and hard on your wallet.

"Look at these!" Cass pounced on a pair of soft baby slippers made to look like cowboy boots.

"Should we just grab one of everything in the shop?"

"I wish we could."

Wye had to admit Cass was showing remarkable restraint, all in all. She had several bags of purchases, but she'd picked up and put down hundreds of items that were just as darling as the ones she'd bought.

"I'm so glad you'll be at Two Willows when the baby is born."

Wye made a noncommittal sound. That was several months away, after all, and despite her conversation with Emerson the night before, who knew what might happen in the meantime.

"Wye? You will be at Two Willows in March, won't you?"

"I... hope so."

"What does that mean?" Cass put down the baby boots.

"I'd like to be. And things are going well with Emerson. But—"

"But what?" She sorted through items on the display table but kept her gaze on Wye.

"Honestly? I don't entirely understand why you'd want me to be." Wye hadn't meant to say that—especially not here—but the truth slipped out before she could stop it. "I mean, we're friends, and it's been fun to have a long visit. I get that. But you've got a husband, a baby coming. All your sisters, their husbands and your father live on the ranch. Why on earth would you want me there permanently, too?"

Cass let the sweater she was holding fall on top of the others, and Wye's heart contracted as her friend's eyes filled with tears.

"Cass," Wye said.

"I forget sometimes how short a time you've known me," Cass said finally, blinking back the dampness in her eyes. "It feels like we've shared so much, but we really haven't."

Cass was right. They'd become close only about a year and a half ago. Wye had known who Cass was, of course, and vice versa, but since Cass and her sisters were homeschooled, they'd never gotten to know each other during their younger years. It was only when they'd both volunteered at a blood donation drive for the local hospital that they'd got to talking and realized they had enough in common to be friends. They'd started meeting for coffee on Saturday mornings, and progressed to lunches and shopping excursions, and soon they'd been talking and texting almost daily. It was hard for Wye to remember a time when Cass wasn't in her life.

"Before I turned twenty-one and Dad finally

stopped sending substitute mothers to watch over us, I rarely got off the ranch," Cass went on. "When one of the wardens, as we called them, was around, we spent all our time figuring out ways to get rid of her. When we managed it, we went to ground trying to eke out as long a period of time unchaperoned as we could before one of the General's spies realized what was happening and got word to him, and he sent someone else. It was like waging psychological warfare. It took up all our time, along with all the chores we were handling ourselves so the General wouldn't realize we'd run off another of his overseers."

"You and your sisters were firecrackers."

Cass frowned, and too late Wye remembered her penchant for explosives. "Sorry." Cass was making it a point these days to feel her feelings rather than set off fireworks to express them. "I mean it, though. You were some fierce teenagers."

"I guess." Cass gazed into the distance at something that was only in her mind. She came to with a start and looked down at the tiny sweater in its crumpled heap. "Fierce and lonely as hell, Wye. I think we're all still making up for that. Those weren't exactly happy times," she added quietly.

Remorse filled Wyoming. "I guess not." She had a habit of making Cass's and her sisters' lives like a fairy tale in her mind, but there was nothing fairy-tale-like about your mother dying when you were a teenager, your father abandoning you and enduring a year's worth of attacks by a would-be drug cartel.

"I value good friends—and company," Cass said. "When you're around, I don't feel so alone."

"How can you possibly feel alone living with so many other people?"

Cass smiled. "I think all of us have holes in our hearts that seem impossible to fill."

Wye thought that over, touching a soft baby towel set. "Maybe you're right. Maybe that's my problem. I have a hole the size of an entire family in my heart."

"I'm surprised you're not more excited to live with us, then," Cass said seriously. "We're a big family!"

"The problem is trust," Wye told her. "What if I let you all in and then you decide you don't want me? I'd be better off not setting myself up to get hurt like that, don't you think?"

Cass touched the tiny sweater again, picked it up and folded it. "I can see why you'd think so, but I don't agree. I think you need to fling yourself at every opportunity for love. Some might not work out, but others will."

Flinging herself at love sounded terrifying.

Cass laughed. "You should see your face. Come on, Wye. I love you like another sister, but like a better one because you didn't spend years trying to buck all my attempts to parent you, like Alice, Lena, Jo and Sadie did."

"It's hard to penetrate that inner circle. You and your sisters." Wye felt her face heat, and she turned away to admire a display of plush toys.

"I guess I can see that," Cass said slowly. "We spent

so much time together growing up."

"And I had no one." Hell, she hadn't meant to say that, either.

"Ward wasn't much of a brother to you when your mom left, was he?"

Wye shook her head. "He stayed as far away from home as he could manage during those years. Joined every sports team he could. Hung out at friends' houses. Slept over as often as he could manage it, which was a lot. I can't blame him; it was no fun at home."

"But you got stuck dealing with your dad."

"Someone had to. Anyway, that's ancient history."

"I'm sorry," Cass said.

"For what?" Wye turned back.

"For not being there."

Wye blinked—and blinked again, tears stinging her eyes. She could have used a friend like Cass back then. "You barely knew me," she said reasonably. "You can't be sorry for that."

"I am, though. I should have known you. I should have invited you to Two Willows. You would have made a good addition to our little guerilla army."

"I would have," Wye agreed.

"Which is why I want you to join us now. Not many people truly understand my past, Wye, but you do. You get me in a way few people do. And you're funny and smart. You make any day better when you're around. You're my best friend. You're family. True family. That's not going to change."

Wye crossed to hug her, which was something, because on the whole she wasn't a demonstrative person. Cass blinked at her, surprised but pleased. "I wish I was your sister," Wye said. "I wish I was magic like you all are."

"You are magic," Cass insisted. "And from now on you *are* one of us." She hugged her back fiercely. "Deal?"

"Deal," Wye said.

"You're awfully quiet, Sergeant," the General said halfway through their drive to Two Willows.

If the General had noticed his mood, he wasn't doing too well hiding it, Emerson thought. "Keeping my eyes on the road," he said.

"Something eating at you?"

Emerson shook his head. No way was he repeating the conversation he'd overheard at the reserve center. The General would wave away his concerns. He'd found nothing to fault in Emerson's service, so no one else should, either, but those men were right; he hadn't seen much of combat. Wherever the General went, he was protected as an asset the US government didn't want to lose, which meant Emerson had been protected, too. That didn't mean his service with the General hadn't placed him in dangerous situations. Exhibit A: his ankle.

It wasn't the first time his service had been derided. He knew rumors had swirled at USSOCOM about his real role in the General's life. Some people thought he must be a relative of the General's, given a cushy position based on his connection. Others thought he was little better than a servant. Still others whispered maybe he shared the General's bed.

He'd never let any of that bother him. Despite what those reservists thought, he'd traveled the world with the General, and he knew his attention to the small details left the man's mind free to hone in on the big ones—the ones that had affected the lives of thousands of soldiers over the years. He hadn't required understanding from the general public—or praise from the General. The job was truly its own reward, to his way of thinking. Knowing that by keeping him safe and happy he was helping to keep all the troops who served under the man safe and happy, too, gave him satisfaction.

Making himself useful. Wasn't that what a man was supposed to do?

"I've got a houseful of sons-in-law now," the General said, cutting through his thoughts.

Emerson glanced his way. The General kept his eyes forward.

"I hope in time I feel about them as I might have felt about sons of my own. I always thought I'd have sons, you know, but Amelia knew we'd have daughters."

Emerson slowed down to negotiate a turn, then accelerated again.

"She told me about them the day we bought her engagement ring. It was as if she could see them. Guess she could," he added gruffly. "That woman saw everything."

Emerson knew Amelia was what one might call fey.

Second sight. The ability to see the future. Amelia had passed some of that magic to her daughters.

"I love my daughters," the General asserted suddenly, and Emerson had to grip the wheel to keep from swerving off the road. He knew the General loved his daughters, of course, but he didn't think he'd ever heard him say so out loud.

Had he?

"I guess I thought I might have an easier time relating to a boy."

Emerson kept quiet. It wasn't often the General talked about his feelings. He didn't want to interrupt.

"That wasn't to be. Like I said, I look forward to getting to know my sons-in-law well enough to feel related to them."

"Yes, sir."

"But I don't have to wait to feel like that with you."

Emerson swallowed. Hell, was the General saying—

"Maybe I'm out of line, but I feel like a father to you. That's why I call you son. I realize I don't deserve to call you that—"

"Yes, you do." The General had been there for him in a way no one else had—until Wyoming came along.

"I want to say how proud I am of you. The job I've asked you to do all these years isn't glamorous. Hell, dealing day in, day out with a grumpy old fart like me—"

"I've been proud to serve with you, sir."

"There must have been times you wanted something more exciting."

Emerson did swerve off the road this time and

parked the truck. He turned to the General. "I haven't regretted a single day of my service with you. It's been all I could ask for, and if I was given my choice of assignments, I'd choose the same thing—even knowing the outcome." He pointed to his ankle. "My father was a man of integrity, and I wish he was still alive, but with him gone, there's only one man I know who could hope to take his place in my estimation. And that's you."

The General kept looking out the windshield. His eyes were dry, but his jaw worked a moment before he said, "That's a lot to live up to, son."

"I know you'll manage it, sir." Emerson started the truck again and veered back onto the road, glad they'd gotten to the heart of it.

"You've got a lot to teach those men at the reserve center. I hope they figure that out."

"Doubt it, sir."

The General guffawed. "Then I guess we'll have to shove the lesson down their throats. You keep showing up. You keep showing them the same dedication you've shown me, and soon enough they'll all give you your due."

Emerson hoped he was right.

"DID YOU HAVE a good weekend?" Wye asked when Emerson and the General arrived at Two Willows. She, Cass, Lena, Jo, Sadie and Alice were all gathered by the back door, pulling on their outerwear.

Emerson nodded, kissed her on the cheek and said, "Let me get the General settled. He needs rest." He eyed the gathering of women curiously.

"We both do," the General said.

"We're heading out, anyway," Cass said. "Be back in a few hours."

"At this time of night on a Sunday? Where are you going?"

"You'll see," Cass told him. "Come on, Wye."

Wye looked back over her shoulder at Emerson and shrugged as she exited the house with the others. She didn't know what this was all about, either. Cass had packed thermoses of hot chocolate for them and told Wye to dress up warm for a long walk.

"What are we doing?" she asked again when she, Cass, Lena, Alice, Sadie and Jo spilled out into the freezing, moonlit night.

"Hunting our Christmas tree, of course," Lena said, picking up an ax that was propped up against the back porch.

"Hunting?"

"That's right," Sadie said. She tilted back her head and howled at the moon. Jo and Lena joined in.

Wye laughed. "Why do I get the feeling you don't do this the normal way?"

"Because you know us too well," Cass said comfortably. "Okay, newbie—which way should we go?"

"What do you mean?"

"The Reed Christmas tree hunt is done entirely on instinct," Sadie said in a mock-professorial voice. "Shut your eyes and let your intuition guide you. Where is the tree of our dreams?"

"Go on, shut your eyes," Cass said.

When Wye did, Cass spun her around until she was dizzy.

"Point," Sadie directed her.

Wye pointed. The other women's laughter had her opening her eyes.

"You're not cutting down any part of the hedge maze, so get that right out of your mind," Sadie said, shaking a finger at her.

"There's forest behind it if you go far enough," Cass pointed out. "Let's go!"

They trooped off, singing a Christmas carol, Wye carried along by their good cheer. When they reached the woods, it was Cass's turn to be spun and point. She did, and her finger led the way deeper into the pines. Soon they were tromping through a heavily scented grove until it was Lena's turn. With every twist and turn, their singing grew more ragged, until Lena began to create new lyrics for the old songs. Lyrics that would have turned her husband's ears bright red if he could have heard them, Wye suspected.

"That way," Jo said when she'd been spun around some time later. Wye's fingers and toes were beginning to lose feeling, but the hot chocolate in her insulated mug was still delicious and her voice was raw from singing and howling along with the other women.

"How do we know when to stop?" she asked. Jo was the last of them; they must be near the quarry, she figured.

"When the tree presents itself," Jo said.

"What the hell does that mean?"

Cass giggled. "You'll see." She linked arms with Wye, which made it difficult to make much progress in the woods. Luckily they didn't have far to go.

"Oh," Wye said, stopping in her tracks a few hundred yards later.

"There it is," Alice said softly.

It was perfect. Far too perfect to be a wild tree, Wye thought. "You all knew exactly where you were going!" she accused them. Someone had tended this tree through the years. Nothing in nature grew so symmetrically.

Lena shook her head. "We had no idea where we were going. We got spun just like you did."

"But these are your woods; you know them."

"That's true, but we don't go marking where the Christmas trees are. It wouldn't be any fun that way," Sadie said.

"It's been trimmed."

The other women laughed. "You got us there," Cass said. "But we're not the ones who do it. Jed Henderson does. He has since we were children. He has a whole host of trees scattered on the property that he kept shaping over the years long after he retired as overseer. If you walk in any direction long enough, you'll find one. The game is to let one find you."

Wye bit her lip, embarrassed it had been so important to her to expose the mundane aspect of their tradition, but the more she thought about it, the more she realized it wasn't mundane at all.

This was the beauty of Two Willows. It inspired everyone who came here to add a little magic to the world. Jed creating Christmas trees all over the ranch was an act of the heart. A man who realized Cass and her sisters had needed some beauty in their lives had made sure they found it.

Cass linked arms with her again as Lena wielded her ax and cut down the tree. "Do you feel like one of us now?"

Wye wished she could say yes, but while she'd enjoyed herself on their adventure, the truth was at the end of it, she felt less a part of things than ever. Cass and her sisters knew each tradition—knew they were welcome to join in, that they were intrinsic to it.

She was a visitor who needed an invitation every time.

"Wye." Cass planted her feet and faced her. "You want to know the secret to everything?"

"Everything?"

"Yes. You keep looking at us like we were born with something you weren't, and maybe we were, because our mother was born with it and her mother was born with it."

"The magic." Wye knew exactly what she meant.

"Yes and no. I'm no more magic than you are. I'm no more special than you are, either."

"Yes, you are."

"I don't see the future or anything like that."

"You hold an entire family together. You hold Two Willows' past and future together, too."

Cass nodded. "You're right, I do. And I suppose that is magical, but the thing about magic—and belonging, too—is that both are decisions, not gifts."

Wye didn't believe her. She hadn't been born with a ranch and a hedge maze and all the other interesting features in Cass's life. Her family wasn't connected the way Cass's was.

"At some point, you make a decision. If you want to have a magical life, you create a magical life. If you want to belong, you decide to belong."

"That's not possible for most people."

"Yes, it is," Cass said vehemently. "It's not *easy* for most people, but that doesn't mean it's not *possible*. First it takes time and imagination. Then it takes focus and determination. The problem is you're trying to make my magic yours, and it doesn't work that way; you have to create your own. If no one has handed you any traditions, it's time to start them. We'd love to participate. If you want to belong to our extended family, you're in. I don't know how much more of an invitation I can give you!" Her feet planted wide to steady her bulky body, her blond hair glowing in the moonlight, Cass was as fierce and striking as a goddess. "Decide, right now, that I'm not lying, Wye. I've never lied to you, and I'm not going to start today. Decide that I really do love you when I say I do. Decide that not everyone is your father, and if anyone starts acting like him, you have the power to tell them to stop!"

"You really think it's that simple?" Wye felt as far from a goddess as it was possible to be. She always had her feet on the ground. Her head on her shoulders.

"Here's another secret," Cass said. "The simplest things are the hardest, but they're also the most worthwhile. Wye, I wish you could see yourself. You look like an angel or snow princess tonight. You *are* magic. You are wanted. You are loved. Look around you—oh!"

Cass gasped when an owl swooped down from a nearby tree and skimmed over their heads on silent wings. She grasped Wye's hands.

Wye could barely breathe—she'd felt a feather trace her cheek as she'd tilted up her head to watch it pass. "It touched me."

"Change," Alice said. "That's what it means—a big change coming your way. Owls are powerful messengers."

Change.

There'd been so much of that in her life these past few years.

Sadie, Jo, Alice and Cass clustered around her.

"What kind of change do you want?" Alice asked. "You want to set your own intentions, or you'll get swept along by someone else's."

Wye took a deep breath, and for a moment she felt it—that she was a part of all this. That she belonged *here.*

"I want love. True love. I want a home. I want work I love. And—I want a family."

A chill wind picked up and made Wye shiver.

"What is it?" Alice asked. "What did you hear?"

How did she know a thought had come unbidden

into Wye's mind? *Be careful what you wish for.*

"Maybe I shouldn't ask for things. Maybe I should be happy with what I have," she said quietly.

Alice shook her head. "That's not it."

"If you don't ask for things, how can you get them? Anyway, you weren't asking—you were stating your goals," Sadie said. "It's okay to have goals, Wye."

"Timber!" Lena called out. The tree they'd chosen hit the ground with a whump that startled all of them. Wye realized it was taller than she'd thought.

"Finish up your hot chocolate," Cass said. "Time to carry this sucker home."

Just like that, the moment passed, but Wye knew Alice's words would stick with her. *You want to set your own intentions, or you'll get swept along by someone else's.* She needed to think carefully about the life she wanted.

With the six of them carrying it, the tree wasn't heavy, but their pace was slow and it was awkward negotiating through the woods. By the time they made it back to the house, it was late, and Wye found she was exhausted but happy.

"Won't the men be disappointed they didn't get to come with us?" she asked.

"They have their own job," Cass said, pointing. While they'd been gone, the men had pulled out the ladder Sadie used to trim the hedge maze and had lit up a tall pine that stood near the carriage house. Now they were stringing lights on the exterior of the house.

"Incoming!" Alice shrieked. A second later, a snowball, thrown by Jack, who was high up on the ladder and had scooped a handful of snow off the roof, whizzed by her head and landed at their feet.

"No fair," Jo called up at him. "Come down and fight like a man—" She cut off with a shout when Hunter ducked out from behind the stairs to the back porch and pelted her with snow.

"Battle stations, ladies!" Cass cried.

"Porch fortress!" Lena yelled.

Wye hurried after the others, who seemed to know exactly what to do. They dashed around the end of the back porch and set to work.

"We need all the snowballs we can get. Lena, can you hold them at bay?" Alice asked.

"You know I can." Lena whipped one snowball after another as Jo placed them in her hand.

"Help me build a wall," Sadie hissed at Wye.

Wye followed her lead, dove to her knees by Lena and began to scoop armfuls of snow into position in front of her. Alice joined them. Cass got down awkwardly and helped, too. When the wall was tall and thick enough to shield Lena and Jo, they worked outward, building a thick bulwark that connected to the side of the porch, so they were sheltered on two sides.

"Bring it around," Sadie said, and Wye kept adding to the wall, wrapping it around to protect their flank, as Alice joined Jo in keeping Lena stocked with snowballs.

"They're mounting an attack!" Jo cried.

Wye looked up, saw the men advancing, Emerson among them, and ducked as a snowball whizzed right by her head.

"Defense positions!" Lena called.

Wye joined the others at the wall. As one, they hurt-led a fusillade of snowballs at the men, beating them back.

The men regrouped, came at them again, snowballs flying thick and fast, but the women had used the respite to make more of their own and threw them as fast as they could. Wye caught sight of Connor ducking away, coming back again a minute later, loaded down with something—were those plastic sleds?

"Shields up, men!" he shouted, tossing a sled to each of them. The men caught them handily. Raised them.

"Make a phalanx," Logan called out. They held up the sleds vertically side by side and began to advance. The women's snowballs hit the sleds and slid off them harmlessly.

"Damn it, it's the old shield-wall trick," Lena said.

"We need a catapult," Jo said.

"Well, we don't have one," Lena told her.

"We need something!" Cass said. "They're coming fast!"

It was too late. Jack vaulted their wall first with a thunderous cry, and a moment later the rest of the men had burst through. They were met with close-quarters hand-to-hand snowball combat, with more than one man receiving a dollop of snow down the collar of his jacket from his wife.

They ended in a tangled heap, lying on their backs in the ruined fort, staring up at the sky, breathing hard.

Wye noticed that Brian had made sure to protect Cass from the worst of the melee, pulling her into his arms and lowering her down gently in the snow. Now they lay together, Cass cuddled in his arms.

"We won," Jack said.

"The hell you did," Lena said. "The whole thing was a ruse to draw you over here so we can have our way with you."

Wye snorted. "Trust a Reed girl to always turn out to be in control in the end."

"You said a mouthful," Brian sighed.

"Why don't we do this more often?" Jo said. "Lie in a heap and look at the stars?"

"It could be a new tradition," Wye said. She looked at Emerson, who'd ended up next to her, and hoped the horseplay hadn't hurt his ankle. She knew better than to ask. His expression was contented, however, as he gazed up at the night sky. All seemed well.

"I'm down for it," Logan said.

"Me, too," Cass said. "And when we get cold, we can head inside and set up the Christmas tree. It'll need to dry overnight, but we can decorate it tomorrow."

"You got any more hot chocolate?" Sadie asked.

"Of course."

"Then let's go."

Chapter 8

"**E**VERYTHING OKAY?" WYE asked Emerson as they trailed after the rest of the party into the house. She brushed the snow off her coat the best she could.

Emerson helped her. "Yeah, I'm good." Really good, actually. After the women had headed outside earlier, the house had seemed unnaturally quiet—until Connor had come and collared him.

"Come on, Myers. We've got work to do." He'd dumped a string of Christmas lights in Emerson's hands and led the way to where Jack, Brian, Logan and Hunter were lugging more of them up from where they'd been stored in the basement. All of them trooped outside where Emerson, Logan and Hunter had worked on detangling the long strings of lights while Brian and Jack climbed the ladder to hang them.

For once Emerson hadn't felt any awkwardness with the other men. They'd ribbed him as much as they had each other. Ordered him around with the same casual goodwill. When they'd spotted the women trudging home with the Christmas tree, it was Jack who'd instigated the snowball fight, but everyone had expected him to join in.

Maybe he'd found a place here after all.

"You seemed a little distant last night," Wye said.

He supposed he had. "Working things out in my head, I guess. Hard to know where I stand around here sometimes." He was feeling more confident about his position now, though.

When Wye tossed her head back and laughed, he stuffed his hands in his pockets. "What's so funny?"

"Cass and the others set me straight concerning that tonight. And I think they're right."

"What did they say?"

"That you can't wait for an invitation to belong. You have to decide that you do. That snowball fight was the first time I stopped asking whether they wanted me around and just assumed they did. It felt good. Maybe we should both stop fighting against this crazy family and let them adopt us."

"I guess. Sometimes I can't work out if Lena wants me around, though," he said. "Or Cass, for that matter."

"Maybe we keep taking every little hiccup too seriously," Wye said slowly. "Maybe the fact that Lena and Cass can tell you how they really feel means they're comfortable with you."

"Maybe."

"And maybe it means sometimes you have to decide what to stand up for and what to let go of."

"Like letting Cass make the coffee for everyone else after I make it for the General."

"Exactly like that."

"What about living at the Park?"

"What about it?"

Following the others, they walked up the back steps and into the warmth of the house. Cass was already making more hot chocolate. Hunter and Jack were struggling with the Christmas tree in the front room. Alice was telling Brian and Logan where the ornaments were stored.

"Might as well pull them out now so we're ready for tomorrow," she said.

Emerson took Wye aside. "I thought it would be good for us to have some distance between us and everyone else, but the General says we should pick a building site close to the main house. What do you think?"

Wye glanced away. "I think that's a conversation to have when we're engaged. If we get engaged," she added hurriedly when he grinned at her.

"*When* we get engaged," he teased, bending to kiss her. Wye let him, glancing up at him through her lashes when he pulled back again.

"Who's up for the skating party tomorrow?" Connor asked, looking up from his phone. "The Night Sky Party is happening in town, and I haven't skated in ages."

"Me," Cass said.

"Me, me!" her sisters chimed in.

"Wye? Emerson?" Connor asked when everyone else had said they'd go.

"I'd love to," Wye said. "It's been years since I've been on skates. Emerson?"

"I don't think so." He tried to be nonchalant. "My ankle probably won't support me."

Wye's face fell. "Of course. We can find something else to do."

"You can still come and look at the stars," Cass urged them. "There will be telescopes set up, too. The Night Sky Party is an annual fundraiser. It's for a good cause."

"What do you think?" Wye asked.

"Sure." But Emerson already dreaded it. What were the chances someone wouldn't suggest he give skating a try—just to see if he could do it after all?

The following night, his prediction came true. He might have known it would be Lena who issued him the challenge. When he and Wye joined everyone at the Night Sky festival, they all took their turns at the telescopes to look at the moon, the Milky Way and a planet. But as soon as they were through, Lena shouted, "Last one on the ice is a rotten egg! Come on!"

Most of the family hurried after her—even Cass. She'd declared that she was perfectly capable of skating calmly around the edge of the rink with Brian to shield her from anyone who lost control.

Wye stuck with Emerson. "Let's check out the bon-fire," she suggested.

But just then Lena turned back to see if there were any stragglers. "Wye, come on!"

"You go ahead," Emerson told her. "I'll watch." He

hoped she didn't know how much it pained him to hold back. He'd always loved to skate. Had played endless rounds of hockey on the frozen pond with all his cousins, an activity his aunt and uncle accepted if all their other chores were done.

"Are you sure? I can stay with you if you like. Or maybe you could give it a try? We could stick to the edge of the rink, like Cass is. You could lean on me."

He bit back a sharp retort, knowing Wye didn't deserve it. He couldn't help feel a stab of betrayal, though. She was with him constantly. She knew he was injured.

"You don't have to," she said quickly. "I've just noticed that when you're not thinking about your ankle, you seem to do pretty well getting around."

"I can walk okay," he told her. "That doesn't mean I can skate."

"You don't have to," she said again, but Lena was still waiting.

"Come on, Myers. You've been walking all over the ranch," she called. "If you can walk, you can skate."

Hell. Was that a challenge? Or did Lena simply want to see him fall on his ass? He had a feeling that though she was trying her best to overlook it, she still resented his closeness to her father.

"Fine," he said to Wye. "Let's try. But if I fall, you'll have to drag me off," he warned her. Humiliation was good for the soul, right? People would keep on pushing him until they saw for themselves the extent of the damage to his ankle.

"I will," she promised him. "Come on."

It took time to rent their skates and get them on, but all too soon, Emerson was limping toward the ice, leaning more heavily than he'd have liked on Wye's shoulder. His gut was tight with discomfort. For all his bravado, he hated the idea of everyone seeing his weakness.

"This isn't going to work," he said.

"Maybe not. I guess we'll find out soon enough."

Easy for her to sound so chipper about it. She wasn't the one who'd be crashing on the hard ice in another minute.

Wye stepped onto the little rink first, got her bearings and then extended a hand to him. "You've skated before, haven't you?"

"Plenty." He stepped gingerly onto the ice with his good foot.

"That will make it easier." Wye supported him as he stepped forward with his injured ankle. He winced as he tried to put weight on it, feeling how weak it was, balanced on the thin blade.

"Easy does it." Hunter appeared on his other side and offered an arm.

"I'm fine." Emerson waved him away. It was bad enough having to lean on Wye.

"Let's make sure of that. Don't want to set back your recovery, right?"

"I'm not a child," Emerson growled.

"No one said you were. Plenty of other grown-ups are accepting help." Hunter pointed, and Emerson lifted his head. Hunter was right; there were several families and groups of friends supporting grown men and women who obviously didn't know how to skate yet.

"I know how to skate. It's just my ankle."

"Which is why I'm here. Lean on me for a minute, and when you don't need me anymore, I'll disappear."

Emerson knew he was being a jackass for refusing help. "Fine." He bit off the word, took Hunter's arm, pushed off and was pleased when his hurt ankle didn't buckle. The exercises he'd been doing daily had helped a lot, and he felt a lot stronger lately. He took a few more experimental glides on his skates.

"Not bad," Hunter said.

"Ankle's improved more than I thought."

"Five minutes. Ten at the most, this first time," Hunter warned him. "Don't screw up things for future Emerson by pushing today Emerson too hard."

"Words to live by," Wye said.

"See you around." Hunter skated off and left them.

"You're steady?" Wye asked.

"Feels good," Emerson confirmed. "This was a good idea," he admitted a few minutes later after they'd made it around the rink twice.

"It was, wasn't it? I'd forgotten how much I like winter sports," Wye said. "I've been a real stick in the mud these past few years."

"When your life gets turned upside down, it's hard not to want to dig in and make conservative choices."

"Is that what you've been doing?" she asked.

He thought about it. "It's what I wanted to do, but instead I guess I'm taking some leaps of faith. Sometimes…" He watched Jack whizz by, executing perfect crossovers as he wove in between the other skaters. "Sometimes it's hard to feel I stack up with the other guys here."

"You do, though. You know that, right?" Wye kept going, though he thought she wanted to stop and face him. He had a feeling she was afraid if they stopped, he wouldn't be able to get going again.

"No," he said honestly. "I'll do whatever I can to strengthen my ankle, and I'll be almost as good as new someday, but I won't be like I was—or like Jack and the other men here still are."

"Your ankle has nothing to do with who you are," Wye said. "Who you are is in your heart, in your words and your actions. You are more man than just about anyone I've ever met, Emerson."

He was the one who stopped. Tugged her to the side of the rink so they wouldn't block anyone. "Don't feel you have to—"

Wye put a hand on his chest.

"Emerson Myers, shut up and listen. I wouldn't hitch my wagon to a lesser man. I deserve the best, and as far as I've seen, the best is you. Own it, already." She went up on tiptoe to kiss him, and Emerson bent to meet her automatically.

The best?

"Are you saying I'm wrong?" she asked when she noticed he wasn't convinced.

"No, but—"

"I know quality when I see it, and you, mister, are

quality. In fact, you rock my world. I've been dreaming about getting home and slipping into your bed all day. I try not to think about you so much, but I can't stop. You're on my mind all the time."

"Really?"

"Yes, really."

"You know I'll give it my all when it comes to you and me—to our family," he told her.

"I know. That's what I'm saying. I know exactly what I've got in you, Emerson."

"Then why aren't you wearing my ring?"

"Because it's too early. I want to savor this part a little, don't you? You're going to be the last man I date, you know."

The breath whooshed out of him. The last man she dated? Did that mean…?

"Kiss me," she demanded.

And he did.

EMERSON WAS STILL flying high from their talk several days later when he arrived in Billings for reserve training with the General. The center was busy today, with a load of new equipment arriving, including new desks, filing cabinets and shelving units for additional offices that had been built recently. Several officers he recognized were guiding the delivery truck into a cramped space close to the entrance of the building to make unloading easier, calling out to each other and the truck driver cheerfully as they went about their business.

The sun was out, although it was bitterly cold. Emerson hustled the General inside, then returned to collect their things from his truck.

"That's it. Let's open her up!" he heard Scott Delaney call as he pushed through the door into the parking lot. A popular young officer, he was always dashing around getting things done.

Showing him up, Emerson thought, biting back a sigh as he watched Scott leap onto the tail of the big cargo truck parked just feet away and pull up its rolling back door. The other men waiting to unload it had moved around the side of the vehicle to talk and joke with the driver, who'd shut off the engine and climbed out.

Scott hopped down again, calling out to them, and Emerson was the only one who caught sight of a large metal bookcase at the back of the truck as it began to tip.

"Watch out!" He leaped toward Scott, pain spiking through his ankle, and his momentum carried them both forward to safety as the metal shelves crashed to the ground behind them. Scott lost his balance and went down, Emerson on top of him, the air knocked out of him as they fell together.

"What the hell?" Scott cried, but a moment later he'd regained his footing and stood staring at the heavy metal bookcase laid out on the pavement. The rest of the men gathered around, muttering in shock. Emerson tried to get up, too, but his ankle wouldn't take any weight.

He bit back a curse word. Hearing him, Scott turned

and offered his hand. "You okay?"

Emerson wasn't sure. He swayed on his one good foot when he was upright again, trying not to think how badly he might have damaged his ankle.

"What happened? What's going on?" The General hobbled out of the building as fast as his cane would let him.

"Emerson just saved Scott's life," Gregory Chant spoke up. "The load must have shifted as you drove, Melton."

"If that bookcase had hit you wrong…" Paul Hunt let his sentence trail off. The heavy metal bookcase was full of sharp edges and pointy corners, and as it fell from the height of the bed of the truck, it had picked up speed. Paul and Gregory were right—the accident could have been fatal.

Don Melton, the driver, had gone pale. "Hell, I thought I had everything in there tight. If something had happened—"

"Well, all's well that end's well, but that load should have been restrained," the General said. "You men, get that furniture sorted. Delaney, take a minute and make sure you aren't hurt. Myers? You okay?"

Emerson wanted to say yes, but the truth was, he wasn't.

"Think I'd better get this checked out." He gestured to his ankle. He wasn't sure how to get to his truck, however. He could drive with his good foot, but walking wasn't going to be easy.

"Here, lean on me," Paul said. "I'll drive you to the

hospital. You'll want to get that looked at quickly so it heals right."

Relief flooded Emerson. His shock was wearing off, and the pain in his ankle was increasing. "I'd appreciate that."

"Hope they get you fixed up," Don said.

"Yeah," Gregory chimed in.

"I'll be back soon as I can," Emerson assured the General.

"Don't worry about me. Take care of yourself," the General said.

It was several hours before Paul dropped Emerson back at the base. The General was waiting for him in his office.

"What's the prognosis?" he asked, sliding his glasses down his nose and peering over them. Judging by the paperwork spread out around him, the General had put his time to good work while Emerson was gone.

"Just twisted it—didn't do any further damage," Emerson told him.

"Good. You'll need to take it easy for a day or two."

"It's wrapped up tight. What do you say we head out?"

"You can drive?"

Emerson nodded. "Didn't hurt my good foot at all."

"Glad to hear it, because I'm ready to be home at Two Willows."

"You and me both."

CELEBRATING THE HOLIDAYS with a big, happy family

was an entirely new experience for Wye. Cass had invited her over the year before, but Wye hadn't wanted to intrude and she'd declined. Instead, she'd stopped by for a quick visit on Christmas Eve before heading to church on her own, and in the morning, she'd had a Christmas brunch with her brother and Mindy, as usual.

This year was different. In the days leading up to the twenty-fourth, she found herself working with Cass to get the whole house in order and to bake dozens of cookies to share, as if she truly were Cass's sister. She joked with the other women and teased the men when they came to steal treats from the kitchen. Emerson had taken it easy for a day or two, but then he'd gotten right back to work on the trailers. Wye was grateful he hadn't damaged his ankle further. She knew how frustrated Emerson had been with it already.

When Ward dropped off Elise on the morning of Christmas Eve, he hesitated in the doorway. "You sure you're okay with taking her today?"

"Just get back as soon as you can. You'll join us for dinner, right?"

"Sure." He was trying not to let his true feelings show, but Wye knew Mindy's continued absence was dragging his spirits down. She felt like he'd gotten into a rhythm with work, chores and taking care of Elise, but he hadn't come all the way to terms with the fact that Mindy wasn't coming back, and he was often distracted. She never saw him these days without his phone in his hand, and she was afraid he'd become addicted to being online instead of being in the present moment.

"It'll be fun, you'll see," she assured him. "We'll have a good meal and attend the candlelight service. You won't have time to be sad."

"I'm not sad." He seemed to recall himself, clearing his throat before he went on. "I'm fine, Wye. Don't fuss. I'd better get to work."

"Of course. Take care of yourself today, all right?"

"Will do."

She watched Ward trudge back to his car, pulling out his phone again on the way, and her heart went out to him, even as she watched to make sure he put it away again before he began to drive. As thoughtless as he could be, he was still human and rudderless without Mindy to give meaning to his days. He was doing his best to hold it together for Elise, but Wye wasn't sure how much more of this her brother could take. She resolved to pay him more attention over the holidays.

"Is he joining us tonight?" Emerson said at her shoulder.

She nodded.

"Good. I don't think he should be alone." He tugged Wye backward to lean against him and put his arms around her and Elise. "I'm glad I found you."

"I'm glad I found you." She sighed as he kissed the top of her head. "Ward needs someone to love, too."

"Don't go matchmaking—it's far too soon."

"I know." Still, she wished there was something she could do to help. When she asked Cass later if it would be okay if Ward and Elise spent the night and joined them for Christmas morning, Cass looked thoughtful.

"Of course. We just need a room to put them in," she said. "I suppose we could put both of them in the nursery."

"I can bunk with Emerson—just for the night," Wye said.

"As if you haven't been bunking with him every night already," Cass laughed. "I'm not blind, Wye."

"Do you mind?"

"Why would I? Please do invite your brother; we're always happy to have one more."

"You're an angel."

"I don't know about that, but I do my best."

The rest of the day was full of last-minute details, including calling Ward to invite him to stay, a rushed trip to the grocery store with Elise and lots of cooking. Wye was putting the finishing touches on the table settings late that afternoon when Ward knocked at the back door.

Cass beat her to open it. "Come in! Oh, you didn't have to do that," she added when he handed her a bottle of wine and a box of chocolates.

"It's the least I can do, crashing your Christmas Eve festivities."

"We're happy to have you. Wye, show Ward where he can wash up. Dinner's almost ready."

Ward took Elise for a quick snuggle, then followed Wye to the bathroom. "You sure it's all right that Elise and I are here?"

"Positive," Wye said, remembering her conversation with Cass and her sisters in the woods earlier that month about deciding to belong. "Did you bring your things to stay overnight?"

"I packed a bag, but I don't know—it seems weird…"

"I know it does, but it isn't good for you to stay home alone. You'll be better off here."

"If you think so."

"I know so. Come on; wash up and let's go eat. Cass and I have been cooking all day."

Chapter 9

EMERSON KNEW IF he didn't stop eating, he'd end up falling asleep at the candlelight service later, but it was hard to exercise restraint when Cass and Wye set out this kind of spread.

"That was good," Ward said, jostling Elise a little, who was sitting on his lap, taking tiny bites of turkey he offered her and chewing them with her limited set of teeth.

"That was stupendous," the General proclaimed. "You outdid yourself, Cass."

"I couldn't have done it without Wye."

"We menfolk will clean up," Brian declared. "Go make yourselves pretty for church."

He was met with good-natured protests, but the women retired happily upstairs, Jo stealing Elise from Ward's arms.

Ward hung back as the other men sprang into action, and Emerson figured he wasn't sure how to help without getting in the way.

"Broom's in the pantry over there," he said. "If you want, you could sweep."

"Sounds good." Ward went gratefully to start the task.

Brian took charge of washing the dishes. Several of the others helped dry and put away. Emerson kept a constant flow of dirty dishes from the table to the sink. Connor put on some music. Twenty minutes later, when they'd put a sizable dent in the work, Emerson noticed Ward had headed outside. Looking out the window, he saw the man bent over his phone, tapping quickly.

Could his wife have gotten in touch? At first, Emerson thought that might be the case, especially as the minutes ticked on, but when Ward finally shoved the phone in his pocket and came back indoors, he just shrugged. "Friends saying happy holidays," he said.

"Thought it might be…" Emerson realized it wasn't a good idea to bring up Mindy. "Never mind." When Ward frowned, he rushed to change the subject. "Want to help me take this tablecloth outside and shake it?"

"Sure."

Ward was back on his phone several more times before they left for church and had it in his hand again during the drive home. Emerson was glad to see him put it away when they reached Two Willows. It was late, and the sky was a sea of stars. Everyone else stopped to look up when they got out of their vehicles.

"I love this part of Christmas best of all," Alice said softly. "The hush before the storm."

"I like opening presents," Jo said. "Always have, always will."

"I like the food," Connor said.

"I like it all," Emerson said, but his gaze was on Ward, who was looking up at the sky as if it had the answer to something that was puzzling him.

"I like you," Wye said and kissed him on the cheek. "And I'm ready to go to bed. I'm exhausted."

"You and me both," Cass said contentedly. "Go ahead upstairs. Get your brother settled for the night."

"Will do. Come on, Ward. Let me show you your room."

"Sure thing."

Emerson was lying in bed by the time Wye had gotten Ward and Elise settled in for the night, and when she slipped into his room, he lifted the covers as an invitation.

"I thought we'd never get to the good part," Wye said, hurrying to join him.

"How's your brother doing?"

"As good as can be expected. Preoccupied, actually," she admitted as she stripped down, slid on a silky little slip of a thing and joined him. "I think he'll do better tomorrow after the morning's festivities. Then it'll be over and life will get back to normal. I think that's easier for him than holidays. I wish he'd put his phone down, though, and pay more attention to Elise. You don't think..." She hesitated. "You don't think he's on a dating site, do you?"

"Maybe." The thought had occurred to him, too. "He's human, Wye. It's hard to be alone during the holidays. You couldn't blame him for reaching out to someone else."

"It's way too soon."

"Probably. Although that never stopped anyone before."

She chuckled. "You're right. As a species, we aren't very sensible."

"Ward is old enough to decide for himself when he's ready to look for love again."

She nodded. "I won't nag him, if that's what you're trying to say."

"I'm not saying that at all. Just thinking out loud. I wish everyone was having as good a holiday as I am, your brother included."

"Are you enjoying yourself?"

"I am."

She snuggled closer. "I think your holiday is about to get a whole lot better."

"Oh yeah?"

"I have a gift for you right here." She indicated herself. "You just have to unwrap it."

"Sounds perfect."

Luckily Wye wasn't wearing all that much to unwrap, and he made short work of tugging off the tiny garment she'd just put on, exposing her to his touch. She climbed on top of him as he palmed one breast and lifted it to take her nipple in his mouth. Teasing her with his tongue, he cupped her other breast, and she arched her back.

He could spend a lifetime exploring Wye's body, Emerson decided as he ran a hand down to skim her waist and settle on the curve of her bottom. Every part of her was art, designed to fascinate him. As she rocked against his hardness, the heat of her quickened his pulse.

"I don't want to think about a life without you," he confessed. "If you ran away, I don't know what I'd do."

"I won't run away," Wye told him. "If I give you my word, I'll honor it."

If. When would that turn into a *when?*

Tomorrow?

Emerson pushed that thought out of his mind, content to stay present with today. As Wye moved above him, her breasts swayed. He brought both hands to her hips, lifting her, pressing against her, wanting her too badly to take much time.

Wye nodded, and he pushed inside her, both of them breathing out in a sigh.

"Why do you feel so damn good?" Wye asked him, taking him all the way in, then lifting and rocking her hips again. "I could do this all the time."

"Good. I can't think of a better way to spend our days."

"Me, neither."

She closed her eyes, and Emerson took that as encouragement. Hands still on her hips, he guided her movements, and her breasts rocked forward and back. He tilted his head to claim one nipple, thrusting deeper inside her while sweeping a hand up to cup the back of her neck.

He needed all of her. Needed to feel her above him, feel the press of her breasts on his chest, her knees against his hips. Needed to push inside her again and again until—

Emerson came with a groan, and Wye cried out above him, arching her back, pulsing around him until he bucked against her, unable to hold back. They kept their rhythm until both were spent, and Wye curled around him, still holding him inside her, clinging to his shoulders as if she'd never let go.

Emerson stroked her body, every curve and dip firing him up again already. With Wye, he felt invincible, and slowly, ever so slowly, he rolled her over and began their dance all over again, taking his turn on top.

He took his time, pushing into her with long, slow strokes, teasing and caressing her body with his hands. When she began to move with him, he linked his fingers with hers and raised her hands over her head. Now he had control, and he wielded it patiently, coaxing pleasure from Wye until she begged him for more.

"Emerson, please," she said, nipping his chin, then kissing it.

"You want more of this?" He stroked into her firmly, and she sighed.

"Yes."

"More of this?" He circled his hips, and she moaned.

"Yes, please."

"More of this?" He pushed up her thighs and encouraged her to link them behind his back. Now he could thrust deep.

"Yes!"

Emerson took mercy on her and began to move in

earnest. Wye tossed her head back and let him ride her, putty in his hands. Her trust moved him more than anything else, and Emerson promised himself he would never let her down. He'd spend his life living up to her expectations. Would—

Wye came with a gasping cry, and all thought fled his mind as her orgasm drew him over the edge. Emerson let his body take over, bucking against her, tensing and flexing until both uttered a final cry.

He gathered her close beneath him, kissed her jaw, her cheek—her mouth.

"Wyoming Smith, I don't care anymore if it's too soon. I love you, you hear me?"

"I hear you. I… love you, too."

SHE'D SAID SHE loved him.

Wye woke up next to Emerson on Christmas morning knowing her life would never be the same. She'd never declared her love to a man. Had never dared to. Her father had laughed at her childish expressions of love for him. Had disappeared the moment she stopped following his every dictate.

When she told Ward she loved him, her brother usually grunted or muttered the words back to her as if under duress. She knew somewhere deep down he cared for her, but he had his own struggles with trust and love.

Since leaving home, she hadn't let herself get emotionally involved with any of the men she'd dated. Her pattern was to go out a few times, maybe even become intimate with a man—and then quickly find a reason he didn't measure up.

Whenever she broke off a relationship, she felt—relief.

Wye sat with that thought a moment as she let her gaze run over the man sleeping next to her. Relief, because... because steeling herself for disappointment or pain all the time was exhausting, and she'd preferred to remain alone rather than to maintain those kinds of defences.

As she watched the rise and fall of Emerson's chest and took in the way his features were relaxed in sleep, her heart warmed.

Last night she'd let her defenses down, and Emerson hadn't hurt or disappointed her. He'd looked her in the eye and declared his love for her.

And she'd said it back.

Part of Wye wanted to hide under the covers. The other part wanted to leap out and dance around the room.

He loved her.

And she loved him.

Could things turn out differently this time?

She didn't see why not. One thing she'd realized about Emerson—he was consistent. He said what he meant. He did what he said he'd do. He was dependable. Trustworthy.

Hers.

A baby's cry alerted her to the fact her niece was already awake, which meant Ward must be, too. Remorse flooded her as she realized she'd been so happy about her own circumstances, she'd forgotten what a sad day this would be for her brother. She didn't want him wandering around in a strange house on Christmas morning, so although she would have been happy to lie in bed with Emerson, wait for him to wake up and talk over what had happened between them, she slipped out from under the covers and reached for her robe.

"Not so fast." Emerson whipped out a hand and grabbed her wrist, his eyes opening. "Don't I get a kiss?" He pushed up onto his elbow. He was even more handsome in the morning light, stubble lining his jaw, his hair tousled with sleep.

"You bet." She tumbled back into bed with him, and it was longer than she'd meant before she pulled away. "I need to help Cass and the others," she said finally, when she'd been thoroughly kissed and caressed by Emerson.

"First open your present." He reached over the side of the bed, grabbed his jeans and pulled something out of the pocket.

Wye sat up when she took in the small velvet box in Emerson's hand. "Emerson."

He sat up, too, and faced her. "Just listen," he said. "You don't have to say yes today, but I can't go a day longer without asking. I know what I want, and it's a lifetime with you. I've never been happier than the weeks we've spent together. I've never felt like I belonged anywhere the way I feel like I belong with you. You're my sun and moon. My everything. Wyoming, will you marry me?"

She couldn't breathe. All her warm thoughts had fled, fear piercing through her chest. Dating a man, sleeping with a man was one thing. Marriage—

That was something entirely different.

She was sure her parents had started off with good intentions, maybe even the kind feelings she was holding in her heart right now for Emerson, and look how that had turned out. Four lives blasted to pieces by the failure of that love to endure.

Every instinct told her to run. Men weren't capable of sustaining their love. Neither were women. Everyone left everyone in the end.

Marriage was surely a precursor to disaster.

And yet—

All five couples living at Two Willows seemed genuinely happy. She'd known Cass and her sisters before they'd married, and she could honestly say their lives had improved.

She loved Emerson utterly. Loved the way he stood up for her. The way he made room for her. The way he cared deeply about what she cared for. The way he'd accepted her brother's presence today. The way he'd created a job for himself down at the Park. The way he always tried to do his best—to *be* his best.

And the way she felt when they were together—she had woken up aching to be with him again. That was new, too. She'd never felt this way for another man. Never could—because she'd never been able to trust one.

She had trusted Emerson last night.

She would love to trust him wholeheartedly.

Wyoming swallowed hard. There was so much danger in opening herself that way. Surely she'd be crushed by disappointment if things went awry down the road.

When they went awry.

But if she said no, that would be the end of her relationship with Emerson. He wanted a life together, a family—all of it. He wouldn't settle for any lukewarm half measures.

It was all or nothing.

She could either take a chance on a future with Emerson or stay in the safe little cocoon she'd built and watch everyone else live full lives.

She took a breath, terror and hope waging war inside her. What if Emerson was different from the other men in her life? Wasn't it worth betting it all if the possible payout was happiness?

She was strong, after all. She'd proved that to herself after her mother's defection and her father's abandonment. If Emerson bailed on her someday, she'd survive that, too.

Even as she thought it, she knew that would never happen. Emerson had experienced loss and abandonment, too, and he would never inflict his wounds on anyone else. He was trustworthy—and he loved her.

"Yes," she said, surprising herself. "Yes, I'll marry you."

A smile broke over Emerson's face as he reached out to cup her chin and kiss her. When he pulled back, her heart was thumping with rush of wanting. He opened the box to show her a beautiful, delicate swooping ring. "It was my mother's. The one thing I have of hers."

Wye let out a shaky breath. "It's beautiful." She knew what it had to mean to Emerson, and something tight inside her chest broke loose a little, exposing a wanting she'd never known she had. All these years she'd thought she'd made herself so strong in her independence, but she craved togetherness—real togetherness—as much as anyone else.

This small token of Emerson's regard for her meant everything in the world.

He lifted it out and carefully slid it onto her finger.

"How does it fit?"

"Perfectly." Just like him. Emerson fit into her heart—and her life—as perfectly as if he was made for her and her for him.

Maybe life could be different. Maybe love could last.

God, she hoped so.

"I know you have to go—"

Wyoming knocked him over and rolled onto her back, pulling him on top of her. She wanted to feel him—wanted the weight of him to make him real. Wanted him to make love to her again to prove how wonderful this all was. "Make it quick," she urged him. "I can't last through breakfast without being with you, but I really can't keep Cass and Ward and Elise waiting any longer."

"I can make it quick," he assured her, already settling into place, nudging against her impatiently.

And he did.

WYE WAS WET and ready for him, and Emerson bit back a groan as he began his task. Make his wife-to-be come? He was down for that any time, and soon Wye's eyes closed and her fingers dug into his shoulders, urging him on, even though he was taking her faster and harder than he'd done before.

She came with a cry he silenced with a kiss, afraid that too many people were awake in the house, not wanting their lovemaking to embarrass Wye later. She lifted her hips, begging him to push deeper, and he did, slamming into her again and again until he, too, slipped into an orgasm and his body took over, wringing pulse after pulse of pleasure from him until he was drained dry.

He collapsed on top of her, then rolled them both to the side, where they stared into each other's eyes, breathing hard. He'd never been happier to possess his mother's ring than the moment he'd slid it onto Wye's finger. His mom had been full of life and love, just like Wye was.

He brushed a kiss over Wye's cheek. Her lips. Her chin.

She groaned. "We're going to start all over again in a minute if you don't stop that. I can't get enough of you."

"I know the feeling. That's a good thing, right?" he asked.

"Definitely." Wye wriggled away and sat up, letting the covers fall as she surveyed the room. When she slid off the bed and reached for her robe, desire pulsed through Emerson again. He wondered if his craving for Wye would ever let up. "I want more of that tonight," she told him as she headed toward the door.

"Every night," he promised her, wishing he could have her again right now. She paused with a hand on the doorknob and waggled the fingers of her left hand at him. "Look, I'm engaged!"

"Me, too," he told her and laughed as she slipped out and shut the door behind her, looking giddy as a schoolgirl.

Hell, he was happy, too.

Happier than he'd ever been since he was a kid.

Finally, his life was heading in the right direction. He lay back down and laced his fingers behind his head, breathing out a breath he felt he'd been holding for years. He could barely let himself imagine the future. A home. A wife. Work he could be proud of. Something bigger than himself to belong to.

All of it lay in front of him, a banquet spread for a starving man.

The door burst open. Emerson surged to a sitting position, took in Wyoming's expression and leaped out of bed, his gut tight.

"What's wrong?"

She was holding Elise in her arms. "Ward's gone home. He told Cass it felt weird to be here on Christmas morning. His note says he'll be back for dinner, but he just doesn't feel comfortable doing an entire family Christmas with people he doesn't know. Do you think I should go after him? He shouldn't be alone today!"

"Why don't you call and check that he's okay?"

He took Elise from her arms, his heartbeat slowing again now that he knew no one was in immediate danger, and he realized from now on he'd be on guard to protect Wye. He kept the baby occupied playing peekaboo while Wye made the call.

"Ward? Where are you?" There was a silence as she listened. "You're not making anything easier; you know I'm going to spend the whole day worrying about you! You should come back." She was quiet a moment. "Oh, my goodness, no one cares if you don't have presents for them; they don't have presents for you, either. And what about Elise? She will notice you're not here. You're her father." Wye sighed. "You'd better be back by dinner. Don't do something stupid and ruin the holidays for me forever. Yes, I'm talking about suicide." She listened some more. Emerson was glad she'd brought up the uncomfortable subject. He knew how hard the holidays could be on someone who was alone. What men were capable of when their hearts were broken. "Okay. Be here by four. I need to be able to help Cass, and I can't do that and watch Elise at the same time. Okay. See you then."

She hung up, shaking her head. "That man. I swear, it didn't even occur to him he'd be missed! Or that I'd worry."

"What did he say?"

"He couldn't sleep last night. Couldn't stand to spend the day around happy married couples, either, so he called a few single friends and made plans to hang out with them. He said they were all grateful to get his call. He seemed almost upbeat."

"He didn't even ask if you were okay with having Elise today."

"You're right; he didn't ask, but I won't hold that against him today. I think leaving her here is his way of not dealing with his sadness about spending the holiday without Mindy. I wonder what she's doing?"

Emerson could only shrug. He reached for his jeans and pulled them on. "I'm going to grab a shower and get dressed."

"Better hurry. Sounds like people are gathering downstairs ready to open presents."

"I'll be there in a minute."

As he showered, Emerson couldn't help but feel bad for Ward, despite the unthinking way he shed his responsibilities onto Wye's shoulders. Marriage was no guarantee of happiness. Had Ward thought he'd stumbled on a banquet only to discover he'd ended up with a plate full of ashes?

What if his marriage to Wye disintegrated around him in a similar way?

Emerson shook off the dark thoughts, letting the hot water wash them away. Wyoming wouldn't run away when times got tough. She was the type of woman who saw things through. And he wasn't Ward, expecting everyone else to pick up the slack.

212 | CORA SETON

When he saw his name on a number of packages under the tree downstairs, he was glad he'd found small gifts for everyone. The General was ensconced in an easy chair, almost beaming at the gathering. Everyone else was seated on a couch or the floor, since there were too many of them to fit on the furniture all at once. Cass kept ferrying in mugs of coffee and tea. Elise crawled from person to person, sitting in laps and babbling at them. Emerson took a seat next to Wyoming on the floor, taking her hand in his.

"We'll eat after the presents," Cass told him. "Jo? You want to hand them out?"

"Jo always hands them out," Sadie said. "I don't think we've ever had this many people here at Christmas. Not since Mom's been gone, anyway."

All the women turned to the General, who cleared his throat and nodded. "Your mother would love a gathering like this."

"I wish she was here," Sadie said.

"We all do," Cass told her gently and perched on the arm of the sofa. "Jo, how about you hand out a few packages?"

Jo got to it, and soon the poignant moment had passed in a flurry of guesses and unwrapping. Wye amassed a pile of hand-knit mittens, books, a calendar and more, while Emerson received work gloves and several fancy tools that were upgrades from the ones in Two Willows' motley collection.

As they were all oohing and aahing over their presents, he realized Wye had twisted her engagement ring to leave a plain band that didn't attract any attention. When she noticed him looking, she put a finger to her lips.

Only when they were done with presents and gathered in the kitchen for a hearty brunch did Wye wink at him, twist the ring the right way around and make a show of reaching for something across the table with her left hand.

"Wyoming Smith!" Cass stood up, scraping her chair back over the wooden floor. "Is that an engagement ring?"

Wye laughed happily. "It is! Emerson asked me this morning, and I said yes!" She fluttered her hand around for all to see.

"Congratulations!" Brian clapped Emerson on the back. "You did it!"

"I told him to," the General said complacently. "I know what I'm doing when it comes to marrying people off."

"That you do," Cass said in mock exasperation. "A toast to Emerson and Wye—may you have many happy years together!"

"Here, here."

Everyone raised their glasses in a toast. Emerson clinked his orange juice with as many others as he could reach.

"When's the wedding?" Connor asked.

"Fourth of July," Emerson said.

"Fourth of July?" The General slammed his drink down on the table. "That's seven months away, Soldier.

If you want to marry on a holiday, marry on New Year's Eve."

Wye, who'd been sipping her orange juice, sputtered, "New Year's? You want me to marry Emerson in six days?"

"I don't see why not."

"But—"

Emerson grinned at Wyoming. He'd be perfectly happy marrying at New Year's, but it had to be her choice. "I'm game. How about you? After all—it's what the stone said we should do."

"But—"

"You might as well give in," Lena said dryly. "I bet Cass already has your wedding half planned out."

Emerson turned to find Cass smiling sheepishly at the rest of them. "Only in my head."

"I saw the wheels turning," Lena said dryly.

"Well, we could pull it off, I'm sure," Cass said. "We've had so many weddings here. But what about family? You'll want to give them time to make plans to attend."

"Family? What family?" Wyoming said, finally finding her voice. "Other than Ward, I'm on my own. You know that."

"Don't look at me," Emerson said. "I'm barely in touch with mine." As soon as he'd left to join the Army, it was as if he'd stepped off the edge of the planet as far as his aunt, uncle and cousins were concerned and he hadn't pushed the connection when it obviously wasn't wanted.

"That's settled, then," the General said and got back to eating.

"It's not settled," Wye protested, then sighed gustily. "You all are impossible, you know that?"

"Amelia used to call me incorrigible," the General said.

All five of the Reed women stilled. Wye understood their surprise. The General wasn't one for reminiscences, especially not such personal ones.

He looked up, saw everyone looking back and cleared his throat again. "Well, she did."

Alice, sitting next to him, patted his arm. "She loved you for it."

The General harrumphed loudly and went to work cutting up his French toast.

Wye thought she felt a touch on her arm and looked up to find no one there, but she couldn't shake the feeling that a presence was nearby. She met Alice's gaze from across the table. Alice had straightened, her eyes wide. Had she felt it, too?

Was it—Amelia?

Cass had often spoken of the way she felt her mother's presence on the ranch, and Two Willows was certainly an uncanny place. Despite all the General's gruffness, his love for his wife ran deep, like a vein of ore in the ground. Amelia's love for her family was evident everywhere in the old house, the maze, the garden...

Now that Wye thought about it, she realized the General and Amelia hadn't had nearly as much time together as they must have wanted. Their happy marriage had been cut short by Amelia's death. Meanwhile, here she was putting off marriage to a man she knew was her soul mate.

Who knew how many years she would get with Emerson. She'd be a fool to squander even a minute.

She felt the light touch on her arm again. A small squeeze, as if Amelia was saying, "That's exactly it." Then it was gone.

"We don't have to rush into anything," Emerson said, breaking the spell. "I can wait as long as it takes."

Wye struggled to find her voice, which had gone shaky and uncertain. "I… I can't wait," she said. "I want to marry on New Year's."

"Are you sure?" Emerson took her hand. "Because it's okay…"

"I'm positive." Wye cut off his words with a kiss.

WYE SPENT THE rest of the morning so excited she could barely breathe. She helped Cass clear up from brunch and work on the enormous dinner she was preparing, while everyone else took turns keeping Elise happy when she wasn't napping. As the time drew nearer for Ward to arrive for dinner, however, Wyoming grew anxious. She was thrilled about her upcoming wedding, but she couldn't expect him to feel the same way. Would her happiness make his sadness harder to bear? Should she take off her ring and tell everyone to keep it a secret—at least for a few more days?

She decided she couldn't do that, not if she and

Emerson were going to marry in less than a week.

She relaxed a little when Ward arrived, looking almost cheerful, until she realized he'd been drinking.

"Did you drive like that?"

"Like what?" He handed her several bags of chips and a bottle of wine. "Sorry. Not much open today."

Wyoming didn't push it, but she decided then and there she'd keep Elise tonight. She doubted Ward would protest.

Cass passed her a mug of coffee with a nod at Ward as he hung up his coat and his back was turned. Wyoming, her stomach tight with worry, passed it to him. "Get your head together," she told him, and he accepted it, making a face.

"Sorry. Did a little too much celebrating, I guess. Had a good time with my friends." He took a long sip of coffee and squared his shoulders. "What can I do to help?"

"Elise is napping, so why don't you ask the men if they need a hand with anything?" She was sure Emerson and the others could keep Ward in line. She just wished they didn't have to. She hesitated before adding, "Ward, I have some news. Big news."

He immediately turned wary. "What is it?"

She took a breath. "Emerson asked me to marry him this morning. I said yes."

For a moment, Ward seemed too stunned to say anything, and Wye braced for the worst, but then a smile spread over his face. "That's wonderful! Wye, that's perfect. You'll have someone to help you—and

Emerson's a good guy. He's not one to leave a woman in the lurch."

"Of course not." Wye was too surprised to say much else. She wasn't sure what she'd expected. Sulking? Barbed comments about not expecting her marriage to last?

Rather than resenting her good news, Ward seemed... relieved.

"When's the big day? I hope you're not going to make him wait a year, like Mindy did me. All that fuss."

"He'll hardly have to wait at all, actually." She steeled herself again. "We're marrying on New Year's Eve—right here. If we can pull it together." Cass had begun to jot down a list of to-dos as they'd prepared dinner together. They needed to find an officiant, send out invitations... Things were going to get busy in a hurry in the morning, but for now they'd both agreed to enjoy every minute of the holiday.

"I'm really happy for you." Ward hugged her, surprising Wye all over again. "You two will be great together."

Just how much had he had to drink? Wye was still trying to take in his reaction as she watched him wander into the living room to find Emerson and shake his hand.

"That went better than expected," Cass said, opening the oven to check on the turkey and side dishes.

"A bit too well," Wye said slowly. Had she misjudged Ward, or was that the alcohol talking? Would he wake up tomorrow in a foul mood and tell her what he really thought?

"Don't borrow trouble. Hey, can you mash the potatoes?"

After that, they were too busy for Wye to worry about Ward.

Wye woke up the following morning bursting with excitement. This was better than Christmas; she got to start planning her wedding today. As she'd expected, Ward had been happy to leave Elise with her overnight and had gone home with a vague plan to return today to pick her up. Wye didn't expect to see him until the afternoon, so she slid out of bed without waking Emerson and went to fetch the baby before she woke up and roused everyone.

Not that anyone slept in around here, Wye thought in amusement as a half hour later the kitchen was full of hungry men and women preparing for a day of chores. Emerson kissed her on the cheek before heading out with the rest of the men, who'd decided to put a morning's work in one of the trailers after their chores were done.

"Sure you don't want to stick around and plan the wedding?" she teased him.

"I'll just get in the way. Text me any questions you have, and I'll try to be decisive," he told her with a kiss.

"Sounds good."

When they'd cleaned up from the meal, Cass set Elise on the kitchen floor with a number of Tupperware containers and wooden spoons. Elise settled down to banging on them happily, while Cass drew out a notebook.

"I've got notes from all our previous weddings," she began but cut off when Wye laughed. "What? I can't help it that I'm organized!"

"Your mother would be proud." Wye had seen the big binder Amelia had left Cass that was full of tips and tricks for keeping Two Willows running.

"I hope so." Cass flipped through the pages. Each section contained a checklist and laminated pages of information. "We start at the top and work our way through."

"Sounds fantastic. Thank you—for everything."

"Are you kidding? Thank *you*! I was afraid no one else would get married and I wouldn't get to use this again."

The day passed so swiftly, Wye didn't even notice Ward hadn't shown up until it began to get dark outside. She went to text him, but he'd already sent her a message.

Be there soon.

He arrived at the same time he would have if it was a workday, and the following morning he dropped Elise off right on time, too, never asking if Wye needed a break since she was planning her wedding. Of course, now the radio station was open, so he was going to work, but Wye couldn't help wondering how hard it would have been for him to take a few days off.

By midweek she was starting to panic. They'd found an officiant, made their guest list and issued invitations. The wedding was to be a small affair, and Cass had taken charge of the dinner plans. The men were putting together a "mix tape," as Connor insisted on calling it, of dance music for the reception. Sadie was going to provide flowers and greenery from her greenhouse, but there were still rental tables, chairs and tablecloths to order, since the company had been closed extra days around Christmas; bouquets and table arrangements to be made; food to be purchased and prepared... and she hadn't even thought about her wedding dress.

"I need to go to Ellie's Bridals," she announced after breakfast toward the end of the week. The men had already left the table, intent on performing some ranch chore Wye couldn't comprehend but that Emerson had delighted in being asked to help with. For once Lena didn't rush off with them. She was savoring a cup of coffee, perusing the internet to find a part she needed to fix a motor she had taken apart and spread over the coffee table in the front room. Jo and Sadie had stayed, too, chatting about Sadie's plans come spring for the walled garden Connor had built her. "Cass, can you come with me and help with Elise while I try things on?"

Cass exchanged a look with Alice and the rest of her sisters that Wye couldn't interpret. Was there something wrong with going to Ellie's Bridals?

"I should have asked you earlier... but maybe you won't want to... or maybe one of you won't want her—" Cass turned to her sisters.

Wye had no idea what Cass was trying to say, but Alice nodded as if she understood perfectly. "I can alter

Mom's dress one more time—unless Wye wants a hoopskirt wedding, too," she added with a grin.

Wye's breath caught in her throat. Alice couldn't mean—

"I'm good with that." Jo nodded, then sighed, "Which means we're in those green bridesmaid gowns again, huh?"

"I'll alter those, too," Alice assured her.

"Sadie?" Cass asked.

"I think it's perfect," Sadie said. "Wye belongs here. She always has."

"I'm good with it," Lena said seriously. "Wye has earned her place here. So has Emerson," she admitted. "At first I didn't think I wanted any more men around, but he's the most trustworthy and least intrusive one I've ever met. You picked good, Wye." She got back to work.

Wye's heart swelled a little, but she couldn't believe what they were offering. "I can't wear your mother's wedding dress."

"Can't or don't want to?" Cass asked. "Alice can make you any dress you want, you know."

Alice nodded again. "Gladly. But Mom wants you to wear her dress, Wye—if you want to."

"How can you know that?" Wye squeaked, but it was just something to say, because she was feeling that presence again—and that light touch on her arm—as if Amelia were saying it was okay to want to belong here, to be a part of it all.

Alice just cocked her head and smiled.

"Say yes, Wye," Cass said gently. "Please."

Wye opened her mouth, feeling like she was about to do the bravest thing she'd ever done. It was like standing on the edge of a cliff and leaping, hoping someone, somehow would be there to catch her.

She shut her eyes.

"I'd love to."

"Yay!" Alice clapped her hands and bounced. "I love altering that gown. It shapes itself to everyone and gets better every time. Come on, we have to go to town."

"What for?" Wye opened her eyes again to find everyone beaming back at her.

"Beads. I'm going to add some beadwork this time. Don't worry. It will be beautiful."

Wye believed her; everything Alice created was beautiful.

"But we need to call the rental company for the tables—"

"I've got that under control," Cass told her. "Go on. Have fun. I'll watch Elise, too."

"Are you sure?"

"Of course I'm sure!" Cass took the baby from Wye's arms. "Go on—shoo!"

They took Alice's truck to town and parked in front of Chance Creek's little fabric shop.

"Will you be able to find what you need here?" Wye asked as they approached the small boutique. There wasn't time to order anything in.

"I'm sure I will," Alice assured her. "Don't worry.

I'll get your dress done in time. It's going to be fine."

"Is it? Can you see that?"

A cloud passed over Alice's eyes, and she took her time answering. "I don't deal in that kind of foresight anymore," she said gently. "I don't meddle in people's lives."

"But you do see the future."

"I've learned to keep to the present as much as possible."

Her answers weren't very satisfying. Wye wasn't second-guessing her choice to marry Emerson, but she did know she was taking a risk hurrying into the arrangement. If there was something she should know, she wished Alice would tell her.

"Look—they're changing the name on Ellie's Bridals," Alice cried, stopping in front of the fabric shop and pointing down the street.

Wyoming looked up to see she was right. A couple of workmen were hoisting a large wooden sign over the door to the boutique that read Ellie & Caitlyn's Creations.

"I'd heard Ellie was bringing her niece into the business in a more significant way. Here's proof of it."

"I bet Caitlyn's over the moon." Caitlyn had been a single mother but was married now and settled in the town. Wye had known her back in school, although they hadn't been close.

"It's good for Ellie, too. Sadie says her arthritis has been slowing her down, no matter how many of her tinctures she takes. Now she has a partner."

"Alice! Wyoming! Good to see you. Did you have a good Christmas?"

Wye turned to see Megan Lawrence coming toward them, a local realtor who'd also grown up in Chance Creek. "It was a wonderful Christmas," she said. "How about you?"

"Good. Quiet but good," Megan said. "I've got to run—I'm showing a house to a client—but I wanted to say congratulations, Wye. You'll pass on to your brother that I'm so happy, won't you?"

"Uh… sure?" Wye stumbled over her words, unsure why Megan had included Ward in her congratulations. Did she think her brother would be relieved Emerson was marrying her?

There was no time to ask for a clarification; Megan kept going, waving at them over her shoulder.

"Alice! Come in!" The fabric store's proprietor came out to meet them, a young, beaming woman, who ushered them inside.

"She loves me because I spend a fortune here," Alice whispered to Wye as they entered the store, but as she told the woman what she needed and they headed to the bead section, Wye thought there was a genuine friendship between them—one creative person to another.

Alice began to describe what she wanted to accomplish. The other woman brought out paper and pencils, and together they began to sketch swirls and flourishes and rosettes. Wye drifted away, realizing the store sold everything a crafty person could want, from fabric to art supplies to how-to books.

"Wye, come look at this," Alice called. Wye's heart swelled again, like it had a hundred times in the past few days. She was going to look at the design for her wedding dress.

And in three days' time, she'd be married to Emerson.

Chapter 10

"I NEED TO drop off Elise a little early tomorrow, if you don't mind," Ward said when he came to pick up the baby.

Emerson transferred the little girl into his arms, disconnecting one of her hands, then the other, from his sweater, where she clutched it as if holding on for dear life. He'd been helping watch the little girl while Wye helped Cass wrangle some household chores that had gotten away from them while they were planning the wedding.

"Emememem," Elise said, leaning toward him as Ward took her. It was her best version of Emerson's name, and every time she said it, Emerson's heart swelled a little. She liked him.

"Daddy's here," he told her. "Can you say, 'Daddy'?"

"Dadada." Elise jerked toward her father, nearly head-butting Ward.

"That's right, Daddy's here." Ward brushed a kiss over her head. "Got all your stuff?" he asked her. He picked up her baby bag and showed it to her. Elise lunged as if to grab it, but Ward snuggled her in closer to his shoulder. "Be careful, little girl."

"I think everything's in there," Emerson said. "Wye's down in the basement with Cass sorting laundry. Want me to call her?"

Ward shook his head. "Just tell her about the early drop-off tomorrow?"

"You know she's getting married in a few days, right?" Emerson couldn't help asking. Sometimes Ward seemed not to notice anyone but himself.

"I know. I wouldn't ask if there was any other way around it." Ward opened the door and maneuvered through it. "See you in the morning."

"See you."

"I think we finished every last piece of laundry, and no one is allowed to make more until the wedding is over," Cass declared, coming up from the basement lugging a brimming basket of clean laundry. She turned the corner and trudged up the stairs to the second floor.

"Did Ward come?" Wye asked, following her, lugging another basket.

Emerson passed on her brother's message, took the basket from her arms and followed Cass upstairs, Wye trailing them.

"I hope he realizes I'm not babysitting on my wedding day," Wye said.

"Or the day after, I hope," Cass put in. "I still think it's a shame you two aren't taking a honeymoon."

"We will in a few months," Emerson assured her. "When the General is steadier on his feet. I'll take you anywhere you want to go," he added to Wyoming. "Let's stop by the travel agency in town one of these days and pick up some brochures."

"Sounds good."

The following morning Emerson was just coming downstairs when Ward drove in, his headlights cutting through the darkness. Wye was up but still getting dressed, so he met Ward at the door to take Elise.

"I've got to run," Ward said, giving his daughter one last snuggle and kiss. "You be good for Wye, you hear me? For Emerson, too." He handed Elise over. "Just wanted to say thank you," he added, not quite meeting Emerson's gaze.

"For what?"

"For taking care of my sister. You will, right—when you're married? You won't go running off at the first sign of trouble?"

"Of course not."

Ward looked him up and down. "You like kids, don't you?" He nodded at Elise in Emerson's arms.

"Yep. Plan to have some of my own if Wye wants to."

"Good." Still Ward didn't go. He bent forward suddenly and kissed Elise's head again. Pulled back. Hesitated. Checked the time. "Hell, I'll be late."

Emerson watched him hurry back to his truck and drive off before shutting the back door. "It's just you and me, kid," he told Elise. "You hungry? I sure am. But first we have to make coffee for the General. Want to learn how?"

It was a long day of preparations for the wedding, interrupted by a quick trip to town for some last-minute grocery shopping for Cass, who'd been baking and cooking since sunrise in preparation for the big day. Emerson and the other men got out from underfoot during the afternoon and accomplished some work down at the Park—but not nearly as much as he would have liked. Buck's trailer was all set, and he'd manage to finish the one for Gary on time—just. But he'd barely started on the three other ones he'd promised would be done by midway through January. He'd have to double down after the wedding.

They came back at dinnertime to find Wye waiting for them on the back porch, Elise in her arms.

"What are you doing out here in the cold?" Emerson ushered them inside.

"Ward hasn't shown up, and he's not answering his phone. I called his work, and they said he took the day off. He didn't say a word to me about it. Did he tell you?"

"No. He just dropped Elise off early, said he was going to be late and took off."

"I'm really worried."

"Should I drive you to town?"

"If you don't mind. I was giving him another ten minutes to show up, but this isn't like him. I mean, I know he's been late before, but he's always answered his phone."

Emerson nodded, his stomach sinking as he thought about Ward's goodbye to Elise this morning. He decided not to say anything about that yet. He didn't want to alarm Wye before he needed to.

Neither of them spoke much on their drive to town. When they reached Ward's house, Emerson stopped Wye from getting out. "Let me look first."

The color drained from Wye's face as she grasped his meaning. "You don't think—"

"No, I don't," he said firmly. "Ward didn't look like a man intent on taking his life when I saw him this morning. I'll be back in a minute. Can I have your keys?" He meant what he said, but he wanted to make sure he was right before Wye came in with Elise.

She handed them over.

Ward might not have looked like a man ready to end his own life when they'd spoken that morning, but now that he thought about it, he had looked like a man saying goodbye to his daughter for longer than one day. Emerson wished he'd paid more attention and asked some questions.

Too late now.

The curtains in Ward's house were drawn, and he expected the door to be locked, but it opened when he turned the handle. Stepping inside, Emerson instantly knew his hunch was right. Something was off.

The furniture was still in place, but the house had the spotless, empty feel of a showroom—all signs of habitation gone. He did a quick circuit of the rooms, checked the refrigerator, the kitchen cupboards and the closets in the bedrooms, then came back to gesture Wye in. She had already gotten out of the car and released

Elise from her seat. She hurried to meet him, the baby in her arms.

"What's going on? Is Ward here?"

"No. He's gone."

"Gone?" Her voice rose an octave.

"Not dead," he hastened to reassure her. "Gone. He's moved out. All his personal belongings have been removed."

Wye blanched. "That can't be right." She pushed past him and strode quickly through the house, opening closets and dresser drawers, her mouth drawing into a thin line as the truth sank in. When she was through, she turned on Emerson. "How could he do this? How could he leave his baby?" She handed Elise to him, pulled out her phone and tapped on it, then lifted it to her ear. "Still not answering." She paced in a circle. "He can't mean to abandon her—not really! He couldn't be such a monster, could he?"

Emerson thought perhaps he could. What's more, he was sure Ward thought he was doing the right thing. Wye loved Elise, and Wye was getting married. Emerson remembered what Ward had said: "You'll take care of her, won't you?"

"What a selfish, horrible thing to do!" Wye exclaimed. "He can't think he'll actually get away with it, can he? The police will track him down, and what about Elise? She'll end up in foster care. It's not like I can just keep her without any kind of authority to do so." She took Elise from Emerson's arms, as if someone might come and rip the baby away from her. "What do I do?

Do I call Cab Johnson? Report Ward missing? Will Child Protective Services take Elise tonight?"

"I don't think you have to do anything if you don't want to," Emerson said, hearing the panic in Wye's voice and wanting to reassure her. "For all you know, Ward will come back tomorrow."

"But—"

A knock on the door startled both of them. Emerson turned on his heel, but the door opened before he could reach it.

"Yoo-hoo, is someone here?" a woman's voice called. Megan Lawrence walked in, evidently as surprised to see them as they were to see her. "Ward didn't tell me you'd be here. You weren't planning to take anything, were you? All the furniture is part of the deal."

"What deal?" Wye asked.

Emerson's stomach sank even further. If Ward had been planning this long enough to hire a realtor and sell his house, he really didn't mean to come back.

"The house deal." Megan cocked her head. "The buyers purchased all the furniture, too. They won't take possession until the end of the month, of course, but when I saw lights on and a truck outside, I stopped to make sure no one was robbing the place. Glad it's only you two. Did Ward forget something?"

Wye looked as if she'd been struck. "Are you telling me Ward sold his house?"

"Of course—that's why I told you to congratulate him," Megan said with a smile. "His house sold in record time, but that's because he listed it so low. I wish he would have taken my advice and tried for a higher price—for his sake, not mine!" she rushed to add. "I've never conducted a sale in such a short time. One week until closing—that's fast!"

"That is fast," Emerson said.

Wye turned bewildered eyes to him. "Closing? How… how long was he planning this?" He could see her working it out in her mind. Knew how sharp her pain would feel. To know someone in your family meant to bail on you—had planned carefully just how to sever the connection—hurt like a knife sliding between your ribs, aimed at your heart. "He knew I was getting married," Wye sputtered. "And he just bailed?"

"Married! Bailed? What do you mean?" Megan asked. She looked from one to the other. "Didn't you know Ward was selling his house?"

Wye shook her head. "He didn't breathe a word."

Megan put a hand to her throat. "I don't understand. Why didn't he tell you? Isn't…?" She took a breath, her eyes going wide as she looked at the baby in Emerson's arms. "Isn't that Ward's daughter?"

Wye didn't answer her. She turned to Emerson. "He's really gone, isn't he? This is exactly what my dad did—sold up and took off and left me behind like I meant nothing! How could Ward do the same thing to Elise that Dad did to us? How can he just—leave her?"

"He must be in a world of pain if that's what he's done." Emerson ached for Wye, knowing exactly how she must feel.

Megan had gone pale. "I'm so sorry—I didn't realize

what was going on. I would never have sold the house if I'd known what he meant to do."

"It's not your fault," Emerson assured her. Wye was shaking, her face drained of all color, and he knew Megan's presence wasn't helping any. "We'll lock up when we go," he said to the realtor pointedly.

"Of course. Wyoming, I'm sorry," Megan said again. "I won't breathe a word of this to anyone. Take all the time you need here." She hurried for the door. "But— you said someone was getting married?"

"We are," Emerson told her and nodded toward the door. She took the hint, slipped out and closed it behind her.

Wye huffed out a ragged breath. "It will be a miracle if the whole town isn't talking about us by nightfall." Her voice was tight and strained, and Emerson realized she was focusing on possible gossip so as not to have to focus on what Ward had done. He was ready when her face crumpled and she began to sob. "Now what are we supposed to do?" she cried, scrubbing her free hand over her cheeks. The tears came faster than she could wipe them away, though. Emerson tried to put his arms around her and the baby, but Wye stepped back, Elise still in her arms. "I don't have time to cry," she told him. "I have to stop Ward. Bring him back. I just don't know how to do that." Her voice broke again.

"I don't think there's anything to do," Emerson said. "We've got to give Ward time. Trust that he'll come to his senses. He's not your father, and I've seen him with Elise. He loves her."

"He sold his house!" Wye exclaimed. "Without telling anyone. He packed up and left, Emerson. No one comes back after doing that!"

"After the wedding we'll track him down. I promise."

"Wedding?" Wyoming stared at him as if he'd lost his mind. "What do you mean after the wedding?"

"Our wedding—the day after tomorrow," he reminded her.

"You think I'm going to marry you? After this?" Wyoming's voice rose. "This is what men do, Emerson. They leave—just when you need them the most. Every last one of them! There's no way I'm marrying anyone now!" She rushed out the door and slammed it behind her, hard.

"I DON'T UNDERSTAND why you won't come back to the house," Cass said later, when she arrived at the door to the room Wye had rented at the Evergreen Motel. "You need people around you. You need to talk to Emerson."

"What's the use? He's a man, isn't he? He'll disappoint me sooner or later, so why not just get on with it?" Wye paced the floor with Elise in her arms as Cass lugged in the baby's portable crib and set it up. When she'd stormed out of Ward's house, she'd found Megan just pulling out and was able to flag her down. Megan was kind enough to wait while Wye retrieved Elise's car seat from Emerson's vehicle and drive her the five blocks to the motel. She'd gotten control of her tears only long enough to book the room and send a text to Cass. Once that was done, she'd sat down in her motel room and sobbed, drying her eyes only when Cass had knocked on her door.

She'd known something like this would happen, hadn't she? She'd known marriage and family and a life at Two Willows with Emerson was too good to be true.

"You're going to hate yourself if you don't marry Emerson," Cass said flatly. "And this isn't like you, Wye. You're the calm one. The practical one."

"Because I've had to be," Wye cried. "No one else was going to take care of me, were they? No one else cared!"

"Emerson cares—a lot."

"He didn't even try to stop me," Wye said. It had hurt her more than she liked to admit that after she'd fled Ward's house, Emerson hadn't rushed out after her. She knew she wasn't making any sense, but none of this made sense. Ward couldn't be gone. She'd called him dozens of times, left message after message until his voice mail was full. She'd even called Mindy's old number, but it was disconnected.

Where could he have gone? How could her brother have dismantled his life so quickly?

"I think Emerson understood going after you wasn't going to help," Cass countered. "He came straight home, you know, and told me he's giving you time to simmer down, but he's frantic, Wye. I heard him yelling at the General before I left. He never yells at the General."

"I'm not going to simmer down! I'm—furious!" Wye burst into tears again. Hell, she hated crying. She'd cried far too many times after her mother left—and after her father moved without telling her. No one cried for her, did they?

Cass took Elise, placed her in the crib and gave her several toys to explore. She came back and sat next to Wye.

"Of course you're furious. The men in your family have let you down all over the place, and so did your mother, but that doesn't mean that Emerson is going to. You know what I think? I think you're so used to people like your father and your brother punishing you, you're punishing yourself. And I think that's stupid!"

Wye reared back. "Thanks a lot! I'm trying to keep from getting my heart broken!"

"You're cutting off your nose to spite your face. You need to talk to Emerson."

"I don't want to talk to him!" That was a lie. She'd give anything for his strong presence at the moment, but she couldn't let down her guard. "I wish Ward was here. I'd give him a piece of my mind."

Cass reached down, picked up one of Elise's dolls from where she'd dropped it and shook it at Wyoming. "Pretend this is him. What do you want to say?"

"Come off it, Cass. Talk about stupid!" Wye shifted on the bed and crossed her arms.

"My name is Ward." Cass lowered her voice to mimic Wye's brother and moved the doll like a puppet. "I just sold my house without warning and disappeared, leaving you with my baby. What do you think about that?"

"Stop it." This was the last thing she needed.

"Come on, Wye," Cass growled in that same low voice. "Give it to me straight. I know you don't have anything better to do than clean up my mess. You should be thanking me!"

"Thanking you?" Wye sputtered. "Cass!"

"That's right, thanking me," Cass growled like Ward again. "You don't have a career. You never go out. You don't do anything fun. You drive off every man who comes sniffing around. It's not like you'll ever have a kid of your own!"

"That's not true!" Wye stared at the doll, shaking with fury. "I'm perfectly capable of having my own children, and I've got plenty to do without your interference."

"Like what?"

"Like look for a new job that's better than my old one. Like help run the rentals at Two Willows and help with the books, too. Like be part of a real family that actually loves me back."

"Ha! What about me?"

"You?" Wye saw Ward as clearly as if he was in the room. "You're nothing but selfish and mean and self-serving! You never think about anyone else! You never notice my accomplishments—or ask me how my day went. You treat me like a couch or a TV set—there to serve you whenever you want and to sit and wait, doing nothing, until you come back needing something else.

Well, I'm not! I'm not a couch! And if you loved me at all, you'd never leave!"

Wyoming lurched forward, grabbed the doll from Cass's hands and wound back to hurl it across the room.

Cass surged up to snatch it, and for a moment they tugged it back and forth until Wye realized what she was doing and let go all at once. She was breathing hard, sobs clogging her throat, tears falling so fast and thick she could hardly see.

Cass stumbled back a few paces awkwardly but caught herself before she fell over. She came to drop down on her knees beside the bed where Wye still sat. "That's the crux of it, isn't it? You're afraid Emerson won't love you?"

"No one loves me!" Wye covered her face with her hands, unable to stop her tears. "No one has ever loved me. I'm all alone!"

"That's not true." Cass set the doll on the floor, leaned in and wrapped Wyoming in her arms, her belly a small mound between them. "I love you. And so does Emerson. So we all do. Wye, sometimes our birth family is just that—our birth family. Sometimes our real family is made up of people who aren't related to us at all. I swear to God, I won't ever leave you, and I hope you won't leave me, either. I've lost people, too," she reminded her. "Please don't make me lose you."

Wye didn't know how to answer her. Couldn't through her sobs anyway. She ached with pain and shock and fear about what the future would bring.

From her crib, Elise pushed up and peeked over the

top bar. "Yiyiyiyi," she called, reaching a chubby arm toward Wyoming beseechingly.

"What am I going to do?" Wye sobbed. "Cass, I'm so scared."

"We all are sometimes," Cass soothed her. "You're going to get through this. You're not alone this time, Wye. You have a whole army on your side—even a General."

Wye laughed, a sound that hitched and edged into a sob again. "Emerson must hate me. I was so awful."

"I think Emerson understands what you're feeling right now better than any of us, don't you?" Cass asked.

Wyoming supposed he probably did. After all, he'd lost his parents, too.

She'd run out on him at the first sign of trouble. "I need to talk to him." She wiped her face on her sleeve.

"Of course. How about you clean up first? I'll get Elise's things together and take you home."

Home. More tears welled up, until Wyoming wondered how there could be any left. She had a home—and she'd almost tossed it away along with the man she loved more than anything.

"Cass," Wye began.

"Yes?"

"Thank you."

"STOP FIDGETING, SERGEANT," the General snapped when Emerson tidied the same pile of paper for the third time.

He dropped the pages on the General's desk and

crossed the room, peeked out the window and crossed back.

"If you touch that stack of paper one more time, I'll have you court-martialed!"

"Sorry, sir."

"Sorry my ass. What's got you so wound up? Where's that girl—Wyoming? And what kind of name is that, anyway? Was Montana already taken?"

Emerson knew the General was trying to help, but his banter was grating on his nerves.

"I already told you she's at the Evergreen Motel, sir."

"Then what are you doing here?"

"Giving her space."

"Women don't want space. If they did, us men would be living on Mars by now. Look, Sergeant, when a woman loves you, and she pushes you away, it's because she wants you to push back."

"I... don't think that's right, General." Emerson moved to a bookshelf and began to straighten the volumes. His ankle ached, and he wondered if he'd twisted it again stalking from Ward's house to his truck after Wye drove off with Megan. He'd wanted desperately to charge after her when she'd raced out the door, but he knew that would only lead to a bigger fight. Wye was the kind of woman who held her anger in until she reached the breaking point, and she had definitely hit that point when she realized what Ward had done. He'd give her time and then do whatever it took to put her life back together. Meanwhile, he wouldn't let himself think about a future without her in it.

"Not push—you know what I mean!" the General exploded. "She wants you to prove that you're going to stand by her, even in the hard times. She's having a hard time, right?"

"Yes." Emerson wasn't sure which made him angrier—the fact that Ward would abandon his child or that he'd assume Wye would pick up where he left off and parent Elise. If Ward hadn't noticed, Wye didn't have a home of her own—or an income outside of what he'd been paying her. That's where he came in, Emerson figured. He was perfectly happy to support his wife-to-be, and Elise, too, but it galled him that Ward thought he could drop his responsibilities and someone would be there to pick them up.

No, more than that, Emerson decided. What bothered him was that Ward acted like there'd be no consequences to anyone else.

To Wye.

"So why the hell are you here when she's there?" the General pushed.

"Because Wye needs time to sort out her feelings, sir."

"That's what you're for," the General told him. "You're her sounding board. You're her support. You're there to provide answers or to just keep quiet if that's what she needs."

"Is that what you've done when people needed you, sir?"

It was a low blow, and the General surged to his

feet, winced and braced himself on his desk. "Yes, I did—with my wife," he growled. "I failed with my daughters. I'm making up for that now. You want to copy my successes or my fuck-ups, Sergeant?"

"Sorry, sir."

"Stop being sorry. Start *doing* something."

"You're right, sir."

"I'm always right. Now, get."

The General waved him out the door, and Emerson made for the kitchen to grab his coat, grateful to finally be taking action, but he came to a stop when the back door swung open and Cass burst inside, lugging a portable crib.

"Emerson."

"Is Wyoming with—"

Wyoming stepped in next, Elise in her arms. It was clear she'd been crying. Her features were drawn, her face blotched red and white.

Emerson crossed the room and pulled them both into an embrace. "Glad to see you safe."

"I'm sorry I stormed out of Ward's place like that. You didn't deserve me yelling at you." Wye leaned against him, and Emerson's heart swelled. He'd do anything to make life easier for this woman. Starting with not pressuring her to sort everything out tonight.

"How about I get Elise to bed?" Cass asked. "Brian? Can you carry the crib upstairs?" she asked when her husband entered the room to see what the fuss was about. "That way you two can talk," she told Emerson and Wye.

"Thanks," Wyoming said. When Cass and Brian had gone, taking Elise with them, she hugged her arms to her chest. "I'm really sorry. I just—"

Emerson touched her shoulder. "We can talk if you want to," he said. "I'm happy to talk all night. Or I can take you upstairs, put you to bed, and we can start fresh in the morning. For the record, I still want to marry you."

"Even if I'm a single mother?" She laughed sadly. "I can't let Elise go into the foster system, Emerson, not when I'm capable of taking care of her."

"I wouldn't expect you to. Wye, look at me." When she lifted her chin to do so, he went on. "You and I both know how important it is for a child to have a loving, stable home. I'm going to be there for you—and Elise—always. I mean that."

Wye's eyes filled again. "I want so badly to believe you. I really do."

He took her in his arms again and let her cry. He knew what she meant. Trusting someone—really trusting them—came hard after what each of them had been through.

"You know what I think? I think you, Elise and I need to take a day off. Let's spend the day together tomorrow doing something normal." He brightened. "I read in the paper about a snow sculpture exhibit in town. How about we go to that?"

"We can't just leave—we're getting married the day after tomorrow."

His arms tightened around her. God, he hoped so.

"Everything is in hand, and I think this is one of those moments when we actually have to trust that our friends are our friends and are willing to help."

Wye laughed, hiccupping a little. "I can almost see Cass quivering with anticipation. She loves to help."

"We've got ten men and women—plus a General—just dying to step in," he agreed. "Let's let them finish the preparations and the three of us go to town."

Wye's mouth curved into a smile. "I don't know."

"I do. Come on, Wye, we need a day off. If, at the end of it, you decide you want to postpone the wedding—or call it off completely," he added, pain shooting through him at the thought, "we'll make that happen."

Wye snuggled into his embrace. "You are a good man, Emerson Myers."

"I'm doing my best."

"HAVE A GOOD time," Cass said the following morning. "Don't worry about a thing, okay? We've thrown so many weddings, we know exactly what we're doing."

"I'm not sure I do," Wyoming told her. "How can I expect Emerson to take on a baby after the way Ward drove off and left her with me? He shouldn't have to pay the price for my brother's selfishness. Honestly, I thought I'd wake up today to find Ward back, demanding to take Elise home. I can't believe he really left, Cass."

"I know. I wonder where he's gone."

"Does he think he's going to start over?" Wye asked. "Surely he has to know that's impossible. Kids don't just disappear because you want them to. I mean, Mom did that to us—didn't it hurt him the way it did me?"

"I'm sure it did. Maybe he thinks if your mom could forget about him, then his child can forget about him, too," Cass said sadly. "But at some level he must know he's wrong."

"I still feel like we should report this to someone."

"I think Emerson is right," Cass said. "Ward is a grown man who's just gone through something devastating. Give him a few days, then report him and go through the proper channels so you keep custody of Elise."

Wye still found it hard to take in. She shifted Elise in her arms, her heart aching when the little girl snuggled against her. She'd been up for hours last night, contemplating the future. One thought had left her breathless.

"If Ward doesn't come back soon, I'm going to stop feeling like Elise's aunt and start feeling like her mother," Wyoming confessed, knowing Cass would understand. "I'm already halfway there with all the time I've been spending with her. And then he's going to find his footing again and come and take her—"

Cass nodded. "I think you're wise to understand that up front. Your brother is sad and scared and lonely and doing stupid, stupid things, but you're right. Likely that will pass. He probably will come back for Elise." Cass smoothed back the baby's hair.

"How do I love her and hold her at a distance at the

same time?"

"You don't." Cass met her gaze, her eyes shining with unshed tears. "I'm sorry, honey, but it doesn't work that way. You love her with all your heart for as long as you can, even knowing your heart will probably be broken. And if Ward pulls himself together and comes home, you do everything you can to repair the bond he broke between him and Elise."

"That isn't fair," Wyoming cried.

"I know it isn't. But that's life, isn't it? Loving when loving hurts like hell?"

"Everything okay in here?" Emerson asked, coming in. "I've got Elise's car seat in my truck. We're all set to go."

"Have fun," Cass said, handing Wyoming a paper towel to dry her eyes. "We've got everything covered here."

"Good morning, little girl," Emerson said, lifting Elise from Wye's hands, giving her time to pull herself together. "Let's go see some snow castles. We need to cheer up Aunt Wyoming."

"I'll be okay," Wye told him as they left. "Cass was just delivering some home truths. Some necessary ones." She filled him in on their conversation.

"I've been thinking about the same thing. It would be easy to think I should step into Ward's shoes, since he's gone and I'm here, but that's not really my place—even if you do agree to marry me tomorrow."

They got into the truck. Wyoming helped secure Elise into her car seat, then climbed into her own.

"Cass says we shouldn't guard our hearts, though."

"I guess she's right."

"It's not going to be easy. Or maybe I should say it's going to be too easy to fall in love with the idea of being Elise's mother. And it's going to hurt like hell when Ward comes back. If he comes back."

"Maybe we should take it one day at a time," Emerson said. "And for today, just be two people who love each other taking a baby to see some snow sculptures."

Wise words, Wye decided. "Okay. That sounds good."

The snow sculpture exhibit was a kind of contest between groups that were competing for a prize in order to raise money for the elementary school's PTA. Different businesses and clubs and sports teams had joined in to create fantastic snow sculptures. Some were funny. Some were pretty, and some downright complicated, like the scale model of Chance Creek's downtown that the business association had commissioned.

As they walked through the town square, viewing the different sculptures, Wyoming relaxed a little. Emerson insisted on carrying Elise and showing the little girl each one up close, giving her a running commentary, which gave Wyoming time to examine her thoughts—and her heart. Caught up in taking care of the baby, Emerson was barely limping today, only a hitch in his step evidence that his wound hadn't entirely healed.

Wye knew she didn't want to lose him, and now that the first shock had worn off, she'd decided that she had the resources to take on Elise's care. In addition to helping Emerson with the trailer rentals and farm bookkeeping, she could look for consulting work or even set up a website to advertise her paralegal services. Maybe she could find some city firm who would hire her to work part-time remotely. She'd help Cass run the house and do the books, and she could easily run errands for the ranch with Elise. She'd find ways to earn her keep.

Meanwhile, she'd trust Emerson when he said he was willing to take on Elise's care, too. She was glad they'd already talked about the difference between fostering Elise and being her parents. They couldn't forget that the baby had a mother and father who were both physically capable of caring for her, even if emotionally they'd suffered a setback. She and Emerson would open their hearts to Elise—but they couldn't depend on forever with her.

Wye was beginning to think she could depend on forever with Emerson, though. Life had thrown a curveball at them yesterday, and here he was, spending the day with her and Elise, trying to convince her that he was ready to spend his life with her.

"Wyoming! It's good to see you out enjoying yourself!"

Wyoming turned to see Megan approaching. The realtor took in Emerson with Elise nearby. "Do you mind my asking what's happening? Did you talk to Ward?"

"No. We can't find him, but we're fairly certain he'll

be back," Wye told her. "Meanwhile, we'll care for Elise as best we can."

Megan watched Emerson showing Elise a snow dinosaur presented by the Chance Creek Athletics Club. "You're so lucky, finding someone like him. I'd love to get married and start my family. I know I've got time, but—I don't want to have time, you know? I want it all right now."

The longing in her eyes tugged at Wye's heart. "I do know. I don't think Emerson and I will wait that long—" She stopped when Megan grinned. "What?"

"I'm so glad you're marrying him after all. I swear I went home and cried last night when I thought you two had broken up in front of me."

Wye's cheeks heated. "I guess I did say the wedding was off."

"You were so fierce!" Megan told her. "And Emerson was so sad. I didn't know what to do."

Wye's heart gave a pang. "We *are* getting married," she assured Megan. "And I'd love for you to be there. I'm sorry I didn't invite you before: it's a small affair."

"You don't need to—"

"I'd like to. I'd like to get to know you better. I'd like to have more friends."

Megan brightened. "Me, too! I'd love to come." Her gaze slid to Emerson and Elise again. "Where am I supposed to find a man like that, though?"

"I could tell the General to send you one," Wye said. "He's the one who ordered Emerson to marry me."

Megan laughed. "I heard about him sending home husbands for his daughters. While you're at it, tell him to send me some clients, too. Your brother's house was the first one I've sold in a while—sorry," she added when she took in Wye's expression.

"I suppose real estate isn't an easy business to get into."

"It isn't, but I'll persevere," Megan said. "Enjoy the snow sculptures, and I'll see you at the wedding. When is it?"

Wye laughed. "Tomorrow."

Chapter 11

"SHE'S ASLEEP," EMERSON told Wyoming when they sat down at a picnic table to drink some hot chocolate. He adjusted Elise in her carrier, wrapped a blanket around the contraption more securely and took the cup Wyoming offered him, careful to keep the hot liquid far away from the baby.

"You tired her out." Wyoming smiled at him. "Thanks for bringing us here. It was a good idea to get away from it all for a bit. Being outside in the fresh air and sunshine puts things into perspective, too."

"I had a good time. You know, when I was living on base, the real world often seemed like a dream. I like it better here in Chance Creek."

"Sounds like you spent a lot of time with the General."

"I did. He picked me as an assistant pretty early in my career."

"Was that a good thing?"

Emerson thought about it. "It was. He taught me a lot about looking at the big picture. That's the hard thing about being a general. Even if you know the details about people and their lives, you're supposed to keep your focus on what's best on the whole, which isn't always what's best for any particular individual."

"Are you sorry you couldn't keep your career?"

"Yes." It felt good to be honest. "I'll make a place for myself helping the General with reserve training, but so far it hasn't felt like the best fit. I need something different." He laughed. "Just figured that out as I was saying it."

"What are you thinking?"

"I like what I'm doing at the Park—fixing up the trailers. I feel like I'll do a good job managing them, too. I've got some savings. Not a lot, but enough to buy one or two more small houses, maybe. Fixer-uppers. Once they're ready, I could rent them. Maybe I can make a career out of property management and repairs. It's flexible enough to allow me to keep helping the General—and helping on the ranch when there's work for me there. Flexible enough to be around to help with any more babies we acquire, too."

"Sounds good."

"What about you?"

She told him about her idea to go after remote paralegal work. "I don't know if I'll be able to find contracts or not, but no harm in trying, right?"

"Right. Sounds like we should be able to cobble together a living."

"A good living," Wyoming said. "I like the idea of controlling my own hours."

"Me, too."

"I like the idea of making a life with you," she added.

"Are you proposing to me, Wyoming Smith?" He took her hand, leaned across the table awkwardly, making sure not to squash Elise, and kissed her.

"I guess I am. What do you say?"

"I say I'd marry you any day."

"How about tomorrow?"

He pretended to think about that. "I guess I could do that."

"Don't sound so enthusiastic," she said dryly.

"Baby, you want enthusiasm, you just wait until our wedding night."

On the ride home, Emerson tried to keep his eyes on the road, but he was having a hard time keeping his mind from picturing what their wedding night would entail. They couldn't leave town for a honeymoon, but Cass had assured him previously she would take care of Elise and make sure they had at least one uninterrupted night, so he'd gone out on a limb and booked a night at one of the bed-and-breakfasts in town, run by Ethan and Autumn Cruz. They'd have a luxurious room and private bathroom, and he'd heard the food was wonderful there. When he'd talked to Autumn, she'd assured him she'd happily deliver them room service. "No need to leave the room if you don't want to."

He didn't think he'd want to.

First he had to get Wyoming down the aisle, though. All he wanted was a quiet night and for everything to go smoothly as they prepared for the wedding in the morning. He trusted Cass would have a wonderful dinner on the table when they got home, as usual, and that most of the work would be completed.

When they arrived at Two Willows, however, Cass met them at the back door, her face troubled.

"It's Ward," she said without preamble. "The General tracked him down."

WYOMING ENTERED TWO Willows' kitchen, Emerson's hand wrapped around hers. He was carrying Elise's car seat in his other hand, the baby fast asleep.

Without a word, Jo came forward and took Elise from him. "I'll be in the living room with her," she said.

"Where's Ward?" Wyoming asked.

"San Francisco," the General said from his seat at the head of the table. "Sit down, and we'll talk this over."

Wyoming sat, her heart in her mouth. Emerson sat next to her, Cass and Brian across from them. Cass's sisters and their husbands filed in, too, as if they'd been waiting for them.

Maybe they had, Wyoming realized. They were family now.

"We're here for you," Cass assured her. "All of us."

"I had some people I know see if they could track down your brother," the General said. "They found him holed up in a motel on the outskirts of San Francisco—with his wife."

"Mindy is with him?" The knowledge hit Wyoming like a punch to the gut. "Are they back together?"

"Seems like they're working on it," the General said.

"They're in counseling?" That would be a wonderful outcome for her brother. Maybe Mindy had grown up a little in her time away—had realized she loved Ward and her baby—

"That's right—and they want you to adopt Elise," the General said.

Wyoming's mouth dropped open. How could he even know that?

"My people sat them down. Talked to them. Laid all the cards on the table. That's what your brother and sister-in-law decided."

"But—"

"They aren't coming back, honey," Cass said. "Ward made that clear."

A chill prickled down Wyoming's spine. How could they not come back?

"They've decided they're not ready to be parents."

Wyoming let out a strangled sound. "That's not something you get to decide after you've had a baby!"

But it was exactly what her mother had decided, wasn't it? And her father had barely done much better. Wye felt sick. Only Emerson's hand clasping hers under the table kept her steady.

"They're prepared to do it legally, so it's binding," the General said. "I told them they owed you that much." He turned to Emerson. "They're prepared to let you both adopt Elise."

Wye turned to Emerson in time to see his eyes widen—his hesitation.

Her world turned upside down all over again. What if he said—?

"Of course," Emerson said firmly. "If that's what Wye wants."

She could barely swallow for the lump in her throat. If Emerson was willing to adopt Elise, that must mean he was in this for the long haul. His fingers tightened around hers for a moment, a squeeze meant to say everything he wasn't putting into words in front of the others.

Everyone waited to hear what she would say, but she didn't need to think it over. Of course she'd raise Elise.

Wye nodded. "I want that," she managed to say, although her head was reeling.

"Your brother is asking a lot of you," Cass said gently. "No one would think ill of you if it was more than you were willing to take on, Wye."

"I want to. I love Elise. And she needs me. I won't let her have the childhood I had." Her words were coming out in gasps, and Wye knew she was barely making sense. She needed to see Elise. To let the little girl know she'd have a mother who'd never leave her now.

As if she'd heard a summons, Jo came back with Elise, slipped her into Wye's waiting arms and touched the back of Wye's hand.

"Love," she said in satisfaction. "Pure love—the kind that lasts forever."

Wyoming let out a surprised breath. She'd forgotten

Jo's kind of magic—the ability to feel what someone else was feeling when she touched them.

Jo had nailed it. Love filled her heart—for Elise, for Emerson and for everyone who lived here, even if sorrow warred within it for all the people who didn't seem capable of that kind of love.

"Thank you," she said to the General. "I'm not even your daughter, and you've helped bring me the life I always wanted."

"You're welcome." The General's voice was rough. "You are my daughter now, even if it's an honorary designation, which means this little mite"—he touched Elise's cheek with a finger—"is my first grandchild. We'll make a fine horsewoman out of her. A real rancher."

Wye snuck a look at Cass to see how she'd take the news that she'd been beaten to the punch, but Cass was beaming with happiness. That was her friend in a nutshell: always the most content when someone she loved was getting what she wanted.

Jo leaned in to hug Wye. "Guess you're a Reed girl now, just like you wanted."

"I guess so." She smiled at Emerson. "For twenty-four hours, anyway. This time tomorrow, I'll be a Myers."

"So the wedding is on?" Brian asked.

"It better be, considering how hard we worked to get things ready," Logan said. Lena shoved him. "I mean, I hope you two worked things out."

"We did," Wyoming assured him, but she kept her

gaze on Emerson, needing him to hear what was in her heart. "I can't wait for my wedding day."

EMERSON WOKE THE next morning with a sense of anticipation he couldn't remember feeling since he'd been a child at Christmastime, and for one moment, he had the uncanny impression that his parents were nearby.

What would they think of how he'd turned out? Would they like Wyoming?

He was sure they would. In all his memories, they were happy, dependable people. She'd fit right in.

He wished they could be sitting in the first row when he made his vows to Wyoming, and he promised himself that if and when Elise chose to marry—or any other child they might have—he'd move heaven and earth to witness it. His parents weren't to blame for their absence, of course, but he wished the rest of his family could have found more room in their hearts for him. He'd never understand why they hadn't been able to do so. Love wasn't diminished by sharing it.

He knew he should try to sleep more, but there was no way he could now that he was awake. This was his wedding day, and his life was about to change forever.

He got up, pulled on some clothes and padded downstairs, needing a cup of coffee. He was surprised to see light shining out from under the door of the General's room. He knocked softly and got an immediate answer.

"Come in."

The General was sitting at his desk, his hair rumpled from sleep, a robe thrown over the pajamas he wore.

"Something wrong, General? Can't sleep?"

"I found this." The General pointed to a large envelope in front of him on the desk. "Woke up as if someone had called me. Turned on the light and saw this tucked behind the bookcase over there." He waved at a floor-to-ceiling bookcase that stood near his bed. "Must have been there for years. Couldn't see it from any other angle in the room. It's for you."

"Me?" Emerson stepped back. "That doesn't make sense—unless it's recent."

"Or unless it's from my wife."

Confused, Emerson opened the envelope.

Dear Emerson, the note inside read.

I owe you many thanks for taking care of my husband when I can't be there to care for him. He may not tell you, but the General is thankful for all you do, too.

It makes me happier than I can say to know that you will find love at Two Willows and remain there, keeping watch over Augustus as well as raising your family.

And it makes me happy to know that in marrying Wyoming Smith—who I know as a darling little girl with a mop of curls, even if Cass hasn't met her yet—you will secure close to hand Cass's best friend, a woman who will prove to be a constant source of comfort to all my girls.

A man with an open heart is my definition of a hero, Emerson. Remain brave no matter what life throws at you. Remember that a good day's work is precious no matter what the recompense.

And know that your parents love you very, very much. Always have. Always will.

Please distribute the rest of my letters to my family, and remind the General my heart is with him.

Love,
Amelia Reed

Emerson looked at the General. "But—your wife has been dead for years."

"Thank you. I'm aware of that." The General sighed. "That's never stopped her before."

"She's sending letters from beyond the grave?"

The General laughed. "Not from beyond the grave, Sergeant—from the past. She wrote that years ago. Hid it where I'd eventually find it."

"But—"

"Don't bother to look for sense, son. You won't find it, not at Two Willows."

Emerson let out a breath. "She said she's happy I'm marrying Wyoming and that we're staying here. She says you're in her heart."

"I never doubted it. She's in mine, too." The General leveled a stern look at him. "Don't ever believe those who pooh-pooh love, Sergeant. It's the strongest force in the universe, despite what anyone says."

"Didn't figure you for a romantic."

"Didn't figure you for an idiot." When Emerson frowned, he went on. "It's not romance; it's common sense. Who do you spend your time with in life? Your wife—your kids. Why wouldn't you give them the best of you? Who else are you going to waste it on—the guys down at the bar?"

"Guess you have a point."

"Of course I do. What're those?" He pointed to the smaller envelopes included in Emerson's hand.

"There's one for each of the girls. And one for each of their husbands," he added as he flipped through them.

"What about me? Hmph." The General sighed. "Guess I had my share of them already."

Emerson remembered the way the General had cherished each one over the years back at USSOCOM. He'd had a whole stack of them from Amelia, each one dated.

"There's one for you, too." Emerson gave it to him. The General swallowed and cleared his throat.

"Well. Would you look at that."

"Want me to hand these out?" Emerson asked, knowing the General would want some time to himself.

"You do that. And get ready. Big day today." The General waved him off.

Cass was awake and puttering in the kitchen when he exited the General's room. He handed her the envelopes for her sisters and their husbands. "They're from your mother."

"Oh my goodness." Cass's eyes filled with tears as she took them reverently. "I'll make sure everyone gets theirs. Who is that one addressed to?" She pointed to the one in his hand.

"Wyoming."

"Better give that one to me, too. It's bad luck to see the bride before the wedding, remember?"

Emerson surrendered it reluctantly. He went back upstairs, gathered his things and came back down. "I'll be at the Park until it's time," he said.

"The Park? Are you sure?"

He nodded. "That way you and Wye can use the whole house while you get ready. Besides, my trailer is nearly ready to move into. Wye and I will be in and out of the main house for a while, still, though, until it's completely done."

"I don't mind that at all," Cass said. "I'm going to miss Wye."

"We'll be less than a quarter mile away," Emerson pointed out.

"That's plenty far enough," Cass said tartly, then softened. "Thanks for being a good sport. It'll be worth the wait to see Wye later at the ceremony."

"I don't doubt it."

He'd expected to spend a quiet morning at the trailer he'd renovated, but when he arrived, he saw an old Chevy truck parked by Buck's trailer. Buck was inside it waiting for him.

"Don't worry—I'm not trying to move in a day early," he called when they both got out of their vehicles. "You mentioned you'd be here this morning, though. Wanted to give you this." He pulled something large and flat from the bed of his truck.

"Hold on; let me drop off my clothes inside, first." Emerson unlocked his trailer, went inside and hung his wedding duds in the closet. He met Buck at the table in the small dining area. "You didn't have to give me anything."

"I wanted to—to say thanks. I was having a hard time finding anywhere to live in my price range that wasn't a complete dump. My girl wasn't too sure about living in a trailer, but when she saw how clean and roomy it is, she was thrilled. She's been telling all her friends and can't wait to move in tomorrow. We're having a party next weekend, if you don't mind. We'll keep the sound down," he assured Emerson. "I heard you two have a baby now."

"Talk gets around, doesn't it?"

"Sure does." Buck laughed. "Open it up." He gestured to the present.

Emerson did and was surprised to find a hand-carved wooden sign inside.

"The Myerses," Buck read out when Emerson held it up. "Figure you can hang it out front and take it with you whenever you two move on. I heard you were thinking of building something bigger up near the main house," he added.

Emerson had to laugh. There were no secrets around here. "Maybe. We'll see." Some privacy sounded fine to him for now. "Thank you for this. It's great."

"You're welcome. I'll leave you be while you get ready. Last time you'll have any peace and quiet for a long time, probably."

"You're probably right," Emerson said happily. "And you can go ahead and start moving in any old time. Wye and I will be at a bed-and-breakfast tonight. Tomorrow we'll start carrying our things over here."

"Sounds good. But I'll wait to move my things over until the morning," Buck said. "You all have enough going on today, I'd say."

"Well, we'll have the other trailers ready for move-in on the fifteenth. We'll finish with the exteriors come spring."

"Sounds good." Buck reached for the door handle. "Good luck today."

"Thanks!" He figured he was already the luckiest man in the world.

"FOR ME?" WYOMING said when Cass pressed a small envelope into her hands. "From your mom?"

Cass was shaking, and there were tears in her eyes. "There were letters for all of us. Wye, I didn't think there were any more to come. When she died, the lawyer gave one to each of us, but that's it. I know she left a stack of them for the General, but I've never seen those."

"Why would she write one for me? How could she even know—?"

"See, you're part of the magic after all," Cass told her. "You have been from the start. Should we both read ours now?"

"Okay."

Wyoming was still in her robe. Sadie had taken

charge of Elise this morning, telling her to rest for her big day. Soon she'd get up and shower and start the process of doing makeup and hair for the wedding. She scooted back to lean against the headboard of her bed and patted the mattress next to her.

Cass joined her, sitting cross-legged on the comforter. She opened the envelope addressed to her. "Go on; read yours," she told Wyoming.

Wyoming opened hers and began to scan Amelia's beautiful handwriting.

Dear Wyoming, she read with a squeeze of her heart.

I wanted to tell you how happy I am that you are in my daughter's life. Cass needed a good friend, and you came along to teach her that she isn't alone in the world and she doesn't have to keep such close watch on everything and everyone around her.

I know she depends on you, and I know having you close by has made a world of difference. I can sense her laughter from here and her sense of well-being; you are a big part of that.

Which brings me to you. It's your turn now to lean on others. Remember that at Two Willows, you are surrounded by those who love you for exactly who you are. You don't need to be tough or independent, although those are fine qualities for any woman. You can express your needs. You can ask for help. It will be given joyfully.

When you took Emerson on as a partner, I'm sure you knew you took the General on as well. He isn't quite the gruff old bear he pretends to be. Your children will bring him as much joy as the rest of his grandchildren, and soon you'll learn what an asset a mellow old man can be to a lively household.

I know you and Emerson will be very happy together. I wish the very best to both of you.

Wyoming, as one who has met you as a little girl more than once, let me assure you that you have always been worthy of love. Your parents' problems are their own and no reflection on you. Go forward with a confident, happy heart and know that you are you—and you are wonderful.

Love,
Amelia

Wye looked up to find Cass in tears, and she set her letter down to hug her friend, clearing her throat before she could speak.

"What did she say to you?"

"That she loves me. That she's proud. That she knows all I did to try to raise my sisters the way she wanted to raise us. That I am good enough." Cass broke down in sobs. "I wish she was here. I wish she could see my baby when it's born."

"I know."

A quiet knock at the door announced Cass's sisters. They filed in silently, closing the door behind them, and climbed onto the bed in a huddle of arms and tears.

"She loved us so much," Jo gasped finally. "Why did she have to die so young?"

"I don't ever want to leave my baby," Cass said. "If

I do, all of you have to promise—to promise—"

Wyoming hugged her harder, then stretched out her arms to try and take all of the sisters into them at once. Squashed together, their tears turned to laughter. "We're all in this together," Wyoming pronounced. "We'll all watch out for each other—and for each other's families. None of us will ever have to feel lonely again."

"Mom said she knows I'm taking good care of the garden," Sadie said, sniffing a little.

"She said she wishes she could have one of my puppies," Jo said. "I wish she could, too."

"She said she's glad I met a man who lets me be me," Lena said.

"I feel like she's here right now," Alice said.

They were all quiet a moment, feeling Amelia's presence. Wye felt Cass squeeze her hand.

"If Mom was here, she'd tell us to get going and get ready for Wye's wedding," Cass said finally. The spell was broken, and they shifted apart, untangling themselves from each other.

"Where's Elise?" Wyoming asked.

"Hunter's got her. They're downstairs," Jo said.

"Go take your shower," Cass told Wyoming. "Time to make you beautiful."

Wyoming folded her letter and put it back in its envelope, tucking it away with her things to read again later.

She was part of the magic now.

And she was happy.

Several hours later, Wye stood in the hall outside the

front room, waiting to walk between the rows of chairs they'd set up for guests and to take her vows. Her stomach was full of butterflies, and she thought she might faint, but Cass, Alice, Lena, Sadie and Jo stood near her, the familiar green bridesmaid dresses making them look younger than their years.

When the General approached, Wye stepped aside to let him pass into the front room, where he could take his seat. To her surprise, he stopped in front of her.

"I wasn't here to walk Cass down the aisle. Or Jo, Sadie or Lena. I regret that. I wish it hadn't taken an injury to get me home for Alice's wedding, either. No more regrets. From now on I'm here for all my girls. That includes you, Wyoming, and my beautiful grand-daughter, Elise, and all the other grandchildren that will arrive at Two Willows. I won't make the same mistakes again."

He crooked his arm, and she took hold of it, tears stinging against her eyelids once more. She'd told herself she wouldn't mind walking down the aisle alone because Emerson was at the end of it, but she was more grateful than she could say for the General's steadying arm.

"Ready?" Cass asked, taking her place at the head of the line. Her sisters arrayed themselves after her.

"Ready," Wye said clearly.

Chapter 12

ALL THE FURNITURE in the front room had been removed, although the Christmas tree remained in one corner. Folding chairs had been placed in rows to seat their guests. An archway, decorated with pine boughs and ribbons, stood at the head of the room.

Reverend Halpern greeted Emerson as he took his place. Brian, Logan, Hunter and Jack came to stand up with him. Connor started the bridal march playing through his phone, which was connected to speakers placed throughout the room, and the music swelled. He took his place next to the other men.

Emerson nodded to Megan, who held Elise on her lap in the first row. She'd insisted on taking charge of the little girl during the ceremony.

A bustle in the doorway from the hall had him straightening, his breath catching when Cass stepped into the doorway in a spring-green bridesmaid gown that Alice had tailored to accommodate her baby bump. She stepped slowly down the aisle between the chairs, followed by Alice, Lena, Sadie and Jo.

Then Wyoming stepped through the door in a wedding gown Emerson knew had once belonged to Amelia Reed. All five of her daughters had worn it.

With its newly beaded bodice and flowing skirts, it suited Wye perfectly as she stepped down the aisle on the General's arm.

The General leaned on his cane as he walked, but he held his head high. When he reached the altar, he placed Wyoming's hand in his.

"I'm happy for both of you," he said and took his seat by his daughters.

Cass moved to the side, and she and Brian stood sentry while Emerson and Wyoming faced the reverend.

"Dearly Beloved," Halpern began.

Emerson's heart thumped loud in his chest as he listened to the familiar words, and when it was his turn to speak his vows, he said them clearly. Every word was true. He did pledge his life to Wye. He would stick with her no matter what happened. He did plan to spend forever and always with her.

Gladly.

This was the woman he'd always dreamed of finding. The life he'd always wanted to live.

He'd found love. He'd found a family.

He couldn't ask for anything more.

WYOMING KNEW FROM the first swell of the music that every moment of her wedding would surpass her wildest dreams. She'd hoped to find a partner with whom to live her life.

She'd never thought she'd find a soul mate, a houseful of sisters and friends, a surrogate father—

She never thought she'd belong anywhere so completely.

Two Willows had pulled her in until she couldn't imagine living anywhere else. Cass and her sisters had taught her what it was to have a family.

And Emerson—

Emerson would still sweep her off her feet fifty years from now, she was sure. He was a hero in the truest sense of the word. Someone to trust utterly. To depend on.

She loved him.

She spoke her wedding vows directly to Emerson, never looking away from his gaze, needing him to know she meant every word. He held her hands, lending her his strength, as always, telling her with his eyes that he'd always be there.

No matter what.

As he slid her wedding band on her finger as proof of his eternal love for her, Elise let out a happy shriek from where she sat in Megan's arms, and Wyoming laughed. Even Elise knew this was right.

"You may now kiss the bride," Halpern declared, and Emerson stepped close, pulled her gently but firmly into his arms and kissed her until Wyoming's toes curled. It was a promise of what was to come tonight and always, she thought.

A promise she couldn't wait to hold him to.

"I love you," he whispered into her ear. "Always will."

"I love you, too."

Epilogue

Seven months later, July Fourth

BRIAN STOPPED ON the way from the barn to the white clapboard house and tilted his head to take in the progress on Hunter and Jo's new home. They'd all been pitching in to get it built, and now its framework stood against the clear blue sky in the early morning sun. In no time they'd have it framed in and roofed, and then Jo and Hunter could take as long as they wanted to finish the interior. It was a funny thing; this time last year, he'd been a newlywed, still so insecure in his place here at Two Willows. Now it felt like the ranch had always been home.

His days here had a rhythm he appreciated more than he could put into words. He got up and worked with his hands, with men and women he trusted and with whom he shared his successes and failures. At the end of the day, he was proud of what he'd done and could sleep with a clean conscience.

He was glad he wasn't some nine-to-fiver, heading off to an office and coming home too late to appreciate his family. He was lucky—so damn lucky—to be able to see Cass and their baby, Emily, throughout the day.

When he'd first arrived here, he hadn't known if he was man enough to love one woman forever, but now he never questioned his relationship with Cass. She was his wife, and that word meant more than he'd ever guessed it could.

He turned and trudged on toward the house, his footsteps quickening when he caught a whiff of bacon emanating from the open back door. He hadn't eaten yet, and he'd already put in several hours of physical labor.

As if sensing his proximity, Cass appeared on the porch in a pair of ragged jean shorts and a sky-blue top, the color of which intensified the blue of her eyes. Her blond hair was pulled back in a ponytail low at the nape of her neck. She held Emily in her arms, and as always, Brian's heart swelled at the sight of his *two girls*.

Four months old, Emily was a tow-headed little ray of sunshine with Cass's pert nose and quick smile, her sweet disposition making her the darling of everyone who saw her. She was spoiled rotten, passed from arm to arm all day until Brian wondered if she'd ever learn to walk given that her feet never touched the floor.

Cass had informed him proudly yesterday afternoon that Emily had rolled over on her own, however. All evening she'd performed her new "trick" to a rapt audience in the living room, looking startled when cheers and clapping greeted each rotation, until Elise, now eighteen months old, had taken umbrage at this hogging of attention and tried to sit on the baby.

Brian grinned at the memory, dashed up the stairs and kissed his wife and daughter. "Breakfast time?"

"Almost. We need to get the show on the road if we're going to make the most of the fair today." She led the way indoors.

"I'll put Emily's portable crib in the truck. I can get Elise's, too, if you want," he said to Wye, who was setting the long wooden kitchen table.

"Thanks, that would be great," Wye said with a smile. She was wearing a long, light sundress dotted with tiny flowers, with capacious skirts that covered her pregnant belly. "Slow down, Elise," she added as the little girl careened through the kitchen, a toy plane in her hand.

"Where are you going?" Brian scooped up Elise and flew her around the room in the same manner she'd been flying her toy, zooming her up and down and then depositing her in Emerson's hands when he appeared in the kitchen a moment later.

"Fair!" Elise crowed.

"That's right, we're going to the fair," Emerson told her. "What's with the plane?"

"Connor gave it to her. He got one for Emily, too," Cass said from the stove. She'd put Emily in her bouncy seat, where she'd be safe to one side of the room, and the baby was reaching for the toys that dangled over her head. "I think he's pushing them both toward a career in the Air Force."

"Navy all the way, right, Emily?" Brian crossed the room, squatted down by his daughter and brushed a finger over her soft cheek.

"Get those cribs packed up and get back here for your breakfast," Cass told him.

"Yes, ma'am." Brian kissed Emily's head and touched one tiny fist. "Gotta do something for your mama. Be right back," he told her and went to perform the errand.

By the time he'd loaded both portable cribs in his truck, the kitchen had filled up. While Jo and Hunter were camping out in their nearly finished house, where the kitchen appliances weren't hooked up yet, they were eating their meals at the main house again. In a week or so the kitchen would be done, and they'd be back to eating on their own. Most days Wye and Emerson ate breakfast and dinner in the trailer Emerson had refurbished but had lunch at the main house since Emerson still helped the General a few hours every morning. They were here for breakfast today just to keep everyone on one schedule.

Lena and Logan had moved into the tiny house Jo and Hunter had vacated. They, too, were planning to build a larger house, but not for another year. They were too busy enjoying their mutual love for all things active and dangerous, as Cass put it, and when their work was done, they spent hours riding, racing the dirt bikes they'd bought or ranging all over Montana to go kayaking, a new obsession they shared. They ate almost all their meals here, grateful for Cass's cooking, since neither Lena nor Logan cared to spend time in the kitchen.

Jack and Alice planned to break ground soon on a home positioned near the carriage house, where Alice had her studio. They'd hired an architect, who'd come up with a plan for a three-bedroom, two-bath home with skylights and wide windows that would drench the interior in light.

Even Sadie and Connor were planning a home, situated halfway between the main house and the outbuildings, with wide verandas and a second-story balcony that would overlook the mountains in the distance. They'd decided they could be patient and wait a year, as well, however. "Two houses built this year and two next year," was the way Connor had put it.

"Everyone's leaving," Cass had told Brian that night when they were alone. Tears had flecked her lashes.

"They won't be far. Besides, we'll fill this house right up again, won't we?"

She'd smiled at that. "I guess."

Now they were on their way, Brian mused as he lifted Emily from her bouncy seat, tucked her into the crook of his arm and took his seat at the table, nodding at the General as the man lowered himself carefully into his own chair. The General was far more limber than he'd been when he'd arrived home, thanks to the exercises Emerson still made him do, but he was tentative when it came to changing position.

"You're looking happy," the General said as Cass set a plate full of bacon in front of him.

"I am happy," Brian said, taking a piece of toast from another platter on the table. "I've got everything I ever wanted, thanks to you, and I'm looking forward to a fantastic July Fourth."

"Someone had to get you back on course." The General snagged several pieces of bacon with his fork and placed them on his plate.

"You did that and more." Brian wasn't reluctant to give the man his due. If the General hadn't interceded in his life, who knew where he'd have ended up?

"Everybody eat so we can get to the fair." Cass took a seat next to Brian. She peeked around him to see Emily. "She looks content."

"I know I am." Brian leaned down to kiss his wife. "As far as I'm concerned, everything is perfect."

She beamed back up at him. "I think so, too."

PERFECT. THAT WAS the word for her life, Cass thought as she watched her family consume the breakfast she and Wye had prepared. Just a year and a half ago, she'd never have dreamed she'd spend her days so happily, her husband near, her baby in her arms, her best friend in and out of her kitchen all day, and all her sisters happily married and moving on with their lives with so much pride and confidence.

It was a miracle that she and her father could sit at a table together, old hurts and feuds gone. Whenever she passed baby Emily to the General, her heart melted to see the care and wonder with which he held her. He liked nothing more than to take her out on the back porch after dinner and rock in one of the old wicker chairs, watching the sun lower in the sky. It made her smile to hear the murmur of his voice as he pointed out the birds, the weather conditions, the state of Sadie's garden and more, teaching Emily all she needed to know about the land on which she lived.

If sometimes she felt a pang of sorrow for what could have been if her mother hadn't passed away so early or her father hadn't been estranged for so many years, the sorrow passed quickly. She had so much now, she couldn't remain unhappy for long.

"It's going to be another hot one," Logan said.

"You all don't know the meaning of the word hot," Hunter drawled.

"Everyone better wear sunscreen," Sadie said and took a bite of fried egg on toast.

Cass bit back a smile to hear such a Mom statement from her younger sister. They'd all grown up a lot in the past year, she supposed. Sadie's farm stand and herbal remedy business seemed to be booming, her garden far lusher and happier than it had been last summer before Connor arrived. She often spotted the two of them standing among her plants in the evenings, Sadie leaning against Conner, the two of them holding hands, pointing to one plant or another and discussing it. She had the feeling that Sadie drew strength from the man who'd won her heart, and after the disastrous relationships her sister had had in the past, Cass was relieved.

Lena met her eye across the table and gently traced one of the bullet groves in the old wood with a finger.

"Seems like a long time ago, doesn't it?" she asked softly. "Sometimes I walk in here and remember, though."

Cass knew exactly what she meant. The kitchen had been lovingly restored. Besides the scars on the table, there were no reminders of the shootout that awful day, but sometimes when she came up from the basement stairs she remembered the terror in her gut when she'd realized she had to make it from one side of the kitchen to the other, passing in front of the back door as bullets shredded it.

She reminded herself she had made it, and she and Lena had survived that fight. "You were so strong that day."

"So were you."

Cass thought that of all her sisters it was Lena's happiness that had healed her the most. Lena might have always been a fighter, but Cass thought she was the most hurt by the General's abandonment of them, and there'd been a time when she wondered if Lena would ever be able to trust a man again.

It was clear she trusted Logan. What's more, they were having so much fun together. They might have had a false start or two when they first met, but now he treated Lena like an equal—and a partner in crime. Cass had never heard Lena laugh so much or so often—and it was wonderful.

Emily let out a little cry in Brian's arms, and Cass bent to see what was the matter.

"Uh oh. That's her hungry cry. Little girl, can't you let your mama finish a single meal without interrupting?" Brian asked Emily fondly.

"Hand her over." Cass felt the usual tingling and pressure in her breasts as Emily began to wail even louder. Brian was right; she did have an uncanny way of getting hungry just as Cass sat down at the table. Good thing she'd gotten expert at nursing Emily and eating at the same time. Brian tugged her plate closer to him as she fiddled with her shirt and nursing bra and he cut up the rest of her food into bite-size pieces before sliding it back in front of her.

"Thanks." She smiled at him gratefully as Emily latched on. It was hard to cut up anything single-handedly. As Emily began to nurse, Cass continued eating. She'd been so afraid of falling short as a mother, it continually surprised her how much she knew how to do already. Taking care of Emily mostly made her feel competent, although occasionally, if the baby didn't settle, she worried that this was the time she'd mess up.

When that happened, Brian was always there to help, as were Wye and her sisters and brothers-in-law. Such a big family could sometimes be a handful but usually was a blessing.

Elise shouted from her highchair, momentarily causing Emily to stop nursing. Wye was quick to hand the little girl more bits of cereal she could pick up and put in her mouth, however, and when the outburst wasn't repeated, Emily got back to work.

When the meal was over, everyone scattered to pull together the things they needed for the day in town, while Wye joined Cass in cleaning up.

"Looking forward to today?" Wye asked.

"I am," Cass said. "I think it will be fun."

"I think we're bringing enough equipment to set up an encampment," Wye said as some of the men trooped past laden down with camp chairs, picnic blankets and more.

"That's all part of the fun." Cass moved faster, washing up at double-time. "We need to load everything into the picnic basket."

"You know we're just going to end up buying food there," Wye protested.

Cass shrugged. "It's good to be prepared."

Wye laughed. "I don't doubt we'll be prepared for anything that could happen."

"Just think, this could have been your wedding day," Cass teased her.

"I'm glad we did it on New Year's." Wye dried a dish and put it away. "I wouldn't give back the past six months for anything. I really thought I'd never find someone I'd want to spend my life with, and then it all happened so fast."

"No regrets?"

"None at all."

Cass hugged her friend. "How about moving to Two Willows? You regretting that yet? You probably do a lot more dishes here than you've ever done before." She gestured to the dishcloth in Wye's hand.

"I'm not regretting that, either, and you know it. I'm glad I met you, Cass. You changed my life."

"I'm glad I met you, too. I think you helped save mine, back when I was so lonely." Cass hugged Wye again, and they stayed like that a minute. Sometimes being with Wye made Cass think of her mother. She had a feeling Amelia approved of their friendship. Had encouraged it somehow in her own magical way.

"I think it's going to be a wonderful Fourth of July," she said.

"We'd better hurry up, then," Wye said and got back to work.

"HOW ARE YOU feeling?" Connor asked Sadie when they'd parked near Chance Creek's town square. The others had spilled out of their trucks eagerly, but he'd noticed Sadie had climbed out more slowly, and now she stood looking at the crowds streaming by with a hint of worry in her expression as he unloaded their things.

"I'm fine." Her response seemed automatic, though. Connor supposed he would have gotten to know his wife well over the past year under any circumstances, but the time they'd spent together on their honeymoon in India had really bonded them together. You couldn't spend twenty-four hours a day with someone on a trip like that without learning a lot about them. Connor had realized Sadie didn't like to bother people with her worries, so he'd made a study of her moods and now could read the signs when something was off.

"You sure? We could find a place to sit down for a while, or I can take you home if you like." He came to stand near her, concerned. Ahead of them, Cass, Brian, Wye and Emerson were surrounded by baby gear, talking and gesturing about who should carry what and what should be left in Brian's truck, while the General was standing off to one side, waiting to get going.

"We'd miss the parade." She looked at him with more of her usual humor. "I really am fine." She hesitated, then moved closer to wrap her arms around his waist and lean against him. Connor ran his hands up and down her back. Something was bothering her.

"Oh," Sadie growled against his chest. "I'm so bad at this."

"At what?"

"Keeping secrets."

He pulled back. "You've got a secret?"

"I do, and I wasn't going to tell you until tonight. I wouldn't have slipped if you hadn't started asking questions."

"What is it?"

"If I tell you, it won't be a secret anymore!"

"I won't pass it on." He linked his fingers in the belt loops of her shorts and tugged her close. "Come on, you know you can't resist my interrogation techniques."

She placed her hands on his chest. "You're right. I'm lousy at that, too."

"Good thing you're good at a lot of other things."

"Too good."

He tilted his head down to look at her in surprise. "How can you be too good at those things?"

She sighed. "Fine. But this would have been a lot more dramatic if I'd spilled the beans while fireworks were going off tonight. It would make a better story to tell later, too."

"I don't care about the story. Tell me the secret!"

"I'm pregnant."

Connor stilled. Pregnant? "Are you sure?" They'd been trying, but they'd had a false alarm once before.

"I'm sure. I just missed my second period. We aren't out of the woods yet, but I know this time it's a go. I can just feel it."

Connor pulled her close, finding it hard to put into words what he was feeling. He knew their time in India had made an impression on Sadie, too. Had steadied her in a way. Seeing so many people with so little had made it clear to them how much they had to be thankful for here at Two Willows. When he'd first met Sadie, she'd meant to leave the ranch for good. Now she had set down deep roots.

He knew he loved it here. He enjoyed traveling and assumed they'd do so again in the future, but he felt he could spend a lifetime exploring all the corners of their ranch. Being with Sadie was enough for now.

But soon they'd have a baby.

All the time he'd spent with Sadie in her kitchen garden and cultivating the new walled garden he'd built for her last year had given him a new sense of time and seasons, and he knew bringing a baby home to Two Willows would be about the sweetest thing he'd ever been a part of.

"Boy or girl?"

"I haven't even had a doctor's appointment yet. Besides, it's too soon to tell. You'll be there when we find that out." She hugged him. "I can't wait."

"Me, either. But we've got a lot to do. We don't have a house—"

"You know what? I think I'm fine living in the main house until after the baby comes," Sadie told him. "Having Cass close by will help. I won't have to take care of a home in addition to a new baby those first few months."

"We'll get our plans finalized before the summer is over," Connor promised her, "and have everything ready to go next spring. By the time the baby's six months old, we'll have our own home."

"That sounds perfect," Sadie said. "How'd I manage to find such a smart man?"

"You didn't. Your father did."

Sadie laughed. "You're right." They turned as one to spot the General, who was now adding his two cents loudly to the discussion about the baby gear. "Who could have thought such an ornery old man could be so good at matchmaking?"

"I thought I'd landed in hell when I got sent to US-SOCOM to work with him," Connor admitted. "Turned out to be the best thing that ever happened to me." He remembered Halil, the stranger who'd saved one of his buddies behind enemy lines in Syria—and who Connor had saved, in turn. On their flight out of that dusty, barren plain, Halil had advised him to "Find a wife. Make her your everything." He'd said it was the secret to his happiness.

Connor had taken that advice. It had paid off in

spades, and before returning his attention to Sadie, he sent a silent thank-you to the universe that Halil and his family had made it safely to Canada.

"You're really pregnant?" he asked again, joy spiking through him in a way that caught him off guard.

"I really am. We're going to be good parents, right?" She snuggled back into his embrace.

"Damn straight. The best." He knew he'd give it his all. "Speaking of which—my parents are going to be over the moon! Dalton, too!" His parents, who had reconciled after a decades-long separation last year, were still together, for which he was very grateful. They'd spent a winter in Texas and were currently in Ireland, where apparently his father was reconciled to his mother's "tiny" farm in a way he hadn't been capable of before now. Connor's brother, Dalton, now officially ran Ard na Greine but welcomed his parents' presence there during summer months.

"I hope they'll all visit when the baby arrives."

"I'm sure they will." He hugged her again. "Uh oh, people are looking. We'd better move along, or there'll be questions. You want to save the surprise until tonight?"

Sadie nodded. "We'll tell them during the fire-works."

"Sounds perfect. You sure you're up for the fair? We could still go home."

"I wouldn't miss this day for the world!"

THIS IS WHAT it felt like to be pregnant, Sadie thought as

Connor guided her with almost exaggerated care to the sidewalk, then went back to collect anything they might need during their day in town. It was far too early for her to feel the baby, but she felt… something. Almost a buzzing sensation inside her, like the processes of her body had gone into overdrive to create this new life. She had a sense she should be a little quieter, move a little more slowly—allow most of her inner resources to be allocated to this important new task.

She thought she might understand Cass a little better now, too. She'd watched her sister all the previous year stop sometimes in the middle of cooking or climbing the stairs and turn inward, as if witnessing something no one else could see. At the time it had felt a little like an affront: like once more Cass was separating herself from the rest of them, playing parent while they all had to remain little girls.

Now she realized it wasn't something you controlled. Your body demanded your attention in a wholly different way than it had before.

"Ready?" Connor joined her on the sidewalk.

"Ready."

They ambled along with the others toward the town square and the fields that adjoined it, where food and game tents would be set up and the Revolutionary War re-enactment would happen later. It was early enough that the day still felt fresh, but soon it would be hot. Sadie was grateful there were a couple of pop-up awnings in one of the trucks they could set up later to create shade for themselves.

"Sadie!" Ellie Donaldson called out from across the street. "Happy Fourth! I'll be by later this week for some more of my tonic."

"I'll have it ready." Sadie was proud of the way her sales had grown this year. Last year, when her garden had failed to thrive and the sense for growing things she'd always relied on to guide her had disappeared, she'd thought she would have to leave her home and give up on gardening altogether. Only when Connor arrived and renewed her belief in people—and love—did her green thumb return. Now her garden sang with appreciation when she came to work in it each morning and had become almost jungle-like in its growth. She thought her love for Connor must be distilled in every tincture and tonic she created because her customers were thriving, too, their small ailments soothed. Her farm stand did a steady business, enough to make her consider adding a second greenhouse to the property. She'd been wondering how much she could grow with a more extensive setup.

Of course, she'd need to balance work and family now, but secretly she dreamed about bringing her child to her garden with her, teaching him or her the names of the plants and the ways to listen to what they wanted. She wondered if her skill at hearing them would blossom in her baby but decided it didn't matter. Connor was becoming a green thumb in his own right, just by spending so much time with her among the plants. He took pride in the fruit trees and flowers they'd planted in the walled garden and was already talking about espaliering peach trees along the wall that garnered the most sun, to see if they could survive the winters.

There was so much they could do together here.

"This looks like a good place," Jo called out, indicating a free stretch of curb where they could sit and watch the parade—the first event of the day. Immediately there was a flurry of setting up camp chairs. Connor opened theirs with a flourish and set them side by side.

He beckoned her into one of them and then pulled out the reusable water bottles they'd filled at the ranch and handed her one. Sadie settled in contentedly. She'd watched this parade every year of her life, no matter how hectic things had gotten at Two Willows, and it never got old.

"I like this," Connor said. "This is what a Fourth of July should be."

"I know. Everyone together. Everyone happy."

Down the road a toddler began to cry.

"Almost everyone," Connor said.

Sadie leaned forward in time to see the dark-haired little mite picked up and lifted to the shoulders of his father, a man she recognized from around town but didn't know well. The little boy's tears turned to smiles instantly.

"All better," she declared to Connor. "All he needed was his daddy."

Connor took her hand. "I'm going to be there for you and this baby forever. I promise you that."

"I know." Sadie never doubted Connor's love, and she thought that was the sweetest part of being married.

Knowing you had found one secure thing. Not that she would ever take Connor for granted, she told herself. After losing her mother so early, she knew you had to value every day you got with the ones you love.

She placed a hand on her belly, shut her eyes and promised her unborn child she'd make the most of every day they had together. She would make sure her baby knew it was loved. That was all she could do.

"I think the parade is coming," Cass exclaimed from a few seats away. "See, Emily? There they are!" She pointed her finger. Emily blinked sleepily.

Next year she'd hold her baby and show her the parade, Sadie told herself. She turned to Connor, who was looking at her with so much love in his eyes she thought her heart would burst. He took her hand and squeezed it. She squeezed his back.

"I can't wait," he told her.

"Neither can I."

And they both turned to watch the first marching band approach.

"YOU REST HERE. I'll go get us some lunch," Hunter told Jo at noon, when they'd found a patch of grass large enough for the family to settle on. Brian and Logan were already setting up the sunshades. Connor had fetched all the camp chairs they'd used earlier at the parade and then returned to the trucks and brought another huge armful he was placing at intervals.

"You know Cass packed a ton of food," Jo said, but she sat down, her large belly making it awkward to settle in the camp chair Connor had set up for her a moment ago.

"I know. Don't worry—I'll eat some of that, too, but I want some butter chicken nachos."

"That does sound good."

"Don't go having that baby while I'm gone." He touched Jo's auburn hair, which was loose today and fell in waves around her shoulders. Her pregnancy sat heavily on her small frame, and it was as if the baby had taken all Jo's reserves for its own use. Her cheekbones were more prominent, her limbs thin while her belly pushed straight out.

Hunter thought she was beautiful, and he marveled daily at the miracle that allowed a woman to produce a new life, carry it safely and tidily around with her for nine months, then birth it into the world, perfect and new.

He couldn't wait to hold his son in his arms. They'd decided to name him Christopher, which Jo declared was a good, strong, sensible name for a boy. Hunter agreed.

As he walked along the row of booths, he wondered what it would feel like in a few years when his boy was tagging along after him. He had no experiences like that of his own to draw on, never having had a father who was active in his life. Thinking back to his childhood made him remember happy days at Heartfelt Ranch with the Franks, the only place he'd experienced any semblance of normal family life. Hunter realized he'd recreated that with the others at Two Willows. At any given time, it bustled with laughter, friendship and family.

He didn't need to worry about his child ever feeling alone. Chris would grow up surrounded by aunts and uncles, a grandfather and cousins galore, by the looks of things. If anything, solitude would be the sensation his boy craved, but there was plenty of room for that on a ranch, too.

One day he'd teach his son to ride, to work with the cattle—to build a house, maybe. He had a lot to offer a child, and that felt good.

Most of all, he had love.

Not love like the hidden, compartmentalized passion his mother had cultivated with her married lover. Open-hearted, acknowledged, reciprocated and celebrated love—the kind he'd always craved.

Maybe it was unfair of him to judge his mother. All the players in that triangle had made their choices, after all. Still, secrecy had consequences, and he shuddered to think how he would have turned out if he hadn't met Marlon Frank, his mother, Sue-Ann, and the rest of their family to stand in for what he was missing at home.

He made it a practice every day to both tell and show Jo how much he loved her. He never wanted her to wonder, the way he had when he was a child. When their son was born, he'd make sure to express his love and pride to him just as often. No child should wonder if he deserved his place in the world.

He wasn't worried about failing as a father anymore.

Expressions of love came easy when you had a wife like Jo. A true partner who sent as much love his way as he sent hers. The days flew by when they were working, playing or just hanging out together.

God, life was good.

He felt no shame when he looked back at all his choices, either. He'd intervened in Marlon's life out of care for his friend, and while that intervention had cost him, it had also brought him to Two Willows.

He approached the food tent set up by the women who ran Fila's Familia. "Two butter chicken nacho plates, please," he said.

"Coming right up."

"I'll take a couple of those, too," a woman called, coming up behind him. She nodded to Hunter. "Sorry—I'm in a hurry." She was dressed in a Revolutionary War–era gown and looked hot and flushed.

"Everything all right, Maya?" the woman behind the counter called. Hunter thought her name was Camila. She was one of the owners of Fila's.

"This whole day has been crazy. I need a bite to eat before the re-enactment gets going."

"I haven't seen it before," Hunter said companionably. "The costumes people are wearing are terrific, though." He gestured to her dress.

"Thanks. You're Hunter Powell, right? From Two Willows? Alice has helped sew a lot of the men's costumes for the re-enactments over the years. Some of the women's, too."

"Maya, here you go," Camila called. "You don't

mind if I serve her first, do you?" she asked Hunter.

"Not at all. Can't wait to see the battle. I've heard it's supposed to be something special this year."

Maya made a face. "It's going to be something, that's for sure." She took the food from her friend and hurried off.

"Here you go." Camila handed him his baskets of nachos. "Make sure you get a good seat for the re-enactment. I'm sure it will be great, even if Maya is nervous. She's part of the crew switching things up this year, and there's a lot of pressure on them to get it right."

"Will do." Mostly he just wanted to get back to Jo. He didn't care if the re-enactment became a riot, as long as he got to spend the day with the woman he loved.

"I'M NOT HAVING this baby anytime soon," Jo announced out loud, still thinking about what Hunter had said. She figured she'd be more than happy when her pregnancy was over and her baby was in her arms, but she wasn't in any hurry. Babies took time and came when they were ready. This one wasn't ready yet.

"Of course not," Cass said, bending to put Emily down on a baby blanket and then setting down everything else she'd been carrying in her arms.

A boy, Jo thought. Soon she'd bring her little baby boy home to her brand-new house, and she couldn't wait. He'd love her McNabs, of course. Isobel would have a litter in the next few weeks, and her child would start life with a puppy companion. What else could a baby want?

Sadie snagged a chair nearby and sat down, looking a little pale. Jo straightened, concerned, and handed her sister a bottle of water. "You all right?"

"The sun's getting to me." Sadie took the bottle gratefully, opened it and took a long swig. "That's better. I'm hungry, though."

"Here's a sandwich." Cass reached into her backpack-style baby bag and drew out a small cooler. "I've got chips, too."

Sadie took both gratefully, but Jo declined her offer. "Hunter's bringing back nachos."

Cass shrugged, not offended. "It'll all get eaten eventually. I know this crew."

That was the thing about having so many men around, Jo reflected. Nothing went to waste.

"What's it like living in your own big house?" Sadie asked her. "Do you miss the tiny house?"

"I think eventually I'll feel nostalgic for it because Hunter and I were so happy there," Jo said, "but even though it's not finished, I love my new home. It suits me just right."

"You and Hunter did a good job on it," Lena put in, pulling up a chair to join them. "Got right to it and made a lot of progress."

"We've had a lot of help," Jo reminded her.

"I have to admit I didn't think you moving out was a good idea," Cass said, settling down with Emily on her lap. "I thought you'd always need me to mother you, but I couldn't have been more wrong."

"I think people always underestimate the youngest," Jo said. It didn't bother her anymore because she'd proven to herself how capable she was.

"Everything has turned out so well. Come sit by me," Cass added to Wye and pointed to a chair. Wye sat with Elise on her lap. The little girl was holding apple slices in each hand and had taken a single bite out of each.

"Sometimes I wake up and for a minute I'm afraid I'm back in the past, the five of us living alone, everything going wrong," Sadie admitted. "Then I remember I've got Connor and everyone's safe and the General's home—" She cut off as the General and Emerson approached. Lena stood up to bring them chairs and grab them bottles of water.

"What's that about me being home?" the General asked.

"I was just saying I'm glad you are," Sadie told him. "I'm glad we're all here."

A murmur of assent ran through the group. Emerson got to work adjusting the pop-up sunshades to shelter as many of them as possible. Cass handed him two sandwiches and baggies of chips. "Share with the General. Brian and Connor will be back with the coolers in a minute."

"Want anything from the food booths?" Emerson asked the General, passing him a sandwich and bag of chips.

"I'm fine with this."

"Wye? Want anything?"

"You know what I like."

He nodded, made sure the General was comfortable and headed off into the crowds.

"A hamburger and fries?" Cass asked Wye.

"You know it."

Jo smiled at the banter going on around her. This was the family her child would be born into. Every one of them could teach him something. He'd learn to care for the horses and cattle. How to ride. How to build a house. How to repair the machinery on the ranch. And most importantly, how to get along with family and work together for the betterment of them all.

When Hunter returned with their nachos and dropped into a seat beside her, she leaned over to give him a kiss.

"What's that for?" he drawled, smiling.

"For being you. For coming here. I'm really happy," she told him.

"Me, too."

LATER THAT AFTERNOON, after they'd eaten and spent more time wandering among the fair's booths, Logan took a seat next to Lena in the crowd that had gathered around the green and handed her a beer.

"I've never been to a re-enactment. Curious to see what it's like," he told her. "Have to say I'm surprised you're not a part of it, what with your interest in the Revolutionary War and all that."

Lena shrugged. "I didn't have time for re-enactments in the past: too busy running the General's overseers off our property. Besides, the Chance Creek version is pretty staid—and they frown on women joining the ranks of the soldiers. Women are supposed to sit around in camp cooking over fires or sewing, and that's the last thing I want to do." She jutted her chin at the tents pitched to one side where women in Revolutionary War–era gowns were doing just that. "Don't be disappointed if the battle isn't exciting. They do the same thing every year."

"As long as you're here, who cares if it's exciting or not?" He should have guessed why she wasn't involved. Lena wasn't one to sit on the sidelines of any adventure. One of the best parts of their marriage had been his discovery that he now had a partner for any crazy activity he wanted to try. He'd had married friends in the past who had to compartmentalize their lives into what they did at home with their spouse and what they did with their buddies. He didn't have to make that distinction. In fact, sometimes he had to scramble to keep up with Lena.

"That's the spirit."

"Maybe we should join the re-enactment committee this year, though. We could think of ways to spice things up, don't you think? You could use that old black powder rifle."

"Maybe. See how you feel after you watch."

"I could make you a soldier's uniform, Lena," Alice put in, leaning forward in her camp chair. "After all, more than one woman chopped off her hair and joined the armies on either side of the Revolutionary War."

"Don't go chopping off your hair." Logan tousled it.

She sighed in a long-suffering way. Logan supposed he'd said that once too often, but he did love her hair all wild and long, especially when they were making love.

"I think the two of you would make a great addition to the re-enactment group," Alice said loyally. "Although I've heard rumors that this year's is going to be different." Her smile made Logan wonder what she knew.

"How different can you make a re-enactment?" Lena asked. "I mean, we all know how the battle is going to end."

"I guess we'll see," Alice said.

"I think they're starting," Jo said from down the line.

Logan turned to look. Jo was right. Warren Hill, who ran the local historical museum and the volunteer society that raised funds to support it, stepped into the grassy space where the re-enactment would happen.

"Welcome, folks. Glad you could all join us," he called out. The crowd hushed to hear his words. "This year we have something a little different for you, and we sure hope you like it."

"He seems nervous," Lena commented.

Alice's smile broadened.

A couple of men and a woman Logan vaguely recognized from around town came forward and took their places as Warren stepped aside. All three were dressed in Revolutionary War garb. Logan settled in as the production started.

"Donald. Rufus. Time for dinner. What news did you hear in town today?" the woman asked loudly. That was Ella Hall, Logan thought, although she was made up to look older than her years. She'd been a real actress in Hollywood before she'd come here.

"A lot of ruckus about the trouble getting closer," one of the men said. Logan thought he was supposed to be her husband. "Some men think there'll be fighting even here."

"Don't you think they're right?" a younger man asked. Their grown son, apparently. As the scene went on, father and son argued about choosing sides while Ella's character was caught between them trying to keep the peace. The scene ended with father declaring the value of loyalty to the monarchy and son voicing his intent to join the rebels—and Ella's character in tears.

"Uh oh," Lena said when the scene changed. "That's Maya Turner and Lance Cooper. What are they doing in a scene together?"

"Why shouldn't they be?" Logan asked curiously. Was he mistaken, or had Alice's smile grown even wider? She kept her hands folded primly in her lap, however, and didn't say a word.

"The Turners and Coopers have been at war since time began," Lena informed him in a low voice. "This isn't going to end well."

"Who's the other woman?"

"That's Avery—she lives on Westfield Ranch," Cass said.

"Hold on to your hats," Lena said. "They're starting."

The scene began with a flourish as Avery threw herself at Lance, who was playing her brother, and begged him not to go off to war. Maya, playing Lance's wife, kept a stiff, heartbroken expression as he went to leave.

"No fireworks so far," Logan murmured to Lena.

"I guess miracles really do happen. The Turners and Coopers are usually at each other's throats."

Both of them straightened as Maya suddenly dashed toward Lance, threw her arms around him and begged him to promise that he'd come back.

"She's a good actor," Cass said, clearly surprised.

"Who can say where the winds of war will blow me, but if it is in my power, I'll be back and never leave your side again." Lance pulled Maya into a kiss, and she went up on tiptoe to meet him, twining her arms around his neck. Their kiss went on and on and on…

Around them the crowd burst into cheers.

"I don't believe it."

Logan laughed at Lena's shocked expression. "Looks to me like those enemies are pretty good friends," he said, but Cass was pointing.

"Look at Liam Turner."

He followed the direction of her finger, saw another man on the sidelines, his arms crossed over his chest, his mouth set in a grim line as he watched his sister kiss Lance.

Logan's stomach sank. Lena was right. Liam was staring at Lance like the man was his sworn enemy.

There was definitely going to be trouble.

THERE'D BEEN A time when Lena had felt she could hold her own in a fistfight with the best of them, and then a later time when she'd been proven wrong and had almost lost her confidence altogether. After nearly a year with Logan, her confidence had returned, but she no longer went looking for dust-ups.

She was grateful, therefore, to see the re-enactment continue with no sign of the trouble she'd been sure would erupt after Maya Turner and Lance Cooper kissed. Liam Turner still didn't look pleased, but the crowd was loving the action on the green. None of Chance Creek's prior re-enactments had included a storyline like this. Lena thought the change was brilliant. By the time the two sides began to line up on the battlefield, everyone in the audience knew the back stories of a number of the soldiers—and cared if they made it through the war or not.

As the redcoats and patriots lined up across from each other, she was truly excited to see how it all played out.

"I think you're right," she told Logan. "I think we should join the re-enactment group next year and be a part of this. It looks fun."

Who would have thought a year ago she'd have time for something like this? Back then, she'd been trying to run Two Willows single-handedly, when she wasn't trying to scare off the General's latest overseer. Bob Finchley had been one of the worst they'd ever had. Thank God Cass hadn't married him like she'd planned to.

"Sounds good. Here we go. Both sides are lined up."

"Something's wrong. This doesn't feel right," Jo said a minute later, leaning forward in her chair.

"No, it doesn't," Hunter agreed.

Lena knew what they meant, and her stomach sank. At first the men on the field had milled about good-naturedly, finding their places and getting ready for the fight. Now, however, it was clear some of the men in the ranks had a real grudge against the other side. Two groups of men glared at each other angrily and stood braced for real battle. Around them, the other partici-pants noticed what was happening, and their banter died down as they shifted in their positions, holding their replica muskets tightly, watching the enemy lines uncertainly.

"I told you," Lena said to Logan worriedly. "There's bad blood between the Coopers and Turners."

The spectators quieted down, too, until it seemed as if everyone was holding their breath.

"They should call this off," Brian muttered.

"Too late," Logan said.

Lance Cooper stepped forward as the Redcoat gen-eral. Liam Turner faced him across the field.

"Oh, hell," Lena breathed.

Lance called out the command to charge.

"At least no one died. But I guess you knew that going in," Jack said as he guided Alice back to the cluster of chairs and coolers that marked their group's territory on the green. The re-enactment was long over, and they'd gone for a walk—and to get more food—before the evening's musical entertainment started.

"You know I try not to look at the future," Alice chided him, greeting the others and settling in her chair as a band began to play on the portable stage set up nearby, "but you're right. I did know that much. Best re-enactment Chance Creek has ever put on, though, right? I think we'll all be talking about it for a long time."

"It's a shame that neighbors can hold grudges for so long. Hope that never happens to us."

"You mean at Two Willows?" Alice looked thoughtful. "You can't have thirteen grown-ups living on one property without a good argument now and then, but we've fought for each other's lives. I can't see us losing sight of what's important." She smiled sadly. "It hurts me to see the Turners and Coopers, though. Those are good people, and they've known so much pain."

"Like you and your sisters?"

"Like all of us."

She was right. He'd sure known his share of hardship—and so had the other men the General had sent to Chance Creek.

"I wonder what my parents would think of where I am now," he mused.

"They were ranchers, too. I think they'd be pleased for you." Alice got to her feet, still graceful although she was seven months pregnant. "Dance with me, husband of mine."

"You think you still can?" he teased her, placing a

hand on her belly.

"You just try to keep up."

Jack gladly took her hand and followed her close to the stage where other couples were swaying in time to the ballad the band was playing. Before he could take her into his arms, however, Cab Johnson waltzed past with his wife, Rose.

"Some dust-up," the sheriff said. "You're lucky you're not on duty today."

"All's well that ends well," Jack said. "At least you didn't have to book anyone."

"Thank God for small mercies. See you at work tomorrow." Cab kept going. Rose smiled and lifted a hand from his shoulder to wave as they whirled past.

Alice snuggled as close as she could get with the bump of her belly between them. Jack sighed. He couldn't get over how right she felt in his arms no matter how long they were together.

"We need to figure out a name for this baby soon," she said. It had been a constant topic of conversation between them for months, ever since they'd found out they were going to have a boy.

"I don't know why you can't take a sneak peek at the future and just tell us what we named him."

"That's cheating. I want to live in the here and now. You know that."

"Edward."

"Too formal."

"Constantine."

"That's even more formal."

"Ned."

"That's just another version of Edward."

"Tertius."

"He's our first child, not our third, silly."

"Augustus."

Alice sighed. "It would be nice to honor the General, but…. That's a mouthful."

"It is." He thought a minute, although he was pretty sure they'd discussed every boy's name ever known to man. "Oliver."

Alice stilled in his arms. "Oliver. Why haven't we thought of that before?"

"I don't know."

"I kind of like it."

"I do, too." He pulled back. Looked down at her. "Did we just pick the name?"

"I think we did."

Jack whooped, then ducked when everyone nearby turned to look at them. "I'd pick you up and swing you around, but I don't want to hurt you."

"Just dance with me." She snuggled into his arms. "Oliver Sanders. It's a good name."

"It is a good name." Jack's heart swelled. "Not much longer, and we're going to have a baby boy to love."

"I can't wait," she told him, "but I love this time with you, too."

"Good." He pulled her closer. "Because I'm not going anywhere." He still found it hard to believe sometimes that he'd created the life for himself he'd always wanted. His work with the sheriff's department scratched the itch to help out and solve problems. His ranch chores kept him moving and strengthened his body. His time with the others at Two Willows gave him the large family he hadn't even known he was craving.

And Alice—she was the best of it all. His magical, beautiful, kind, funny, creative wife.

"I've got something to tell you," she said, tilting up her chin to look at him. "Kate O'Dell got in touch. She's ready to move forward and hire me for her Civil War movie. She loves the costumes I created."

"What about Oliver?"

"I'll have to hire some helpers. I'll fly out to California now and then, but I've told Kate I'm having a baby, and she knows I won't move there permanently. She doesn't care. She said she'd do whatever it takes to accommodate me so she could have the best." Alice wriggled with pleasure. "That's me. I'm the best."

"Yes, you are. At everything. And I love you for it."

THE PRIDE IN Jack's voice told Alice all she needed to know. He wasn't threatened by the new project she was taking on, and he wouldn't hold her back. He would continue to be the partner she'd come to rely on in the months they'd been married.

Some men would have expected her to put off her dreams because of the baby. They would have complained if care for the newborn impinged on their daily schedule.

Jack wasn't like that. He'd been interested in every stage of her pregnancy, exploring the new contours of her body as it changed, delighting in the feel of the baby's first movements within her. She had no doubt he'd be a dedicated father—and one who'd be careful to keep his love free and clear from any hint of a need for reciprocity. Jack loved his adopted parents and was sure they loved him, too, but Alice knew he'd feared abandonment as a child if he didn't measure up to his adopted father's expectations. Alice liked to think she was helping to heal those old hurts, just as he was helping heal hers.

They were good for each other, she thought. And Chance Creek, for all its quirks and ups and downs, would be a good place to raise their family. She hoped in the end the Turners and Coopers could see that. Chance Creek was worth fighting for. So were family and friends. Sometimes you had to get through hard times to get to the good.

Alice was glad the events of this past year had brought her to a place where she had better control over her flashes of foresight. She didn't want to live half in the future anymore, especially now that she was pregnant, and definitely not when her baby was born. She wanted to be firmly in the present, aware of each moment she got to spend with Oliver—and Jack.

"We should celebrate," Jack said. "You got your dream job."

Alice's heart swelled. "I did, didn't I?" She let out a shaky breath. "I'm going to make the most beautiful dresses anyone's ever seen. And then I'm going to get to do it again and again. Kate O'Dell's movie is the kind that will make a splash, and I'm sure I'll get hired for other lavish productions. I did it, Jack." The realization came over her in a rush. She'd worked for movies before, of course. And wonderful plays and musicals. But this really was her dream—the kind of production that would tax the range of her talents. "I didn't know how competitive I am. How much I wanted to be the best—and have a lifetime of projects to work on."

"You couldn't before. You can't reach for the stars without a solid foundation beneath your feet."

"Your right; my foundation was pretty shaky until recently." Alice didn't like to think back to those times—she and her sisters trying so hard to hold it all together while everything was falling apart. "Now it's strong." She hugged him.

"And it's not going anywhere." He tightened his arms around her, and she leaned into him. Jack was the bulwark between her and everything difficult, and she appreciated that more than she'd ever thought she would. It worried her from time to time that his work put him in the path of danger, but she'd learned to let those fears go. Jack was careful, thorough and not the kind of man to take reckless chances. Like he said, he wasn't going anywhere.

"We're going to have so many kids underfoot at Two Willows soon," she said.

"I'm glad. No one will be lonely."

She ran her hands up his back, feeling the strength

of the man she'd married. He was right: none of them
need be lonely anymore. "So much togetherness but so
much space, too. We'll have to keep building everyone
little personal places to get away and dream. I don't
know what I'd do without my studio."

"I wonder what kind of space Oliver will want when
he's old enough. What will he want to create or special-
ize in?"

Alice shrugged. "I don't know. And I'm so happy
about that."

He squeezed her back. "I'm happy about everything."

"TIME FOR DESSERT," Cass declared when everyone was
back together waiting for the fireworks to begin. "I've
got fruit cups and brownies. Take your pick."

"Sit," Emerson told her as she got up. "I'll pass
things around."

"Thanks. Fruit cups are in that cooler, and the
brownies are in that Tupperware over there."

As Emerson made his way around the group taking
orders, he had to smile at how many of them there
were. Next year there'd be even more, he thought in
satisfaction, including the child he and Wye would bring
into the world around Christmastime. Their son.

Every time he thought about it, his throat thickened
with emotion. They'd gone to the doctor just two days
ago and found out their baby's gender, and he was still
astonished by the experience of the ultrasound and the
news.

A boy.

He'd welcomed Elise into his life with an open heart, and each day with her and Wye brought him more joy than he ever could have expected, but Elise, at eighteen months, had made it very clear that she was, as Lena put it, "a girl's girl." She loved everything pretty. Begged to put on new outfits several times a day and had definite opinions about what she wanted to wear. She was never happier than in Alice's studio, surrounded by heaps of beautiful fabrics, and Alice had declared that soon she'd make Elise her apprentice. She might be joking, but Emerson thought there was a good chance her prediction would come to pass. He'd seen Elise in deep concentration separating fabrics out of a large pile Alice had provided her with, matching them together in smaller sets, and it was clear even to him that the combinations she came up with were pleasing to the eye.

Emerson didn't begrudge her any of it and hoped he'd always be the kind of dad to support his children in whatever their passions turned out to be. Maybe one day Elise would help him decorate the interiors of the houses he refurbished.

What would his son like to do?

Emerson longed to find out. Would he take to the horses that Emerson loved to ride? Emerson had bought one of his own, a bay gelding that loved to explore the ranch as much as he did. Would he like to build and fix things with his hands, activities that brought Emerson more satisfaction than he could have expected?

Whatever it was, Emerson promised himself he'd be by his side. Every child in his care would get as much of him as he had to give. Life was precious—and precarious—and he wouldn't miss a moment if he could help it.

"Fruit cup or brownie?" he asked Logan when he reached the man.

"Yes."

Lena swatted her husband, then grinned. "Actually, I'll take one of each, too."

Emerson updated the tally in his head, and soon he was making his way back around handing out the food.

"You have an amazing memory," Wye told him when he handed her the brownie she'd asked for and settled down with one of his own. She took a bite and groaned with pleasure. "Oh, Cass has always made the most amazing brownies. I think it's Amelia's recipe."

He took a bite, chewed and swallowed. "That is good. As to my memory, that's part of the job I used to do. Getting the details right so the General could see the big picture. I guess it's a skill that's hard to shake."

Wye glanced at the General, who was sitting nearby, working his way through a fruit cup, a brownie perched precariously on the armrest of his chair. "The General seems content these days."

"Don't tell anyone, but we're going to try a ride tomorrow."

"On horseback?" Wye clapped a hand to her mouth and looked around to make sure no one had heard her.

"Really?"

"Really," he confirmed. "He's been diligent about his exercises, and his doctor gave the go-ahead. The General doesn't want an audience watching, though."

"Of course not."

"We'll give it a try quietly, and if he's successful, we'll tell the others."

"That's amazing. And it's all your doing. You know that, right?"

Emerson shrugged. "He's the one doing the hard work."

"At your insistence. I think everyone here owes you more than they know."

"Hey, don't talk like that." Emerson leaned in close. "They've given me so much."

"You've given them back their father."

Maybe she was right, Emerson thought, but being at Two Willows had worked a magic of its own on the General. The man was mellowing. Still feisty enough, he supposed, but becoming the kind of father he had a feeling the General always wanted to be.

It helped that there were so many men on the ranch. Emerson knew the General had always been more comfortable around men than women, and he still blustered and fussed around his daughters sometimes but not nearly as often as he had at the beginning.

He was wonderful with Elise and Emily, too. His pride in their accomplishments was genuine, and in getting comfortable with praising the babies, he'd become more comfortable with praising his daughters, too.

Several months ago, the doctors had given the General the okay to drive, and his independence made him a new man. He'd begun to reconnect with old friends, grabbing a burger with his buddies or a beer on a Friday night. Emerson still drove him to Billings for their reserve work but was no longer at his side all day. The General could fend for himself for the most part, and Emerson and Wye had bought two small houses in town he was refurbishing in preparation for renting out now that all the trailers in the Park were done. The work kept him busy. Sometimes Wye came with him; sometimes she stayed home doing remote work for a large law firm in Billings or helped Cass.

Elise, who had been snuggling in Wye's lap, lifted her arms. "Daddy."

Emerson picked her up and transferred her to his lap. "Ready for the fireworks?"

"Fireworks!" She nodded her head vigorously, although her eyes had the droopy look that signalled she'd soon be asleep.

"What about you?" he asked Wye, taking her hand. "You ready for all this?" He hoped she knew what he meant.

"Definitely."

WYE COULDN'T THINK of anywhere she'd rather be than sitting in the middle of the town square waiting for the night sky to light up with fireworks. She needed to pinch herself every morning when she woke up to make sure it was all real. She wasn't alone anymore. She had a husband. A child. A baby on the way. She shared a ranch with her best friend, and her days were filled with interactions with people she'd come to love—to think of as family.

That was the true revelation of life at Two Willows. She, who'd never felt part of a real family, now felt embraced by one every minute of every day. It had taken several months before she stopped second-guessing how everyone really felt about her. Cass was still her best friend, but she'd begun to spend a lot of time with Alice in her studio, since Elise was so enamored of the fabric there. Alice enjoyed the little girl's company, and to pass the time while the two were busy, Wye had even started an embroidery project, something she hadn't done since she was a little girl. The small creative act had awakened a part of her she'd forgotten existed.

Some days she rode out with Lena, who had discovered her riding skills weren't very advanced and who'd taken it as a personal challenge to make Wye a regular horsewoman. "If you don't learn now, you won't be able to keep up with your kids," was how she'd put it, and Wye thought she was right. Elise loved the huge animals and cooed with delight whenever Emerson put her in the saddle and let her "ride." Besides, Lena adored every inch of Two Willows and enjoyed showing her obscure corners of the ranch that Wye figured she'd never have seen otherwise. Sadie and Jo, who'd seemed so young to her when she'd first met them, had grown into companions who turned out to have much to teach her, too. Sadie was convinced she needed a garden at the trailer cabin and had spent long hours with her this spring drawing up plans and getting to work on it. Emerson had helped them install a stone terrace, where their picnic table and grill could go, and they'd filled the borders with perennials and bulbs that were pretty enough this year but that Sadie claimed would be wonderful when spring came around again.

Emerson had been right about the trailer: he'd made it look like a cozy cabin, and her heart swelled whenever she came home from a day's work at the main house. The reservists Emerson had rented the other trailers to had turned out to be young, fun neighbors. All but one had a wife or live-in girlfriend, so weekends were lively, and there was always someone around offering to throw another hamburger on the grill if you wanted to come to dinner. Wye enjoyed their active social life, but she also appreciated that Sadie had insisted on carving out a private space near the rear of the trailer cabin, where bushes and small trees gave cover to a seating area they'd created around a fire pit. When she and Emerson wanted to sit alone after Elise had gone to bed, they came out here, leaving the door open so they could hear her if she woke up, and lit a small fire. They could cuddle together on the wicker outdoor couch or sit on the swing and gaze up at the stars—without their neighbors being able to see their every move.

Maybe someday they'd build a bigger home on another parcel of the ranch's land, but for now, Wye was content.

A burst of fireworks lit up the sky in shades of red, white and blue.

"Ahhh!" said the crowd right on cue, and Wye nestled her head on Emerson's shoulder.

"Love you," she said.

"Love you, too."

"GOOD NIGHT, GENERAL."

"Good night," Augustus said and firmly shut the door to his first-floor room as Emerson turned away. Much as he appreciated the young man's solicitude in checking to make sure he had all he needed before he left for his own house, Augustus was completely capable of getting himself to bed these days.

Thanks to those infernal physio exercises, he'd regained much of the mobility in his hip and moved around without his cane. He was surprised at how spry he felt sometimes, although at the end of a busy day, he tired sooner than he would have liked.

Tomorrow he'd get on a horse and ride for the first time since the blast. Much as he hated to admit it, he was a little nervous, but he knew as soon as he was in the saddle, his muscles would remember what to do. He'd practically been born astride a horse, after all.

It was almost time to consider the future. He'd spent the last year feeling like an old man with his injuries, but in reality it had been all the desk work he'd done in the past decade that had aged him before his time. Men were meant to be moving, and he'd determined he was going to get back to fighting trim. There was lots of work to be done on this ranch, and he'd be damned if he'd let the younger generation do it all.

He enjoyed his work at the reserve training center, too, and had a feeling more opportunities were coming his way in that vein now that people knew he was gaining strength. He looked forward to new career challenges, but he meant to be careful not to be pulled away from the ranch too much.

He had grandchildren now, and they needed him to be present in a way he hadn't been able to be for his own daughters. He wanted to keep up with them, which meant changing the way he viewed himself. He'd let himself get far too curmudgeonly before his time.

Now it was time to age backward, as Emerson liked to say, and as much as he growled at the younger man when he spouted nonsense like that, Augustus had decided he was right. This summer he meant to swim in the creek, ride his horse, go to fairs and celebrations, spend time with old friends and new grandkids.

He meant to live life to the fullest.

He certainly felt blessed.

As he turned in, he thought of Amelia, as he always did. She'd led him back here, and she'd helped him create a small, busy community at Two Willows. As alive as she was to him still, and as present as she was on this ranch, he felt a softening of the connection between them. It would always be there, but she'd walked her path on this mortal coil and lingered here to help him go a little further on his own, knowing he hadn't been ready to be without her. Now her work here was done, and he was strong enough to move forward alone. She needed to move on, too.

Augustus swallowed, the familiar ache inside him still sharp, but sweet, too. He had many years ahead of him. A family to surround and support him. A career to continue in various incarnations. Someday he and Amelia would be together again. Until then, any number of adventures still lay ahead.

And he was ready for them.

Emerson and Wye found their happily ever after, but the Turners and Coopers are too busy feuding to find love—or are they? Want to know how the Turner/Cooper feud got started? Why Lance Cooper and Maya Turner are kissing? And what really happened at the July 4th Reenactment? Check out Cora's next Chance Creek series, **Turners vs. Coopers**, beginning with *The Cowboy's Secret Bride*.

Be the first to know about Cora Seton's new releases! Sign up for her newsletter here!
www.coraseton.com/sign-up-for-my-newsletter

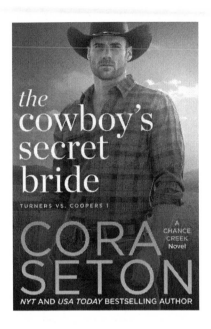

Read on for an excerpt of Volume 1 of the **Turners vs. Coopers** series – *The Cowboy's Secret Bride.*

Present day

THIS WASN'T THE place.

Carl swept his gaze across the pastures before him, took in the squat, ugly house perched close by and shook his head over the dilapidated barns and outbuildings some distance away.

"I know it doesn't look like much, but Hilltop Acres is a bargain," Megan Lawrence, his realtor, said. An earnest young woman, she was relatively new at her job and very enthusiastic.

"It's small," he countered.

"It's a ranch. Not many of them for sale around here."

"You're telling me." He'd spent years on and off looking for the right one, and he was beginning to wonder if he'd ever find the property he wanted. He'd always been able to picture it in his mind: a stately home perched on a rise of ground, fields and pastures sloping away around it to a tremendous view. Plenty of acreage for a large cattle operation. A prosperous place like the ones featured in the movies he used to watch with his father when he was young.

Not a stunted little spread like this one.

His dad had spent summers on a ranch when he was a kid and always talked of the day he'd retire to one, but that hadn't happened before he passed away. It was up to Carl to make that dream come true.

"If you're not interested, I guess we'd better leave. I've got another appointment." Megan pulled out her cell phone, frowned at something on the screen and tucked it away again.

Carl adjusted his hat, wishing his father was still alive to help with this search. "Someone else is looking at this property?" He didn't want it, but if there was nothing better available…

"No—it's Camila Torres. She just wants a little place in town."

"Camila—?" Carl cut off, his chest tightening. "Camila's looking for a house?" An old, dull ache pulsed to life within him. He couldn't believe he'd let her get away. He still lay awake some nights thinking about the conversation they'd had in DelMonaco's three years ago and wondered what he could have said to make the outcome different.

After that disaster, he'd ended up spending six months in California and had considered giving up on Chance Creek, but the place had a hold on him, and he kept coming back. He hadn't found a woman to replace Camila, though, and now and then, when he saw her in a store or on the street, the ache in his chest made him wonder if he ever would.

Meanwhile, Whitfield Tech had soared in valuation, and knowing a good opportunity when he saw one, Carl had sold it for a princely sum last year. He never needed to work another day in his life if he didn't want to. The experience had required many more trips to California, and all the flying back and forth began to wear on him. He was always living out of a suitcase. Running to catch a plane.

He was ready to settle down.

For good.

And Chance Creek kept calling his name.

He'd finished the period of consulting work required of him as part of the deal with Whitfield Tech's new owners. He'd kept mentoring Sven as his friend and ex-employee expanded the robotics business he'd started on the side a few years ago, too. That had occasioned more flying back and forth, but Carl owed Sven for all his hard work at Whitfield Tech.

Through it all, he'd worked with the Coopers on their ranch whenever he could, soaking up everything there was to learn about running a cattle operation. He knew a hell of a lot more about ranching now than when he'd first tried his hand at it years ago. Maybe it had been for the best he hadn't been able to find a spread yet, but he was ready for his own place now. Soon Sven wouldn't need him so much, and he'd stop flying back to California all the time and be able to devote all his energy to his new ranch.

If he ever found one.

"That's right. Camila," Megan said, interrupting his thoughts. "She's looking for something with two bedrooms, one bath. Close to her restaurant."

"For her—or is she with someone?"

Megan shot him a curious look. "Just for her. I haven't heard that she's with anyone right now. I think she works too much to date."

Carl nodded. For all she'd given him a hard time about his dedication to his company, it seemed like she was always working when he stopped by Fila's for a meal. Which wasn't very often these days—it was too damn awkward.

But after her workday was over, Camila went home every night. He supposed that made all the difference to her way of thinking. She'd been right three years ago; it wasn't fair of him to think she'd wait around for months on end every time he had to put out a fire in California. She'd known it would be years before he was really ready to settle in Chance Creek—if ever.

Still, some part of him had always hoped they'd find their way back to each other.

"I guess she's sick of waiting for her knight in shining armor and has decided to slay her own dragons," Megan said.

Carl turned on her but realized she had no idea he and Camila had ever been a couple.

"Guess so."

The idea of her buying a house ate at him, though.

"Something wrong?" Megan asked.

Everything was wrong, Carl thought. He didn't have a ranch. Didn't have a home to offer Camila so she didn't have to buy her own.

Didn't have Camila.

And damn it, he still wanted her.

Bad.

"Carl?" Megan was peering at him curiously.

"It's just—" He broke off. He couldn't explain any of this to Megan. She wasn't the woman he should be talking to. He needed to find Camila. Tell her they'd both made a mistake. Tell her he was ready to make that promise she'd asked for.

Hell, he'd never leave Chance Creek again if it meant he could be with her.

It was as if Megan's words had torn the scab right off the wound Camila's refusal had left three years ago. He was kidding himself if he thought he was over that. If he thought he was ready to give up on the idea of a future together.

He wasn't over it, and he wasn't going to give up.

"I need a ranch," he said.

"I know—that's why we're here."

Megan must think he was an idiot.

Carl scanned the property in front of him again. It was small, but it was a working ranch. The house was a hovel—but he could tear it down and build a new one.

"Are you going to the Spring Fling Fair today?" Megan began to trudge back to her vehicle.

Spring Fling Fair? Carl hadn't thought about it, but now he did. Camila would probably be there, running a food concession tent with Fila. He could bump into her casually. Strike up a conversation.

Ask her out and take the first step toward a future he was ready to fight for with everything he had.

"Yeah, I'll be there. Listen, I want to make an offer on this place. First thing tomorrow," he added when Megan turned in surprise.

"Really?"

"Really." He was done screwing around. Done waiting to start this new phase of his life.

Done standing by while Camila moved on without him.

He'd hesitated once—and lost his chance to be with her.

He sure as hell wasn't going to let that happen again.

THIS WASN'T THE place.

Camila tried to hide her disappointment as Megan extolled the virtues of a kitchen so small its oven and fridge were three-quarters size. The house's two bedrooms were hardly big enough to hold beds. It lacked hookups for a washer and dryer. The living room faced north, gloomy as a crypt on this beautiful spring morning.

"It's in your budget," Megan reminded her when she was done praising the scant two feet of chipped countertop.

"I guess I was hoping for something… more."

Something that felt like home, at the very least. This place felt as temporary as the cabin she was renting from the Turners. She knew she should be grateful she could afford anything in Chance Creek, and she expected to buy a fixer upper.

It wasn't the house that was depressing her.

It was the fact she'd be purchasing it alone.

Somehow, she'd always assumed she'd marry before purchasing her first home. Once she'd even thought she'd found the man she wanted to be with—

But Carl hadn't been ready to settle down.

She'd done well for herself since. Improved her own business. Widened her circle of friends. She was staying right here, for good, and any man she chose to be with needed to be as committed to Chance Creek as she was.

Which was why she was house hunting alone. She'd never found met a man who'd replaced Carl in her heart. Hadn't been trying all that much, if she was honest.

"Are you and Carl Whitfield an item?" Megan asked.

Camila swung around at the unexpected question. "Me and Carl?" Had Megan read her mind?

"He asked about you this morning. I didn't know you two were friends."

He'd asked about her?

Camila couldn't say why the thought left her breathless. Against her better judgment, she pictured him in this kitchen, bumping against the counter in the too-small space, trying to maneuver around the table she'd have to add. He wouldn't fit.

Which didn't matter, she told herself firmly. Carl would never be in this house.

And she didn't want to live here, either.

"I wouldn't say friends. More like acquaintances." She looked around the kitchen one last time, ignoring the pain her words conjured inside her. It hadn't worked between her and Carl, and when something didn't work, there was no sense trying to force it. "I don't want this house," she added.

Megan sighed. "I'll see what else I can find and set up more viewings. Are you going to the Spring Fling Fair?"

"Fila and I are running a food booth." Camila looked at her watch. "Better get a move on—she'll wonder where I've gotten to. Thanks for showing me the place, even if it's not right for me." She hurried for the door.

"I'm not giving up," Megan said, following her. "Sometimes you look all over and then find the perfect one is right under your nose!"

CARL SWALLOWED HIS uneasiness as he waited in line at the fair later that afternoon for a chance to talk to Camila, who was turning skewers of chicken on the grill in the food tent in front of him. Now that he was here, he wasn't sure what he was going to say to her. He wished he'd gotten Megan to write up his offer on Hilltop Acres today. He wasn't the only one in town shopping for a ranch, and he'd feel a lot better making his play for Camila if he could tell her he was in the process of purchasing a home in Chance Creek.

Everyone in town was here at the fair, he reminded himself, settling his Stetson more comfortably on his head. No one was searching for real estate today; the grounds were as crowded as this food line was long. Didn't look like Camila would have much time for talking when he reached the head of it, either, which maybe was a good thing. That would give him less time to screw it up.

Carl chuckled at himself. Look at him, nervous as a schoolboy asking his sweetheart to the prom. He knew Camila, and she knew him. There was nothing to fear in the coming conversation.

Unless she turned him down again.

He let out a sigh. He hoped she didn't. He couldn't wait to be close to her once more. Now that he'd given himself permission to think about pursuing her, all his pent-up desire for her had burst free. He'd been keeping it at bay through sheer doggedness, and his self-restraint was fraying fast.

He and Camila had always worked together that way, even if they'd dated only a few months. Since they'd split up, he'd missed hanging out with her, going to hear live music at the Dancing Boot and pulling her close on the dance floor, taking drives on snowy country lanes and talking for hours. But it was the thought of their nights together that haunted him when he couldn't sleep.

Could he get her alone so he could ask her on a date without everyone else hearing? Fila was working in the back of the tent. Maya Turner was taking orders—which was a problem Carl hadn't anticipated. When he and Camila had been dating, the Coopers had just returned to town after several years away, and the ancient Turner/Cooper feud had been on a low simmer. It hadn't interfered with their relationship, even if they'd lived on the rival ranches.

Since then, the feud had heated up. Carl didn't know the details. Wasn't sure if it really mattered. Whenever you talked to a Cooper about the Turners, all you got was a laundry list of complaints, some that dated back over a hundred years and others as fresh as last week. Now the conflict was as hot as the eighty-five-degree temperatures that were nudging Chance Creek into an early summer, and everyone knew it would take only one spark to really set off a blaze between the families. Carl had heard about a minor altercation at the Dancing Boot between Lance Cooper and Liam Turner last weekend.

He'd have to watch what he said in front of Maya. No one needed a fight on a day like this.

He had eaten his breakfast around sunup, and by the time he made it to the counter of the concession stand, where Maya manned the till under the large white canopy, he was ravenous. And hot. A trickle of sweat made its way between his shoulder blades under his black cotton T-shirt.

Fila came to deliver a plate of food to another customer, flipped her long black braid over her shoulder and said, "Hey, Carl. How are you doing?" She was sensibly dressed in a light cotton sundress. The heat didn't seem to bother her.

"I'm great."

Fila raised her eyebrows at his enthusiasm. "Finally found a ranch?" she quipped.

Hell, what was that supposed to mean?

He told himself to calm down. Fila's question was innocent; it was no secret he'd been looking for a long time. "Actually, yeah, I did."

Fila blinked in surprise, leaned closer and asked, "Does that mean you'll finally ask her out again?" She nodded almost imperceptibly at Camila, still manning the grill, and Carl bit back a groan. He wasn't ready to take this show public.

"Ask who out?" Maya chirped. "Who's caught your fancy, Carl?"

Camila looked up from the grill, caught Carl's gaze and swiftly looked away. Had she heard Maya?

She must have.

Carl sent a pointed look Fila's way. "No one. Mind your own business, Maya."

"Fine. Next." She looked past him to the man standing behind him and waved him forward.

"Maya. Carl's a paying customer." Fila shook her

head. "What'll you have, Carl?"

"A plate of your butter chicken nachos."

"Good choice." Fila leaned closer again. Lowered her voice. "Sorry about that."

Carl made sure Maya was busy talking. "I may not be a Cooper, and Camila isn't a Turner, but it wouldn't do to rile up that crowd."

"You think your landlords care who you date?"

"They do if an honorary Turner is involved." He glanced at Camila again. She was doing a good job pretending not to notice the conversation, but he had a feeling she was trying to listen in. He raised his voice again. "Anyway, I'm putting in an offer on a ranch first thing in the morning. Plan to settle here for good."

"It's about time," Fila said in an equally loud voice before whispering, "You're lucky no one else has come along to steal her heart, you know."

"Who's heart?" Maya asked, startling both of them. Her customer had stepped to the side to wait for his order, and she'd bent closer to hear their conversation.

"No one's," Carl growled.

"It could happen, you know," Fila told him with an admonishing shake of her head. "There's a lot of fish in the sea."

He knew that all too well. Had been bracing himself for three years against the possibility Camila might pair up with someone else. Get married.

Be lost to him forever.

"Who. Are. You. Talking. About?" Maya demanded.

Carl paid for his order and stepped aside to wait for

his food without answering her, and Maya let out a little huff. "Coopers," she said derisively.

"Carl's not a Cooper," Fila told her.

"He might as well be. He worships them. And he acts like them, too. Stubborn as a mule."

Carl kept his cool. He'd never understood the feud between the two families or how someone as level-headed as Maya could fall under its sway.

But all the Turners were like that. Dead set against the Coopers. And vice versa.

Was that why Camila wasn't looking at him? He knew she got a great deal on rent from the Turners. Maybe she didn't want to put that in jeopardy just to chat with him.

Or maybe he was too late.

Fila leaned toward him again. "Do you want to talk to her?" she asked in a low voice, keeping an eye on Maya, who had waved another customer forward.

"Hell, yeah."

"Hold on." Fila moved to Camila's side and said something to her. Camila shook her head, but Fila kept talking until Camila finally straightened.

"Fine," he heard her say.

"Here you go. One plate of butter chicken nachos," Fila said a moment later, delivering his meal, a satisfied gleam in her eye. "She'll meet you over there in ten minutes. Keep out of sight of the booth." She pointed in the direction of the portable toilets set a discreet distance away from the rest of the festivities. "Next," Fila called out.

Carl walked away. The portable toilets might not be his first choice as a rendezvous spot, but who cared? This was his chance to repair the damage between them—and he meant to make the most of it.

He'd gone only about twenty paces away from the food tent, however, when something sharp prodded him in the side.

"Carl!"

"Hell!" Carl nearly dropped his nachos as a sharp-eyed, gray-haired woman poked the tip of her umbrella into his rib cage again. He sidestepped her third attempt to spear him. "Virginia—you nearly made me lose my food!"

Carl's anger didn't faze her. Nothing fazed Virginia Cooper, matriarch of the Cooper clan and his landlord at Thorn Hill. Since he'd moved onto the spread, he'd come to enjoy the younger generation of Coopers, despite their ready tempers, but Virginia was another matter. Virginia would try the patience of a saint. It wasn't her age—her eighty-four years hadn't slowed down her keen acumen, her fast stride or her sharp tongue.

She was simply mean.

Carl had learned to stay out of her way. Luckily for him, most of the time he could do that. Virginia might still own Thorn Hill, but she currently resided at the Prairie Garden assisted living facility in town, where she happily tormented the other residents and staff.

"I've got a proposition for you!" she announced, ignoring his protest. "Did you hear about the prize?" In her three-quarter-length gray skirt and flower-patterned blouse, Virginia was neat as a pin. Her hair was pulled back, braided and coiled into a bun. Her fingers gleamed with several large rings, but none of them circled her ring finger. Virginia had never married.

"What prize?" Carl looked back to catch a glimpse of Camila, but too many people blocked his view.

"Weren't you paying attention to the announcements? It's only the biggest piece of news to hit Chance Creek in over a hundred years!"

Now she had his attention. "I just got here. What's going on?"

"The city's giving up the Ridley property. Giving it away to the winner—which will be us!" Her eyes shone with determination.

Carl was lost. "Where's the Ridley property? And how would we win it?"

She poked him again with her umbrella. "The Ridley property is a ranch that straddles Pittance Creek to the north of Thorn Hill and the Flying W. It was given to the city by the Ridleys in 1962 and kept in trust since then. Those fools thought the town center would spread to encompass it. Must have figured Chance Creek was the next Chicago." She shook her head to show what she thought of that. "It's been sitting there unused ever since."

Carl was beginning to understand the significance of the announcement. If the Coopers won it, they could double the size of their ranch.

"Think of it." Virginia jabbed with her umbrella for

emphasis, but Carl dodged it. "Twice the land—and control over Pittance Creek," she said triumphantly.

Clarity crashed over him. There was the rub. The land was one thing, but the water could be even more important. The Turners' ranch—the Flying W—also depended on Pittance Creek. Both ranches had wells, of course, but the creek was valuable, nonetheless.

"Virginia, you're incorrigible. You wouldn't deprive the Turners of their water, would you?"

"Maybe. Maybe not. Depends."

Hell, he wanted no part of this. "Well, good luck. Hope you win."

"That's all you've got to say?" Virginia lifted her chin. "Fat lot of help you are, after everything we've done for you."

Carl sighed and checked over his shoulder again. No sign of Camila yet, but he needed to get going. "What do you have to do to win it?" he asked, because he knew Virginia wouldn't let him pass until she'd told him.

"Provide the biggest boost to civic life during the next six months. Whatever that means."

Carl could have laughed. It meant the Coopers would have to do something good for the town at large—maybe for the first time in their lives. The family wasn't known for its civic mindedness. "Like I said, good luck." This time Carl really meant it. If vying to win the Ridley property motivated them to become model citizens, he was all for it. He liked the Coopers, but they were a wild bunch.

"That's where you come in."

"What do you mean?" He should have known she'd try to rope him into something.

She jabbed him again. "Pay attention. This is important. Like I said, I've got a proposition for you."

"Spit it out."

"You need a ranch. I need that prize. Help me win this contest, and I'll make sure you get the property of your dreams. You must be sick of living in our little cabin. A millionaire like you," she added.

"You'll sell me the Ridley property?" That was interesting. He tried to picture the land to the north of Thorn Hill. All he'd seen from the road was a tangle of brush and scrub. Were there any buildings on it? He couldn't say. At least it was close to town.

Virginia bristled. "I'm not selling you Cooper land. I'm talking about another ranch. A big one. It's not for sale yet, but it will be soon. I can get you access to the seller before anyone else even knows about it. If—and only if—you help me win."

A big ranch for sale no one knew about? That would be a miracle. Prosperous spreads in these parts stayed in family hands for generations. The ones that did come on the market were too dry, too rugged, too far from town, too one thing or another. Multiple buyers competed for them anyhow. Before today, he'd almost given up hope he'd ever find a decent place. Hilltop Acres barely qualified.

He didn't doubt Virginia's word, though. Living at the Prairie Garden put her in close proximity with dozens of pensioners who might be ready to dispose of a property. Hell, it seemed like she kept tabs on everyone in town.

"If we get a jump on this civic stuff, no one will be able to catch us. Give my family a leg up, and I'll see you get your ranch," she said.

"You want me to donate money to some charitable cause?" He supposed he could do that much and hold the ranch Virginia knew about in his hip pocket, in case something fell through with Hilltop Acres or if he wanted to upgrade at the end of the year. He'd been meaning to contribute more here in Chance Creek anyway. After all, this was his town, too.

"Money isn't enough," Virginia said. "Anyone can donate money to the town. We need to donate something big. Something everyone will remember forever."

"Like what?" His ten minutes were ticking away. He needed to shake Virginia if he wanted to meet Camila.

"If I knew, I wouldn't waste my time asking you." Virginia pursed her lips. "Something that goes back to our roots. We Coopers built Chance Creek's first elementary school in 1898, which means every generation since then owes us gratitude for their education. Maybe we'll build a new high school."

"The town already has a high school," Carl pointed out.

"And a sorrier piece of work I've never seen. The Turners were responsible for that travesty. Now the roof leaks in a dozen places, the auditorium is much too small and it's ugly."

Carl frowned. If Virginia tried to tear down a Turner

building and replace it with a Cooper one, the two families would be brawling in the streets before construction even began. At the same time, he remembered a conversation he'd had with Sven recently about how the lack of technology in schools in poorer districts meant that kids were being left behind before they even graduated from high school. That gave him a better idea.

"Chance Creek doesn't need a new school. It needs a way to train its students for the future. You can fix up the current high school—and offer kids a better education at the same time."

Virginia snorted. "You can gild a trash can, but it won't smell any better."

"Hear me out." Carl warmed to the idea. If he was going to give back to Chance Creek, this was a good way to start. "Schools these days are changing. They've got 3-D printers in the computer labs, tablets in classrooms, technology everywhere. The workplace is changing, too. Not all our students are going to be ranchers. The rest need to be ready to work in an automated world—and I doubt Chance Creek High is doing much to prepare them. You could fix that. Launch a program that really sets our high school apart from the others."

"Like what?" Virginia sounded skeptical.

Carl thought about it. "You'd still need to repair the building, but once that's done, you need something that makes people sit up and take notice." He thought of Sven again. "Like… robotics. That would get press like you wouldn't believe."

"Robotics, huh?" Virginia mused. "I like it. No one will see that coming." She nodded as if it was settled. "I'll need the proposal next week."

"The proposal?"

"That's right."

Carl laughed but faltered when Virginia's chin lifted in anger. How had his role escalated from pitching possibilities to overseeing the project? "Virginia, I'm just giving you ideas, remember?"

Virginia smacked her umbrella on the ground. "I thought you needed a ranch."

"I already found one. Going to put an offer in tomorrow." He'd like to help bring Chance Creek High into the twenty-first century but on his own terms.

Her eyes narrowed. "What ranch did you find?" she demanded.

"Hilltop Acres, over by—"

She snorted. "Hilltop Acres is a dump. The ranch I told you about is ten times as big."

Ten times? Carl's hands curled into fists in his pockets. He could do a lot with a property like that.

But Hilltop Acres was for sale today, and Virginia had already said she wouldn't tell him about the other property until they'd won the prize—which would be months from now, if ever.

"Maybe so, but I can't wait around, because—" he wasn't about to tell Virginia about Camila "—I've already waited long enough," he finished lamely.

"But you haven't bought it yet?" Virginia watched

him silently for a moment, and Carl couldn't begin to guess what she was thinking. "I have a feeling you'll come around," she said finally, then turned on her heel and walked away.

"YOU'D BETTER GET going," Fila said under her breath. "It's been ten minutes already."

"Carl can wait." Camila didn't know why she'd agreed to talk to him in the middle of the lunch rush, but Fila hadn't given her much choice, nagging at her to give him a chance to say his piece until it was clear she wasn't going to take no for an answer.

"Go."

"Fine. Be back in a flash," she said loudly for Maya's sake. "Just heading to the bathroom."

She quickly undid her apron and left it folded beside the grill, then ducked out and made a beeline in the direction of the portable toilets. She slowed her steps when she spotted Carl ahead of her. He was standing with his uneaten plate of nachos in his hand, watching Virginia Cooper stalk off to the craft stalls. Camila walked right by him, wondering if he'd follow.

Had he really found a ranch? Would he actually buy it? What did it mean that he'd come to her food tent and announced it like that?

It wasn't like they were together anymore. She was over him—

No. That wasn't true, no matter how hard she wished it was. Somehow she couldn't shake her feelings for the man. It had been that way ever since she'd met him. A friend of hers, Mia Matheson, had told her how helpful Carl had been when she was opening her event planning business. When Camila confessed she had some questions about her restaurant, Mia had gotten them together over coffee to see if Carl had answers. He'd definitely given her some good advice—and when he'd called later to see if she'd like to meet again, she'd said yes, unsure if he was simply being friendly or had other things in mind. Back then she'd been nervous around the millionaire, but she'd soon relaxed. Carl was a good listener, and he took his time to explain everything to her, down to the smallest detail, treating her restaurant as if it was as important as the tech company he owned.

She'd fallen for him during those conversations, and she still craved his company after all this time. She hated herself for the hope that had flared within her when Fila told her he wanted to talk to her. Surely a woman her age knew life didn't give you second chances. Besides, even if it did, Carl had hurt her once. What would stop him from hurting her again?

Her thoughts tangling in her mind, Camila picked up her pace until she was out of sight of her booth, hovering near enough to the row of portable toilets that anyone who saw her would assume she was waiting for her turn but far enough away the smell wasn't too bad. Butterflies jittered in her stomach as she prayed Carl wouldn't keep her waiting long. She needed to get this conversation over with and get back to her life—before he broke her heart all over again.

"Victoria Cooper could talk the paint off a barn," Carl said by way of apology when he joined her. He'd made short work of his plate of nachos in the past few minutes, and he tossed the remains in a nearby trash can. "And Maya Turner sure is nosy. Thought I'd never make it here to talk to you."

Camila was too busy studying his face to pay his words much attention. The past few years had left their mark on him. New lines framed the corners of his eyes. His time outdoors had given him a deep tan. He was more muscular after years of helping out at Thorn Hill, his black T-shirt emphasizing his shoulders and biceps.

How had she ever thought she was over him? She was growing hot under his direct gaze, desire threading low in her belly just from his proximity. Did he ever think about their nights together? She did, no matter how she tried to wipe them from her mind.

Suddenly Camila was sick of keeping her feelings for Carl buried. Maybe instead of turning him down, she should have gone all in instead, and trusted him to keep coming back to Chance Creek no matter what happened with Whitfield Tech. After all, here he was—buying a ranch. She could have spent the last three years with him.

Instead, she'd spent them alone. Busy with her work and friendships, of course, but climbing into an empty bed night after night.

What a waste, when she still wanted him as badly as she ever had.

She glanced back at the food tent, knowing how

Maya would react if she saw her standing so close to Carl. She'd need to keep this conversation under wraps.

"Are you really putting an offer in on—" She couldn't even bring herself to say it, as if she could jinx his purchase merely by saying the words out loud.

"That's right." He looked around, reached out and took one of her hands. Tugged her closer. Checked again to make sure no one was watching. "First thing tomorrow, but I was wondering—"

"Wondering what?" She ached to nestle into his arms the way she had so many times before. The distance between them was killing her. She'd been such a fool giving him ultimatums and destroying both their happiness.

"If you'd like to come see it first."

Camila's breath caught. Why would he want her to come see it, unless—

He still wanted her.

She looked up to find him watching her. Even if she thought she knew the answer, she still had to ask.

"Why?"

"You know why," he said firmly. "Nothing's changed on my end, Camila."

Her stomach flipped as if she was riding a roller coaster. If he still felt the same about her, then she wasn't a fool for craving him so badly, but if he was still torn between California and Chance Creek—

Did it matter if he was? Camila tried to look into her own heart. Was having Carl some of the time better than not having him at all? Because not having him at all had been—

Lonely as hell.

And she didn't want to be lonely anymore.

"When can I see it?" she heard herself ask, wondering if she was being brave or utterly irresponsible. All she knew was that she wanted to be close to him, and going to see a ranch meant a ride in his truck, time by his side—

"Tomorrow. First thing. I'll clear it with the realtor, but I know it'll be all right," Carl said. "Meantime," he added, "everyone's going to be at the fireworks tonight. You want to watch them with me? Seems like a good way to celebrate. It'll be dark." He lowered his voice. "I'll make sure no Turners or Coopers see us. I'd like the chance to hang out. I've missed our talks."

She'd missed a hell of a lot more than that, but he was right; she'd missed their conversations, too. Carl had been one of the first men in her life to truly treat her like an equal. Her traditional father had expected her to take a background role in life. Her brother had seen her as a competitor. The more she'd gotten to know Carl, the more she'd appreciated the hours they'd spent together talking about nothing and everything. Carl was well read. Interested in learning new things. A true entrepreneur. He loved hearing about her family, made her teach him words in Spanish, laughed at her impersonations of everyone they knew.

Why had she thrown all that away?

"O-okay." Camila smiled shakily, ignoring the little voice inside that urged caution. That said she might get hurt again. "I'd better get back, though," she told him. "Before Fila and Maya get overwhelmed."

"See you later." He gave her hand a squeeze and let her go, although Camila had a feeling he wanted to do more. She sure did. But they were in a public place, and there were Turners and Coopers everywhere. As much as she ached to touch him, run her hands over those delicious biceps, go up on tiptoe to meet his kiss—she tore herself away from him and said goodbye.

As she walked back to the food booth, her heart beating hard, Camila realized things were about to change. Carl's declaration that he was buying property in Chance Creek was a clear message: he wasn't looking for a fling. He'd made it plain when he proposed to her three years ago he wanted to be married. To have a family. If she gave him another chance, she had to be ready for that possibility.

"What happened? What did he say?" Fila whispered when Camila rejoined her and Maya at the booth.

Camila checked to make sure Maya was busy. "Carl asked me to watch the fireworks with him. He really is buying a ranch," she added. "He wants me to come and check it out tomorrow morning."

"That sounds serious."

"I know."

Camila tied her apron back on and moved toward the grill. She could feel Fila watching her. "I want details—"

"Oh, man. Here comes Uncle Jed," Maya called from the front. "Brace yourselves."

"Later," Camila promised Fila. "Not here."

"Maya, I've been looking for you," Jedediah Turner boomed from the far side of the counter, making Camila jump. Jed was one of the orneriest men she'd ever met, but he was her landlord, which meant she had to watch her manners around him.

"Hi, Uncle Jed," Maya said cheerfully.

"Hi, Jedidiah," Camila echoed. "How are you today?"

"I'll be fine as soon as we've won the Founder's Prize." He must have once stood tall and square shouldered, but time had taken its toll. At eighty-five, he moved stiffly, but he was as proud as ever.

"Founder's Prize?" Camila exchanged a look with her friends, but they were as mystified as she was.

"Didn't you hear the big announcement? The winner will be chosen on Halloween. A lot of land riding on that contest. Land that should belong to us Turners."

Camila just nodded. She wasn't a Turner, but living at the Flying W seemed to make her an honorary member of the family, which she usually appreciated. The Turners were known for being upright, trustworthy members of society, and for the most part, they lived up to their reputation.

Until the Coopers got involved.

Then they seemed to lose their minds.

"What land?" Maya asked.

"The Ridley property."

"The Ridley property?" Maya's eyes grew wide, and she turned to Camila to explain. "That property forms the northern boundary of the Flying W and Thorn Hill. It's on both sides of Pittance Creek. If we own it, we control the creek, right?" she asked Jed.

He nodded.

"Of course, the Coopers will want it, too. What do we have to do to get it?"

"Be the biggest contributors to civic society in town. Which we already are and always have been. It's a slam dunk," he said smugly.

Camila glanced at Maya. Was it? The Turners were good people, worked hard, went to church sometimes, participated in town events, but as far as making a contribution to civic society… didn't that require something more?

Jed must have sensed her skepticism. "We built the high school," he exclaimed.

"Back in 1953," Maya returned. "What have we donated since then?"

"How many high schools does one family have to build?" Jed answered huffily.

"It might be a case of 'What have you done for me lately,'" Fila put in.

Camila was grateful to her friend for saying so. Jed was better behaved toward outsiders than he was to Turners—real or honorary.

"Bah!" He waved a dismissive hand. "I served on the town council for forty years. I've done my bit. I'm a shoe-in for the prize."

"If you say so," Camila said slowly. She didn't like any of this. It was a set up for trouble, pitting family against family for such a valuable prize. Everyone in town would want to take a stab at it, which was probably the point. The council would get an unproductive piece of land off their books and possibly get some free upgrades in exchange for it.

Jed turned on his heel and strode off, mumbling under his breath.

"Hi, ladies. How's it going?" said Maya's sister, Stella, slipping into the booth from the back. "Sure looks busy." Twenty-seven years old, with dark curls and bright hazel eyes, she scanned the customers waiting for their turn.

"We've had a lineup for most of the day," Camila confirmed.

"Uncle Jed's on a tear," Stella said to Maya. "I'm here to hide for a minute."

"About the Founder's Prize? He was just here telling me about it. He'll be mad if someone else gets that land," Maya said. "He's pretty sure he deserves it just for being born."

"You think the Coopers will try for it?" Stella asked.

"Of course they will," Camila told her. "Everyone's going to try for it, don't you think?"

"I guess," Stella said. "But I don't know what we can do. It's not like we have any spare cash to donate another school." She bit her lip, caught Camila watching her and smiled. "Doesn't matter. The Coopers are worse off than we are. Still, the next six months might get messy. This might be the right time to move out— not that I want you to leave," she hastened to assure Camila. "I've loved having you around the place, but didn't you say you had an appointment with Megan Lawrence about buying a house this morning? How did that go?"

"Not so well, but I'm going to view another place tomorrow." She didn't mention Carl was the one thinking about buying it. She caught Fila's eye and shrugged. "I have high hopes about this one."

She prayed those hopes didn't go down in flames.

End of Excerpt

The SEALs of Chance Creek Series:

A SEAL's Oath

A SEAL's Vow

A SEAL's Pledge

A SEAL's Consent

A SEAL's Purpose

A SEAL's Resolve

A SEAL's Devotion

A SEAL's Desire

A SEAL's Struggle

A SEAL's Triumph

Brides of Chance Creek Series:

Issued to the Bride One Navy SEAL

Issued to the Bride One Airman

Issued to the Bride One Sniper

Issued to the Bride One Marine

Issued to the Bride One Soldier

Issued to the Bride One Sergeant for Christmas

The Turners v. Coopers Series:

The Cowboy's Secret Bride (Volume 1)

The Cowboy's Outlaw Bride (Volume 2)

The Cowboy's Hidden Bride (Volume 3)

The Cowboy's Stolen Bride (Volume 4)

The Cowboy's Forbidden Bride (Volume 5)

About the Author

With over one million books sold, NYT and USA Today bestselling author Cora Seton has created a world readers love in Chance Creek, Montana. She has twenty-eight novels and novellas currently set in her fictional town, with many more in the works. Like her characters, Cora loves cowboys, military heroes, country life, gardening, bike-riding, binge-watching Jane Austen movies, keeping up with the latest technology and indulging in old-fashioned pursuits. Visit **www.coraseton.com** to read about new releases, contests and other cool events!

Blog:

www.coraseton.com

Facebook:

facebook.com/coraseton

Twitter:

twitter.com/coraseton

Newsletter:

www.coraseton.com/sign-up-for-my-newsletter

22686833R00215